DESTINY

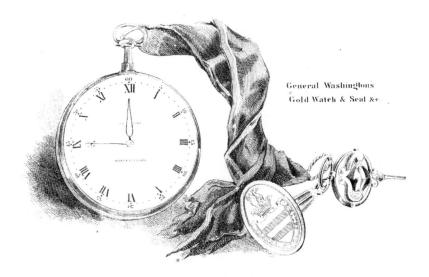

General Washingtons
Gold Watch & Seal &c.

by
Sylvia Clute

Sunstar
PUBLISHING LTD.

Destiny
by Sylvia Clute

© United States Copyright, 1997
Sylvia Clute
5511 Staples Mill Rd.
Suite 102A
Richmond, VA 23228-5422

Cover Design: Therese Cross
Text Design: Elizabeth Pasco

LCCN: 97-066695
ISBN: 1-887472-21-5
Printed in the U.S.A.

Portions from *A Course In Miracles*® © 1975
Reprinted by Permission of the
Foundation for Inner Peace, Inc.,
PO Box 1104
Glen Ellen, California 95442

This novel is a work of fiction and any resemblance of the characters, names, events, dialogue or plot to actual persons or events is coincidental. They are the exclusive product of the author's imagination and are fictitious.

To my loved ones,
for having chosen to share
the destiny of our lives together.

Lessons I have learned from *A Course In Miracles* are reflected
throughout this novel. As I teach, I also learn.

ACKNOWLEDGMENTS

I would like to express my gratitude and my love to the following people:

My husband, Eric Johnson, and our children, Andrea, Weston and Danielle, for being the inspiration of my life and giving unceasing spiritual and physical support to me.

Suzanne Soule, who, through her dependability, loyalty, commitment, and love has made many undertakings accessible to me, of which this book is but one.

Lavonne Michaelli, Darla Blatnik, Anne and Vernon Sylvest, Michael H. Brown, Karl E. Bren, Michael Fowler, and Wendy Innis, all exceptional friends, for their guidance and for giving me kind words of encouragement.

George and Annelise Petry for being there, sharing their journey and spurring Eric and me on our own.

My sisters, Marianne Pearce and Patty Johnson, and my brother, Eddy Clute, for having given in so many ways to their little sister, and Ray Pearce for demonstrating how supportive in-laws can be.

My mother and father who, even after life on Earth, continue to support and love me.

Kenneth Johnson, my brother-in law, for his generous permission to use pieces from his collection of old lithographs of Washington in this work.

Nancy Cherry who introduced me to *A Course in Miracles*, and the Foundation for Inner Peace, Inc. for its generous permission to use material from *ACIM* in this manner.

And special gratitude to Elizabeth Pasco, my editor, who also was my teacher, and Rodney Charles, Managing Editor of Sunstar, for having faith in my work from the beginning.

CHAPTER ONE

"**B**utchery! Pure butchery! Could this guy have done a worse job?" Christi exclaimed aloud as she reviewed photos from the firm's client—a plastic surgeon who specialized in reconstructive surgery. Open wounds on the woman's chest where her breast tissue had been removed in a mastectomy. Folds of skin lay to the side of each open wound, skin that would be used to cover the flaps of abdominal muscle tissue the surgeon would use to construct the new breast mounds. More photos of the assisting microsurgeon attempting to connect the tiny blood vessels near the woman's shoulders to bring blood to the transplanted tissue. And finally, the dead flesh that had not received an adequate blood supply—reconstructive surgery at its worst. And an unhappy patient.

"This guy had a license to mutilate, not heal," Christi said under her breath. She pulled her arms around her chest and hugged herself, thinking, "I'd feel better if this woman was my client, not this butcher." But she had no choice. Christi Daniel was an attorney in the civil litigation department of Harp, Harrison & Humphrey, a large Washington D.C. firm best known for its insurance defense work. Twelve years as an anti-trust attorney with the Department of Justice hadn't prepared her for these attacks of conscience in private practice. In thirteen months she had moved from lead attorney on an important employment discrimination case to the firm's primary female attorney defending male clients against claims brought by women. The female attorney versus the female plaintiff.

In this case the plastic surgeon was charged with medical malpractice and fraud. Prior to this particular operation, he told his patient he had successfully performed the free flap TRAM procedure a dozen times. Yet something went wrong. The procedure took hours longer than had been expected and the available blood supply had been exhausted before the operation was completed. When one flap had failed, the result was serious disfigurement and thus more surgery to repair the damage. More medical bills. And now litigation. The woman's lawyer claimed the surgeon had never actually done the procedure before; that his client was the first, and probably the guinea pig used to gain experience in this lucrative field of breast reconstructive surgery.

When Christi was assigned the case, two years after the fact and following several trial date postponements, the surgeon had still not located the paperwork to verify he had performed the procedure before this failed attempt. The plaintiff's attorney was demanding a reply. Christi's review of the documents confirmed her worst suspicions. If there was no evidence the surgeon had successfully performed the procedure, where was her case? The surgeon's lame excuses regarding the missing paperwork wouldn't cut the mustard.

Life at Harp, Harrison & Humphrey had its challenges—physically and morally. There were certain basic rules known to all attorneys at the firm—first and foremost, never admit liability on the part of the client. No matter how she did it, she could not admit guilt. Just cram some facts into a theory that exculpated your client, like stuffing the stepsister's foot into Cinderella's shoe. Block out the plaintiff's suffering and bring out the anger against the woman who submitted to a surgical procedure that was cosmetic.

But Christi was bothered on another level, as well. There would be no sexual stimulation for the woman with these mounds of tissue; no child would take nourishment from the fake nipples. Why did women think they needed these protrusions on their chest to be whole?

She realized she was judging again. Judging the woman for wanting to be normal, and judging the surgeon who performed the mutilating task. Just tell the insurance company to cut the check and move on. But this was not an option at Harp, Harrison & Humphrey.

Christi stuffed the file into her leather briefcase, squeezing it in next to the Smith file, another equally disturbing case. Her homework that required a more settled environment to digest.

She switched off the light in her office and stepped into the oak paneled hall. Several people were leaving the office of Winston Harp, one of the senior partners. Willard Smith was among them, the same Smith of the file that was stuffed in her briefcase. "Some coincidence, the week before trial," she thought. Christi paused as the others passed her. As she walked to the elevator, she heard Harp call her.

"Christi, wait," he raised his voice to assure her compliance. Harp, a short balding man with an expanding midsection, was affectionately known as "Win" by those who were of his stature. Christi felt the muscles in her back tighten as she pivoted to face him. Another dreaded after-hours encounter with Harp.

"I didn't see you at the rally this morning," he said as he approached her. "Were you there?"

"No," Christi responded firmly. "I'm swamped. Preparing two cases for trial, you know. I'm even taking work home." She patted her briefcase and tried not to look him in the eye.

"Maybe next time," he said gruffly, rearranging his tie. "Christi, I need your help with some new attorneys we'll be training on Monday. Can you be there?" He drew close to her. She instinctively began to button her coat.

"Yes, certainly, Mr. Harp," she responded coolly. "I can rearrange my schedule to be there."

He reached up and touched her hair, then kissed her cheek lightly.

Christi stepped back, recoiling from his touch. "Please don't," she said sharply. Then in her most professional tone of voice she asked, "What time is the training session?"

"What's the matter, dear?" Harp asked. "I was just showing you how much I appreciate you. I've been so busy forming this new political party that I haven't seen you for some time. You do know I'm fond of you."

Christi glared at Harp, forcing him to look at her face that betrayed no emotion. She was the professional waiting for a response.

"The training session begins at 8:30 a.m. sharp in conference room C. You'll be our representative of the gentler sex, you know. Show the new attorneys we're an 'affirmative action firm,' right from day one." Harp smiled at Christi, undaunted by her coolness. "You're such an appealing specimen of the gentler sex."

Christi didn't respond. Instead she turned toward the elevator.

Harp added, "Say, how about some dinner tonight so we can discuss the two trials coming up. My wife's busy with her Rebel Republic ladies tonight. We can work all night if you like."

Christi faced him again and responded bluntly, "Sorry, Mr. Harp, but I really have too much work to do on these cases. And I need to get in those extra billable hours. Got to keep up the quota, right?"

She heard an office door open down the hall and another attorney stepped out. As he approached Harp, and before Harp could protest, Christi took this as her cue to walk away. She reached the elevator door and quickly stepped inside by herself.

This was an easy escape, more so than some. Harp had been wearing her down since she arrived at the firm thirteen months ago. Diplomacy had been ineffective in deterring him. His interest in her went beyond her abilities as an attorney. Even in the company of her peers he had made advances toward her or embarrassed her with his sexual comments, which she did her best to ignore.

At first she took Harp's behavior lightly, trusting her profession-alism would overcome this occupational hazard. But his persistence, despite her cool demeanor, was overwhelming. She had become tired of the exchange and even began to question her own behavior. "What am I doing to encourage this?" she began to ask herself when he confronted her in this way.

Christi pulled the collar of her wool coat closer to her face as she stepped into the cold January wind that swept down between the office buildings. She had planned to take the metro home but when she saw a yellow cab approaching she hailed it. Too cold, too much to think about.

She stared out the cab window, turning her thoughts from Harp to the Smith file in her briefcase. Here was a man accused of molesting the young daughter of his live-in girl friend over a four-year period. She had to defend him despite his own admission that he had touched the girl on one or two occasions when she had supposedly asked him to. Of course, his recent description of events was in stark contrast to the medical evidence and testimony of the girl.

She had traded the Justice Department and life in a basement apartment for this. Now she could afford the high-rise apartment in Crystal City and the wardrobe to go with the position at Harp, Harrison & Humphrey. But the stakes were higher than she had imagined.

When she arrived home there was a message from Tom on her answering machine.

"Hi, Chris. Got some great news for you. I got the assistant professor position in the physics department. Can you fly up this weekend to celebrate? Call me A.S.A.P. Love 'ya."

"If only," she thought. Any celebration would be a welcome distraction, but hard to imagine at this moment. Maybe if Tom was in Florida instead of Cambridge she would be more inclined. No, it wasn't the weather that kept her from going. It was the two files in her briefcase and her integrity. No matter what. Even if she was working for Harp.

She picked up the phone and dialed Tom's number.

His voice was animated, his excitement spilling out like a kid on a merry-go-round. "Can you come up this weekend?" he asked. "There's a Beethoven concert in Boston. We could have dinner at Giovanni's."

Christi was buoyed by his enthusiasm. Dinner, a concert, Tom's warm embrace and gentle touch. "Sounds divine, I'd love to, but... there's no way I can come this weekend. I've got a trial the end of next week and I still have to review the depositions, outline my opening statement and prepare witness questions. Then there's this medical malpractice case and discovery answers are due on Tuesday. The client just brought me the information today. And to top it off, Harp wants me to spend Monday as an ornament in a training session for new attorneys."

"Sorry, Christi, you sound pretty stressed out. Anything I can do to help?" Tom asked.

Her defenses were pierced. Tom could do this to her. She grabbed a tissue and blew her nose.

"Okay, so I'm disgusted. The legal system is rotten. My life here stinks. And I'm wondering if I have the guts to change it."

"But this was your dream job, wasn't it, Chris?" Tom asked.

"So much for dreams."

"What could you do that would be as prestigious as this job?"

"I now know prestige means nothing without principles."

"Has Harp been after you again?"

Christi paused, fighting back her tears. "Maybe what I need is to be my own boss. No one to tell me how to do my job. Just a quiet little practice in the country, litigating property line disputes and doing real estate closings."

"If that makes you happy, Christi. Do you think they need a physics professor in the country?"

"Doesn't have to be forever," she added. "I just need a break. I'm sick of everything around me, of everything I do every day. I'm even sick of what I might become if I stay here."

Christi was surprised she said that. Was that what was scaring her? That eventually she would become one of them. Hard nosed. Callous. Deceitful.

"I'll be all right, really," she said. "You know I have to go through these episodes every so often. If I finish my trial in time next week, I'll catch the shuttle to Boston on Friday. I promise. We can celebrate then. I'm happy about your new position. Don't worry, I have lots of work to keep me sane."

"Okay, Chris, I'm looking forward to seeing you here. Just take it easy on yourself. I know you'll work it out."

Christi put the receiver down and paused. First some dinner then work. Without thinking she picked up the remote and turned on the TV. The screen flashed on in the middle of the evening news. The announcer was reporting the morning political rally—the one Harp had expected her to attend.

"The newly-formed Rebel Republic party held a rally at the Pentagon this morning. Several thousand demonstrators demanded the government ban homosexuals in military service. The spokesperson for the party, Winston Harp, called for a return to family values."

Harp, flanked by his wife and two young adult daughters, appeared on the screen. "We demand change in this Nation," Harp yelled, pounding his fist on the podium. "A return to the days when two parents raised decent kids, when millions of babies weren't murdered by abortions. We must stop the decay of the American family."

Christi hit the off button on the remote. It was bad enough that Harp was contributing to a rotten legal system. Now he was embroiled in politics. Family values!

She pulled her knees to her chest and buried her face. Smothering her sobs, she cried, "God help us! There has to be a better way."

S aturday morning meant an early start for Christi. Drafting answers to extensive discovery in the surgeon's case, she reluctantly accepted his assertion that the records of prior procedures had been lost by inexperienced staff. But she believed otherwise. This new explanation had surfaced only after a round of golf between the surgeon, the insurance risk manager and two senior attorneys from Harp, Harrison & Humphrey. She nonetheless knew the surgeon would be convincing when he described this unfortunate turn of events in his upcoming deposition.

Next it was depositions taken in the Smith case. As she read page after page, she could not dispel the image of her client—shifty dark eyes, a jaw that came to a point just below the mouth. Perhaps that's what made him seem so loathsome. The bow tie he always wore and his unkempt moustache didn't help.

His words, too, were embedded in her memory. Smith denied molesting the little girl, but said he had a friend who was intimate with his daughter and claimed it was the best sex he ever had. "Good and tight," Smith had said with contempt.

Smith claimed his girlfriend's daughter had run around in her night gown, begging for his attention. She tried to lure him into sex to get back at her mom, but he resisted, knowing sex with a minor could get him in trouble. Christi believed his story even less than the surgeon's. "How can I win such a case?" she thought. "And why would I want to?"

Working steadily, on to Sunday morning. The words still wouldn't come for her opening statement to the jury in the Smith case. Instead she turned to a detailed outline of the evidence in the case prepared by her legal assistant, Mark Reuben, and her strategy for questioning each witness at trial.

At last it was Sunday noon. She was meeting Shenandoah Adkins, her closest friend and former college roommate, for lunch. After graduating, they were both drawn to graduate studies in either law or history. They decided to determine the path each would take by the flip of a coin. It was heads, and Shenan now worked as an archivist at the Smithsonian Institute, specializing in American Indian artifacts. Christi was now the lawyer.

Over lunch, Christi lamented that Harp made her feel like a cheap sex object, an admission she was embarrassed to make, even to her confidante. But it was Christi's description of the child molestation case that elicited the greatest sympathy from her friend.

Shenan's high cheek bones and bronze skin belied her American Indian lineage. Her diminutive stature was offset by her strong face graced by long black hair and penetrating dark eyes. "I would refuse to handle such cases," Shenan declared.

Christi shook her head. "Too risky, I'd be fired. . . . You know what I really want?" she asked. "I want to be my own boss. Have a quiet little practice in the country."

"Yeah?" said Shenan as she peered at Christi over her coffee cup. "So do it."

"You make it sound so easy, but it's not."

"It can't possibly be more difficult than defending sex perverts! And anyway, what's a blue-blooded liberal like you doing in the midst of Republican Rejects? That's what I call that new party." They laughed.

"You're probably right," Christi admitted. "But it wasn't so bad when I first joined the firm. I knew it was conservative, but this Rebel Republic stuff didn't surface until several months later."

"We have a few R.R.s, even at the Smithsonian," Shenan disclosed. "There's one man who tries to force everyone to accept his views. If you don't, he gets angry. You're some sort of traitor, like it's a sin to disagree with him. It's alarming how quickly they're gaining support."

"And how fast they're raising money," Christi added. "But so many people are dissatisfied with the status quo, they make easy targets for the R.R.'s simplistic answers. I know there has to be a better way, but for the life of me, I can't see what it is."

Lunch ended too quickly and the sisters-in-spirit parted, promising to meet again soon.

It was midafternoon when Christi arrived at the office. Two secretaries typed busily on appellate briefs. Junior attorneys milled about. Harp was in New York on a fund-raising trip for the R.R.s.

Christi entered her office with a sense of doom. She scooped up two large notebooks of evidence in the Smith case and carried them to a small conference room several doors from her office—out of the way and quiet. An antique walnut table, about eleven feet long with ornate pedestal legs, dominated the room. The old table was out of character with the modern, straight-lined veneer furniture that filled the rest of the law firm, but it had become Christi's place of refuge. It offered not only additional work space, but a place to clear her mind.

When Christi joined the firm she immediately felt drawn to this table, an attraction she couldn't explain. Curious about its origins, she could only garner that it had been Harp's conference table in his first law office a quarter of a century ago.

As she entered the conference room and dropped the notebooks on the table, her attention was drawn to an engraving of George Washington that hung on the wall above the table. She had never noticed it before. He was wearing a small apron decorated with curious symbols. His gentle eyes scrutinized her. Oddly, the first President seemed alive.

Dismissing these thoughts, she focused on the Smith file marked "Plaintiff's Records," records covering the four years of alleged abuse of the little girl. Gynecological records from the exam after the abuse was reported. Each drawing of the young plaintiff's hymen indicating the locations of scarring consistent with attempted penetration. Each birthday and Father's Day card given to Smith by his alleged victim, most of which were signed "I love you, Debbie."

She held a letter to her client from the young plaintiff, the measured cursive of a grade school child thanking him for permitting her and her mother to live in his house, for the nice things he did for them. The letter closed with the plea, "Please don't ever make us move away, even when my mommy makes you mad." Christi perceived an ache in her heart and lightly touched her chest.

She turned to the window ignoring a headache that was beginning to throb in her temples. As she stared, she thoughtlessly rubbed her hand over the grain of the wood in the old table. "What secrets do you hold?" she wondered. "Who has sat here over the last century, perhaps even the century before? What stories could you tell me?"

Six a.m. Monday the alarm clamored. Christi's stomach knotted at the prospect of the day and the week that lay ahead. She wished this cup could pass her by.

She stood in the shower, hot water running over her shoulders, loosening the knots in the muscles at the base of her neck. Her legs felt weak, but she straightened her shoulders and briskly stepped out of the shower. Her wish could not be granted; she had a job she must do.

Minutes before the training session was to begin, seven new associates were still meeting firm attorneys, munching donuts and sipping coffee. Nervousness filled the air. Christi quickly made her tour of the group, introducing herself and shaking the hand of each neophyte.

One new attorney named Virginia Goode, an attractive young woman, highly intelligent, and an ardent fan of Harp, especially caught her attention. Virginia had been President of the Young Republicans at the University of Virginia Law School, but felt alienated by the Republican Party's softness on major issues, like abortion and military spending. She admired the Rebel Republic's firm commitment to principles of patriotism and family values and unabashedly admitted she had sought employment at Harp, Harrison & Humphrey for political motives.

Christi quizzed Virginia, "Isn't 'family values' just a code word for religious doctrine that some want to impose upon others, using the power of government to achieve this end?"

"You must be a liberal. No values. You wouldn't understand," Virginia retorted.

As the training session was about to begin, Harp stepped toward Christi and whispered that he had made luncheon plans for them; he would meet her at noon. She quickly sat in the nearest chair to consider her strategy.

The morning session began as usual. A welcome from each senior partner, a description of firm hierarchy, an outline of the training provided new attorneys. It ended with a senior attorney explaining the billing system. He opened with a joke. "A line of people was standing at the gates of Heaven as St. Peter called the roll. St. Peter asked each new arrival his age. As a recently-deceased attorney approached the front of the line, St. Peter asked, 'How old are you, sir?' 'Fifty-two' replied the attorney. St. Peter checked his record book and looked at the attorney. 'According to the billable hours you charged your clients, you have to be a hundred and two'." Everyone, including Christi, politely laughed.

Then he explained the rules regarding billable hours, a routine only too familiar to Christi. "Every associate must average forty billable hours per week. That's eight hours a day, five days a week, for a total of 2,000 billable hours per year. Not all hours are billable, so associates are expected to spend sixty hours a week on cases, and possibly more, to meet the quota. Vacation time is allowed, if billable hours are current. A senior attorney will discuss any problems encountered with the billing arrangements.

"It might sound oppressive, but I have some helpful suggestions," he continued. "When an insurance company sends us a case that you're assigned to, our reputation for thorough work must be upheld. At Harp, Harrison & Humphrey, we fully develop each case so the client can be accurately advised of its strengths and weaknesses. You never settle a case too soon. Our policy, to protect against mistakes of course, is to never settle until at least 150 hours have been billed on a case, and most cases never settle. This gives you ample opportunity to make your billable hours."

The litany about padding your bills to keep the firm's doors open had Christi's head swimming. She welcomed the lunch break, until she recalled Harp's plans.

Harp's secretary met Christi at the conference room door. Harp was waiting for her in the firm's limousine. She pulled on her coat as her assistant, Mark Reuben, reminded her that jury instructions in the Smith case were due tomorrow.

"I've done an initial draft I hoped you could review during your lunch break," he said.

"Sorry, Mark. Harp is waiting downstairs for me. Leave them here and I'll look at them this evening. I'm sure you did a good job." She picked up a legal pad and headed for the elevator.

It felt like the onset of flu as Christi leaned against the metallic elevator wall. Pounding headache, queasy stomach, weak knees. But she had to admit it was apprehension about the impending lunch with Harp, minimized only by knowing they would be in public which she hoped would assure his good behavior. As she approached the black limousine, Harp opened the door from the inside and motioned for her to get in the back seat next to him.

"How's the training going?" he asked.

"Fine. Looks like a good group of associates coming on board. Two of them are married which might make it hard, with all the time they have to spend at the office. But they seem eager to begin, especially Virginia Goode who hopes to work for the R.R. party."

"Is she the pretty U. VA. graduate?" Harp asked.

"Yes, I think that's where she said she attended law school."

The long black car sped through the city streets toward the northeast side of town. It pulled up in front of the Jefferson Inn, a new motel about a mile from Capitol Hill.

"Here we are. Curtis, wait for us here," Harp instructed the driver.

Harp grabbed his briefcase as he and Christi exited the automobile. They entered the registration area where Harp approached the man at the desk who gave him a key. Harp then said they were going to a room on the second floor. They entered the elevator. "Is anyone else going to join us for lunch?" Christi asked, standing as far from Harp as possible.

"Yeah. They're on their way. Come with me," he directed as the elevator doors opened. The key slipped easily into the door of Room 213. Harp opened the door for Christi to enter. It was a large suite with a king-size bed, a chair near the door and a table by the window. He closed the door and followed her into the room.

Christi felt her stomach knot as she scanned the room. "When will the others be here?" she asked as she reticently walked to the closet where she hung up her coat. As she began to turn, Harp was directly behind her.

"We don't need anyone else. I've been thinking about you all morning," he said, loosening his tie.

Christi slipped around him and began to back up. "Mr. Harp, I don't know what you have in mind. This doesn't look like a place to have lunch," she protested. "You invited me to lunch, not to a motel room."

"Ever heard of room service? We'll have lunch, but first we'll mix a little business with pleasure." He threw his coat on the chair. "Just relax," he ordered, approaching her.

She was cornered. The bed was behind her and Harp blocked the door. "But there's no meeting going on," she continued to protest, her mind swirling. She glanced at the bed behind her. Instantly he grabbed her hair and forced her mouth against his. The taste of cigarettes and alcohol penetrated her. She pushed him away, but he lunged back. The bed jerked as they fell upon it. His body molded itself on top of hers, squeezing out her breath. He pulled up her skirt, his hand against her thigh. His penis pressed against her pelvis. His cold fingers ripped her panties.

The struggle began to move in slow motion. Christi felt herself slip out of her body and peer down on the attack. As she watched herself struggle, the fervor of his attack intensified, stirring his erotic response.

A surge of strength coursed through her. She turned on her side. He rolled away. She ran to the phone, began to dial 911. The phone flew from her hand and she careened toward Harp. The back of his hand crashed against the side of her face.

"Who the hell do you think you're calling?" he demanded savagely. "Do you know what opportunities are available if you cooperate? I can give you whatever you want in the firm. I can make you a partner in a couple of years, but you're such a stupid bitch you haven't figured that out. Some pristine princess, is that what you think you are?"

Christi's rage equaled his. She stared at him with contempt. Her voice swelled. "I'm not your property. I'm not a piece of dirt for you to spit on, to wipe your feet on. I'm a lawyer who works for your firm but that's soon to be past tense. I'm disgusted with you, with your firm, with your low-life, lying clients."

Her words sobered Harp. "Christi, you know I didn't mean any harm. I just find you very attractive, that's all. You know, it's just a thing I have for you. I know you find me attractive too. You never told me you didn't."

"How could he utter such words?" she thought. This man who stands for everything she despises. She straightened her clothes and grabbed her coat from the closet.

There was a knock at the door. "Room service. Are you going to order lunch?" came the voice from the other side.

"We don't want room service," Harp yelled back. "Put your coat on. We'll just forget this ever happened." He put the knot in his tie then picked up his briefcase. "Curtis is waiting for us. What happened isn't important."

Christi bolted for the door and ran to the elevator. Outside she welcomed the gust of cold air. In the limousine she huddled in the corner, her arms tightly folded across her chest as Curtis drove them away.

"Ready for the Smith trial?" Harp inquired, as if pleasantries were in order. "Very important case."

"Why was Harp even aware of this case?" she wondered.

"Willard, he's a good old guy," he continued. "Started out with nothing. Selling guns out of his home, then out of the trunk of his car. From that to one of the biggest gun dealers in the country. Now he owns gun stores up and down the east coast. Probably a million-aire many times over. Worked like a dog, provided a good home for that woman and her daughter. And that's the thanks he gets— accused of molesting the kid. That's a money-grabbing scheme if there ever was one."

She remained silent.

"Christi, you have to win Willard's case," Harp implored.

"I never gave him any guarantees," she replied coolly. "The other side has some strong evidence and he doesn't make a good witness."

"I'm telling you—you have to win that case." Harp raised his voice. "It's not a case we can afford to have you lose. Who's the judge on the case?"

"The judge?" she thought. Was he thinking of contacting the judge, pulling strings? "We won't know until the day of trial," she replied, unwilling to yield this information.

Curtis brought the limousine to a halt in front of the law firm. "Remember, nothing happened," Harp said under his breath as he slid out the door then disappeared into the building.

Curtis opened the door for Christi. "Are you all right, Ms. Daniel? You look upset."

"I'm fine, Curtis. Thanks." She waited a moment to give Harp time to catch an elevator before entering the building. Going directly to the restroom she examined the reddish blotch on her left cheek. A few touches of blemish remover and it was passable.

The associate training was in session as she slipped into her chair. She leaned her head against her left hand hoping to hide any evidence of the noontime assault. An hour was all she could bear. She used the urgency of the Smith jury instructions to justify leaving early.

In her office the pages of jury instructions swam before her eyes. She bundled them together and hurried down the hall to the small conference room, to her special table. She touched the surface with both hands and again pondered its history. She looked up at the engraving of Washington for clues. He smiled silently.

When at home at last, she drew a tub of hot bath water and began to soak her way through the events of the day. Should she call the police? She hadn't been raped. No evidence to be taken at a hospital. No witnesses. Evidence of Harp striking her face would be gone by tomorrow. What of the other partners? Little chance they would act, other than to dispense with her, now a liability to the firm. Before it was over she would be the perpetrator, having pursued Harp. There was nothing she could do. Harp had committed the perfect crime.

Venue for the Smith case was the Winchester Circuit Court, a Virginia court to the west of D.C. It lasted an endless day and a half. Christi was shocked by the mother's testimony of the little girl's early reports of the sexual abuse, reports the mother had ignored believing they couldn't be true. The courtroom was silent as the young plaintiff described how the abuse developed from what she believed was play to hurtful penetration with his finger, oral sex and ejaculation on her stomach. All but rape.

The jury's quick verdict for the plaintiff was a relief to Christi. She might never collect the judgment, but at least Smith's victim had been validated. Smith was enraged and immediately demanded the case be appealed, that his good name be vindicated. Christi advised him of procedural errors the judge may have made, grounds for an appeal and another shot at victory.

Hurriedly Christi returned the boxes of trial materials to the law firm and caught the shuttle to Boston, the last passenger to board. Tom met her at the airport. As they drove to his apartment, she confided in him.

"I'm leaving the firm just as soon as I find a house in the country," she announced. "My grandmother's inheritance will serve as the down payment and I have savings to live on for awhile, until I establish a practice."

He looked at her through his wire-rimmed glasses with surprise. But it was not until after dinner that Christi disclosed Harp's assault on her.

"Why didn't you call me?" Tom asked solemnly.

"What could you have done?" She glared, rolling her napkin nervously as she spoke. "No one will do anything about it. It's gone on for centuries with impunity. This wasn't the first time Harp has taken a woman to 'lunch'. If it wasn't a female attorney, it was a paralegal or a secretary, a client. I know it's happened before and will happen again—many times in many firms by the many Winston Harps of the world. They think they are all-powerful while women are powerless, property for men to use as they please. And worst of all, Harp doesn't believe what he did was wrong."

"But Chris, how do you expect me or anyone else to help if you take a defeatist attitude like that?" Tom asked impatiently. "All men aren't like this. Maybe you should report it to the police, or at least to the EEOC as sexual harassment."

"So I can become another EEOC case file, lost in the backlog, blackballed among D.C. law firms?" Christi retorted. "What good would that do? No.... There's only one thing I want. If I could get it, it might all be worth it."

"What do you want, Chris?" he asked.

"An antique walnut table that's in a small conference room down the hall from my office. If Harp would give me that table, I'd walk away and be happy."

"Maybe you can make a deal with Harp," he suggested. "The table for no police report and no EEOC complaint."

"Maybe. I can't trade a criminal charge for anything," Christi advised. "That's extortion. But I could settle a civil claim for sexual harassment in exchange for the table. I wonder if Harp would.... Even if he would, what would I do with the table? Where could I put it? It's huge!"

CHAPTER THREE

Christi was consumed with pursuing her claim against Harp. Any confrontation meant an end to her career at the firm, a trade she was willing to make for the table. In any event, her career at Harp, Harrison & Humphrey wasn't worth much now. Mark Reuben was the only attorney in the firm whom she trusted.

Monday morning, following her weekend with Tom, she commenced execution of her plan. First, gather the evidence. She summoned Mark to her office and closed the door.

"Mark, I need to discuss something confidential with you.... When you've been in meetings with other firm attorneys and Harp was there, do you recall any sexist comments Harp has made to me in your presence?"

"Which ones?" he asked. "I don't recall a conversation with Harp when he didn't make insulting comments to everyone, but especially you. It's pretty hard to stomach."

"I know.... I have a difficult question I must ask. No matter what your answer is, I'll understand. I'm asking, not demanding," Christi began tentatively. "Consider it a request from a friend, not the attorney who supervises you. Mark... if I were to bring a sexual harassment claim against Harp, would you be willing to testify about the remarks you've heard him make to me?"

Mark's back straightened. He looked at Christi wide-eyed. "How could I do that and still work for the firm? Christi, there's not a single person in this firm who would testify against Harp. If I did, I'd be the only one, and everyone else would testify that both you and I were lying. Are you sure you want to do this?"

"No, Mark, I'm not at all sure. I'm just considering my options," she replied, knowing her options had just narrowed.

"My wife and I have been discussing our future," Mark continued. "I really enjoy working with you, and if I didn't have to be around the senior partners, and especially Harp, I could manage to be happy here. The hours we're required to work are barbaric, but I'll probably face that in any firm where I'm just an associate. What I dislike most is what the firm stands for. But I've only been here about a year and I need at least a couple of years before I move on. You know, looks bad on the resume. My wife and I are planning to have our first child. We've decided I have to stay, for the time being at least. I can't stay here, Christi, and testify against Harp. I'm... I'm sorry."

"I understand, Mark. Understand completely. Sorry I even asked. We both know the truth. Maybe that's the best we can do."

"Our legal system leaves a lot to be desired, doesn't it?" Mark said, looking at the floor, elbows leaning on his knees.

"The language I use to describe it is a little stronger than that," she replied jokingly to disguise her disappointment. "Thanks, Mark, for understanding. Someday things will be better. They have to be."

His head hung low, shoulders slumped as he turned to leave.

"Mark," she said softly. "Don't feel like you just sold your soul. Sometimes we gotta do what we gotta do. Look at me.... I defended Smith against that little girl. Hey, the bills have to be paid, right?"

He grinned feebly and left.

Any action would now have to be taken alone. Christi stood up, tucked her appointment book under her arm, and marched to the desk of Harp's secretary. "I'd like to make an appointment to see Mr. Harp," she said firmly. "Please."

Surprise crossed the face of the middle-aged woman dressed in a gray wool shirt dress, hair pulled back in a bun at the nape of her neck. "What about?" she snapped.

"It's a personal matter."

"Mr. Harp doesn't see junior attorneys about personal matters. You'll have to take it to the personnel department."

"It's also a legal matter." Christi was determined to get her appointment. "I'm confident Mr. Harp wouldn't want me to take this matter to the personnel department."

The secretary's eyes narrowed as she looked at Christi. "I can pencil in a fifteen-minute appointment at eight in the morning, but Mr. Harp will have to approve it."

"Thank you," Christi said. "Please tell him it's about what happened last Monday. I don't think he'll object to seeing me personally. I'll expect your confirmation."

Feeling her knees might buckle beneath her, she quickly returned to her office and dropped into her chair. She wiped the perspiration from her brow as questions tumbled through her mind. . . . What risk does this action pose to her legal career versus the statement she wants to make? What about the time and money she and her family have invested in her legal training? . . . But it's the lack of courage to do what must be done that has caused the system to be the way it is. . . . No choice. She would stand her ground.

Christi spent a restless night. The image of Harp's rageful visage was mixed with guilt over feeling intimidated. . . . Visions of herself as a child. . . . Voices from the past. "You're selfish—always thinking of yourself—this wouldn't have happened if it weren't for you. . . ." Her instinct to fight back. But I'm not a child. I'm a grown woman. There's nothing Harp can do to me now—except fire me. . . . "You should have tried harder." The night drummed on until sleep at last brought relief.

She selected a dark suit and large jewelry as attire for the meeting. Harp's reception area was empty when she arrived minutes before eight o'clock. She knocked on his door. No response. Another knock. The door angrily swung open. Harp ordered her inside.

She marched to the chair in front of his desk and sat down. He stormed to his high-backed red leather chair and sat facing her. His large imposing desk was the battlefield separating opposing armies about to charge.

"It's about your assault on me last Monday." Christi cleared her throat.

"What the hell are you talking about?" Harp sneered, his face reddened. "I didn't assault you or anyone else last Monday."

"I'm referring to what happened in the room on the second floor at the Jefferson Inn last Monday," she said resolutely. "When you pushed me on the bed. You tried to rape me."

"You're delusional. What is this, some sort of blackmail attempt? Have you taken leave of your senses? I'm not crazy enough to try to rape someone, much less a female attorney in my own firm. And the attorney who handles our sexual harassment cases, at that. Who's going to believe such a preposterous allegation? What evidence do you have to support your claim?"

"I have my knowledge of what occurred, Mr. Harp." She was unwilling to yield an inch. "My testimony is my evidence, and I am willing to testify to what occurred, precisely because I am the attorney who handles the sexual harassment cases. I know how difficult these cases are to prove. But I also know how important it is that those who perpetrate such wrongs be held accountable." She looked Harp straight in the eye. "I may not prevail, but you're not going to walk away without some accountability for what you did to me."

He looked away. "What do you want? What is it you want for your trumped-up claim?" The tables had turned.

"Not much," she said confidently. "I'll settle all claims I have against you and the firm in return for the old walnut table that's in the small conference room down the hall from my office."

"What!" Harp exclaimed. "Now I know you're crazy."

Christi felt her heart sink. How foolish for her to have assumed Harp would part with the beautiful table from his first law office.

"My partners thought I was crazy to keep it, but it had sentimental value to me," he continued. "We got it into that conference room by lifting it with a crane through the window. There's not an elevator that it will fit in."

Was he yielding ground? "I think it's a fair exchange, my sexual harassment claim for the table," she argued. "It's not used much, anyway."

"What on earth would you do with that huge table?" he asked. "It's a piece of junk."

Christi's heart jumped for joy. Now act fast. "If you'll give me the table, this is what I'll do. I will leave as soon as my cases can be turned over to other attorneys. I'll give you a signed release for any and all claims arising before the date of the release in return for you conveying the table to me and moving it to anywhere within a hundred miles of here within six months. If I don't claim it within six months, I lose my right to it."

"Draw up the release and get out," yelled Harp. "We don't want you here any longer."

She started to get up, but hesitated. "And one more thing," she added, her elbow resting on the edge of his desk. "The engraving of Washington that hangs above the table goes with it."

"Get out of here. Draw up your release and take your bits of trash."

"I'll prepare it immediately," Christi said. "The table and the engraving."

"Before you go, what cases do you have that have to be transferred?" Harp asked, sounding almost conciliatory.

"It won't be hard to make the transition. The associate who works with me can handle much of my work. A couple of major things. The appeal for Willard Smith. The appeal brief and appendix will be due in a couple of months. My associate, Mark Reuben, can do an excellent job on that."

"That Jew boy?" bellowed Harp. "Smith would never work with a Jew. The only reason we hired him was because he graduated near the top of his class at Harvard. Harrison's idea. Said it would look good for the firm. Reuben isn't going to touch Smith's appeal. Smith didn't even want a woman handling his case, but I told him he had to. You know, it looks better to the jury on a sex case if he's represented by a woman. But you lost. He's mad as hell."

Christi ignored the pain of his insults. "But an appeal isn't like a trial," she protested. "Smith won't have to work closely with Mark. Mark will be working exclusively with the transcript of the trial. He doesn't have to prepare witnesses to testify, like I did. Smith wouldn't even have to see Mark."

"Absolutely not," Harp said smashing his fist on the desk. "Willard Smith doesn't even know we have a Jew in this firm. I'll assign his appeal to Virginia Goode, one of the new associates. She's bright and can do a good job. I'll sign the pleadings and argue the appeal before the court. That takes care of that case. What else do you have?"

"I'm preparing for a medical malpractice trial involving breast reconstructive surgery that ran into problems. It's set for trial in about four weeks."

"Harrison can handle that," snapped Harp. "He's our medical malpractice expert. He'll get a continuance based on change of counsel. We've already done that several times for the doctor."

"Yes. Well, everything else is farther down the road." Christi said, cutting her answer short. "I'll make a list of the cases, a brief description of each and leave it for you. I'll pack up and leave as soon as the release is signed."

Christi stood but Harp remained firmly planted in his chair. "This is best for everyone," she said, turning toward the door. She let herself out of Harp's office and headed directly to the small conference room, to the mysterious old table. She slowly rubbed her hand across its smooth surface, hardly able to believe it would now be hers.

She walked around the table and stood before the engraving of Washington, admiring his gentle strength. He gazed down at her. "Please be my guide, wherever this path may lead," she pleaded softly.

CHAPTER FOUR

The moving van wound its way along the narrow country road. "Read me those directions again," the driver said to his assistant sitting on the passenger side of the cab.

The young man squinted at the paper. "Pass the exit to Mount Vernon on your left. Continue on Route 235 about three miles until you come to Route 321. Turn right and continue until you come to a mailbox with 'Daniel' painted on the side. Turn right into the drive and continue up the hill to the old, two story brick house at the end of the drive."

"Damn, I think we just missed it," the driver said, slapping the steering wheel. "Better turn around as soon as there's a place that's wide enough."

The old farm house was beginning to take shape. Its hand-made bricks hewn in the mid-eighteenth century, no doubt by slaves, had provided solid construction that remained reasonably sound. The slate roof had recently been repaired and the interior smelled of fresh paint. The plumbing was in poor repair, but Christi deemed it livable until she had funds to do more.

Originally part of a much larger estate adjoining George Washington's land in northern Virginia known as Mount Vernon, its most recent owners ceased their renovations when they divorced. After nearly three years on the market while the feuding couple fought and finally filed for bankruptcy, Christi's purchase had spared it from the auction block.

Too large for her needs and requiring more renovation than she desired, it was nonetheless a better buy than the more modern homes she had been shown. And most importantly, it had a formal dining room that could easily accommodate the eleven foot antique walnut table of which she was now the proud owner.

"Here they come," shouted Tom as Christi came around the corner of the house. It was spring break and he had come for the week to assist with her move.

Christi stopped by the apple tree in full bloom in the front yard. "Finally. I hope the table made the move intact."

Tom put his arm around Christi's shoulders as they watched the truck lumber up the drive. "I don't understand the fascination with a table," he said.

"Don't feel bad, I don't either. I can't explain it, it just felt right. Maybe I wouldn't have carried through with this crazy idea if I hadn't felt so strongly that the table and I belonged here. I knew, as soon as I walked through the door."

The truck pulled up in front of the house, turned, and edged its rear next to the front steps. The two men descended. The driver looked around, checked the front door. "Guess it all has to go up these steps. No problem except for that big table. Any chance your friend there might help us get it in, when we get to it?" He motioned toward Tom.

"Sure," Tom said. "I'll help with all of it."

The smaller objects were quickly moved to their designated locations. The heavy walnut table was the last item to be removed from the truck. The three men worked in unison, while Christi balanced one of its huge legs. The men strained as it slid up the steep steps on its side, taxing the make-shift skid beneath it. The old table squeaked and moaned.

"It goes on the left, through the double doors. In the dining room," Christi directed.

At last it was gently tilted upright in the middle of the magnificent room. It fit perfectly. Christi was pleased. While many aspects of her new life made little sense, she nonetheless knew this was right.

She surveyed the table's new setting. The large bay window facing the west provided ample light. Wide panels of cut glass above the window acted as prisms in the afternoon sun, creating multi-colored streamers of light across the ceiling. The room was newly painted in a light Wedgwood blue with cream trim. The ceiling was adorned with a decorative cornice, carved tassels hanging in each corner. A wide chair rail encircled the room.

On either side of the dining room fireplace were ornate wooden panels that stretched from the floor to the ceiling. A small doorway to the left of the fireplace joined the dining room to the kitchen.

The decorative marble surrounding the fireplace intrigued Christi—two crossed keys suspended below a five-pointed star. Above the mantel she carefully hung the engraving of Washington. She stepped back to admire how well it looked in its new home.

She paid the movers and directed them to a shortcut back to D.C. Then Tom's stomach rumbled. "Poor Tom. You're too thin to lose any more weight. We've eaten a lot of peanut butter sandwiches this week, but this evening we're going to celebrate. We're having tuna fish on rye under the apple tree," she announced. "We'll dine in its fragrance and be sprinkled with falling petals."

She placed the sandwiches and drinks in a basket and handed it to Tom. She grabbed a blanket and took his arm as they strolled toward the door. They stopped momentarily to admire the table as the first rays of the late afternoon sun fell upon it. In this light, it was more beautiful than ever.

"Do you think your neighbor will come visit you?" Tom asked as they descended the front steps.

"What neighbor?"

"You know, your neighbor George Washington."

Christi laughed. "Oh, that neighbor. Of course. In fact the man who owns the little lumber yard in town said every now and then he rides from Mount Vernon over here in a carriage. Several people have seen him. It's a ghost carriage, of course. Do you believe in ghosts?"

"I don't know. Perhaps."

"What, a physicist who believes in ghosts!" Christi spread the blanket on the ground under the large apple tree. "I thought if you scientists couldn't see it and weigh it and bombard it, it didn't exist."

Tom set the basket on the blanket. "Not any more." He sat down, propping his back against the trunk of the tree. "In fact, in quantum physics we deal mainly with phantoms. Far more exists that we're unable to see and measure than that which we can. There may even be six or more dimensions that we know virtually nothing about."

"Six dimensions!" Christi sat on the blanket and took the food from the basket. "I thought there were just three—up, down and sideways."

"Oh, no, not any more. You're back in the Newtonian Age. We thought we lived in a four-dimensional world, the three you mentioned plus time. But now we believe there are at least ten dimensions, six of which we know little about."

Christi handed Tom a sandwich. "So where are the other six? I can't imagine!"

"Probably right here, curled up inside of the four we experience every day."

"What! What are you talking about? You mean other dimensions are curled up inside of you and me?" Christi took a bite of her sandwich.

"Maybe. Probably, in fact. There's still so much we don't know about our Universe. There's even a lot of matter that we can measure, but we can't identify its location. About ninety percent of all mass is still unexplained."

Christi opened her soda. "That's bizarre. So is that where you think ghosts live?"

"Probably not, but so many things we used to believe were true have fallen by the wayside. You have to be open to almost any possibility. Maybe people who see ghosts have just developed the ability to communicate with one or more of these other dimensions. Perhaps they have somehow overcome the barriers between dimensions that limit most of us."

"Tom, please eat. I know you're hungry," Christi admonished. "The last big development in physics I heard about was the Big Bang. What ever happened to that?"

Tom bit into his sandwich. "It's now widely accepted, although a new theory that's been proposed attempts to explain what happened before the Big Bang."

"So what was there before the Big Bang? Have you found God yet?"

"Well, now that you mention it, that is a pretty good description of what may have preceded the Big Bang. According to this new theory, infinity was filled with vibrations of infinite frequency and amplitude in every direction in time. That's about as close to omnipotent and omniscient as you can get!"

Christi thought a moment. "So why did this infinite energy become finite? Why not just stick with God, instead of messing it up with all this stuff?"

"That's what the philosophers since the beginning of time have been trying to figure out—why did God bother to create us? It's now hypothesized that the act of creation was the blocking of these infinite waves by some kind of interference to form waves of finite frequency and amplitude. When that happened, matter was formed."

Christi looked at the sunset as it filled the horizon. "Maybe that wasn't the act of creation. Maybe that was the act of separation. I mean, when we separated from God."

"Hmmm. You might have something there. But we now know we aren't actually separate. There's this string theory, the theory that something resembling bands of energy, like strings, actually fills the Universe and connects everything. That's why we say the spin of a molecule can thunder through the Universe. Nothing happens without affecting everything else. Even thoughts are a form of energy. In reality, we are so interconnected that even our thoughts affect one another. Your every thought affects everyone else on this planet—the whole Universe, in fact."

"So we didn't really separate from God? We just created the illusion this had happened, then believed our own illusion?"

"Yeah, as a matter of fact. You pick this stuff up real fast." He took a gulp of soda. "Now there's even evidence that in order for anything to exist—matter, energy, anything—there has to be an equal counterbalancing vibration. I mean, an anti-universe has to exist to balance the matter in this Universe."

Christi poked Tom's arm. "You mean there might be another United States somewhere? Just like this one?"

"Not just like this one as far as what's going on there. It just has to have the same mass as this one. And it has to be spinning in an opposite direction in time."

"Wow! It's a good thing I studied law." Christi laughed. "I don't know if I can deal with time going forward and backward at the same time. Is this Physics 101 or is it graduate level stuff?" She munched on the last of her sandwich.

"It's not all that difficult. Just think about it like this. Time is actually spinning. But for there to be balance, when it spins in one direction, an equal amount of energy must be spinning in the opposite direction. If time is moving in one direction, which we know it is, it has to also be moving in the other direction or everything would spin off, out of control. It's actually a simple concept. It's just that we were stuck for so long in Newtonian physics, it's hard for us to let go of those old ideas. We wanted to believe like Newton, that it was as simple as gravity causing the apple to fall off the tree onto the ground. But that left too many unanswered questions."

Christi smiled. "Now you sound like a college professor, Tom. But I still don't see how ghosts fit into all of this."

"Well, with all these discoveries and the new information that's being reported every day, perhaps what we call ghosts is actually communication in some fashion with a parallel Universe. It's just a thought. It's not what I teach my students."

"I'll have to think about it. It's pretty interesting, actually. Maybe there's a quantum physics book for lawyers that I can read."

Tom nodded. "You lawyers could use it. A little quantum physics might help our system of justice find some balance. Sure needs it."

Christi lay back on the blanket and stared into the distant sky. "I know. If we continue the way we are we'll destroy ourselves." The sun slipped below the horizon. A chill breeze blew around them and she pulled the blanket over herself. "When laws are used for personal gain or to benefit a few at the expense of the greater good, we're doomed. There must be a better way. And time—which ever way it is spinning—time is of the essence."

CHAPTER FIVE

After more than two weeks in her new home the water pipes continued to spew rust. Christi lugged her basket of laundry out to her car. It was midmorning when she arrived at the laundromat. Alone, she loaded clothes into two washing machines, dropped her quarters into the meters, then headed up the street to visit the local plumber, Billy Waldrop.

There was no problem getting new plumbing installed on credit, as long as a sizeable deposit was paid in advance. In this rural area, much of Waldrop's work was done on credit. Problem was, he couldn't get to it for another month. "Patience is a virtue," he told Christi as she left.

She returned to the laundromat, still uninhabited, but two other machines had clothes churning around in sudsy water visible through the window in the doors. Her wash was finished. She put both loads into the over-sized dryer then set out on foot toward the county courthouse. There were a couple of law offices on the courthouse square she wanted to visit.

It was a pleasant walk to the courthouse, just a couple of blocks, past the local businesses on the short main street. Directly across from the courthouse entrance was a small, white frame building with a sign hanging above the door.

Patrick Hayes, Esquire

Attorney at Law

a.k.a. "Happy"

Pleased to be of service!

"Quaint," she thought as she opened the door and stepped into the small reception area. The musty smell of old books greeted her.

The metal desk sitting a few feet from the door was empty. A short hallway off the reception area led to two doors across from each other.

"Yoohoo. Anyone here?" she called.

"I'm back here," answered a man's voice. "Please come on back."

The voice came from the doorway down the hall on the left. Christi ventured into the small office. Behind a large oak desk sat an elderly man with a ruddy round face. She smiled at how he resembled a leprechaun. His right hand lay on the page of an open book.

"Hello. My name is Christi Daniel. I've recently moved here. I'm an attorney."

He turned toward her but his milky white eyes with faint blue irises could not see. He was blind.

"Happy to make your acquaintance," he said standing, extending his right hand in her general direction. His handshake was firm. "Please have a seat. Everyone calls me Happy. Hap for short. I heard a big city lawyer had moved into the old Tyler place. That must be you."

"Has to be me. I just came to town on a few errands. Thought it was time I started meeting people. It's a big change from D.C., but I love it here. At least I think I'm going to love it here."

"What brings you way out here?" Hap asked jovially. "As you said, it's a far cry from practicing law in the Nation's Capital."

"I'd about had my fill of that. If it can't be any better than that, I don't want to practice law. How do you like it here?"

"Well, my wife is my assistant. She reads the cases and statutes to me. I can get a few things in braille, but mainly I rely on her. I probably couldn't practice in the city. But here, people are pretty accommodating."

Christi leaned back in her chair. She felt at ease with this gentle man. "What type of cases do you mainly handle?"

"Everything from A to Z. Traffic tickets, wills, real estate closings, some divorces, although I try to steer clear of those fights. A little criminal work, mostly misdemeanors. Kids getting into mischief and ending up in Juvenile Court. That sort of thing. Every few years we might have a murder. You planning to do any legal work around here?"

"I hope to. Eventually. If I can round up some clients."

"What type of work did you do in the Capital?"

It seemed so long ago and far away, Christi had to think. "I did civil litigation. Mostly insurance defense work. Any need for that type of work around here?"

"Nope. I reckon you can't be too choosy if you want enough cases to pay the mortgage. You better plan on learning how to write wills and settle estates. Most everybody is related to everyone else so we generally try to work it out some other way. But you can count on people dying from time to time."

"Do you know anywhere I could rent an office? Just something small?"

"Sure do. Got one right across the hall. Since my partner died, it's been mostly used for storage. But if you're not looking for anything too fancy, it's a law office."

"But you don't even know me. I can get you references."

"I've got a pretty good feel for people. I wouldn't have offered if you didn't qualify."

She beamed. "It would certainly fit in with my plan to practice in the country. I don't know much about writing wills or settling estates. But I can learn."

"And I can teach you, with June's help, of course. June is my wife."

Christi hesitated. Could she trust making such a decision so quickly? Perhaps she could just let her instinct govern, like Hap did. "Yes, I think I'd like to do that—to rent your spare office. How much is the rent?"

"Well, I can't provide you any secretarial help. June answers the phone and does my work, but I'm so dependent on her she couldn't help you much. Seventy-five dollars would be more than enough."

"Seventy-five dollars a week isn't much rent," objected Christi.

"Not a week, a month. My rent for the whole office is only two hundred a month. This is country."

"Mr. Hayes, I mean Hap, you just got yourself a tenant. But I have to split the rent with you, at least pay a hundred a month. I have a computer, so don't worry about secretarial help. I don't expect I'll be writing many long briefs. And I'll put an answering machine on my phone."

The front door opened and closed. "That's my wife June.... June, guess what," Hap called down the hall. "You went to lunch and I got us a tenant. How's that for good work!"

A slender gray-haired woman with soft blue eyes entered the office. "I'll have to go out more often," she said. "I'm June Hayes. Happy to meet you."

The women shook hands. "My name is Christi Daniel. Pleased to meet you, too. I just moved to the old Tyler place from Washington, D.C. I'm looking forward to practicing law in the country for a change."

"That office will have to be cleaned up, but June can help you," Hap offered. "It's already furnished, if you don't mind early attic decor."

"I don't mind a bit. I'm sure it will be fine and will help me look the part of a country lawyer. I like old things." Christi flinched at her choice of words, but Hap and June both laughed.

"Then you'll like both of us," June said. "Hap was worried about who could pick up some of his caseload. We're not as fast as we used to be. We're pleased to have you join us."

"Can I start next week?" Christi asked. They agreed and the deal was closed with a handshake.

Christi briskly crossed the courthouse green. "Can this be real?" she wondered. Is it possible for major decisions to fall into place so easily?

Returning to the laundromat she found her clothes neatly folded in piles on the folding table. Someone else's clothes were spinning in the over-sized dryer. A quick inventory of her clothes and they were all there. "This is like living in a different world," she thought. Had she traveled to one of those other dimensions Tom had described?

On her way home Christi stopped at the local grocery store for a few items, including bottled water. As she was checking out, the young woman tending the cash register said she had heard someone had moved into the old Tyler place. "The Tylers were only there for a couple of generations, but that was a mite longer than the Cobbs, who owned it last. So we still call it the ol' Tyler place," the young woman explained in a distinctive southern dialect.

Christi confirmed that she indeed was the new owner of the old Tyler place.

"You know, you don't have to buy drinking water," the young woman continued. "We mostly sell that to tourists who pass through. Whenever anyone around here has trouble with their water they go to Sam Taylor about a half mile up the road. He has a spring and gives water to anyone 'round here who needs it. If you got the containers, you can git your drinking water there 'til the pipes in your house git fixed."

"Pipes fixed!" thought Christi. How had news she was having trouble with her water pipes traveled so quickly? Did the cashier also know the color of her underwear—a tidbit shared by whomever had folded her clothes at the laundromat? Attachment to secrets apparently had no place here.

Her last stop was the hardware store. A new shovel, rake and hoe, and packages of seeds for the old garden plot behind the house. It was planting time.

Christi spent the remaining hours of the spring afternoon pulling dead weeds from the past and turning the rich soil with her new shovel. A serious backache might be the price she would pay, but no matter. She was as close to Heaven on Earth as she could imagine.

As the afternoon waned, she put the tools in the shed. She ate supper sitting at the old table watching the sunset. Multiple rainbows created by the cut-glass panels above the bay window danced across the ceiling. "Confirmation," she thought. This is a special place, indeed.

CHAPTER SIX

For three days Christi pulled weeds, worked the ground, and planted neat rows of flowers and vegetables. Every muscle in her body ached, but she was pleased to have completed her initial round of planting. After soaking in hot, rusty water, she went to bed early, reading for a short time then falling into a deep sleep.

At some point during the night Christi awoke, startled. She couldn't see in the darkness, but she could hear men's voices coming from downstairs. Someone had surely broken into her house! Christi could hear her heart beat; her limbs were cold. She lay motionless in bed, listening, trying to discern what was being said. . . . How bizarre? It sounded like a normal conversation. And no property was being disturbed.

Her courage bolstered, she slid off the side of the bed, then stood motionless for a moment to see if she had been detected. When the men's conversation appeared unaffected by her movement, she inched her way across the bedroom floor, hoping it wouldn't squeak. Each time it did, she froze and again listened to see if anyone was coming up the stairs.

The discussion continued. Whoever was in her house had probably not detected her presence, yet. If they did, they weren't interested. Her courage grew. She slipped through the door and tiptoed toward the top of the stairs. As she stood near the railing, she could barely make out some of their words. It seemed several men were in the dining room, gathered around the table having some sort of meeting.

One man, apparently in charge of the meeting, was referred to as "Worshipful" and another as "Venerable." The others were referred to as

"Dear Brother" or "Very Dear Brethren." Was some sort of church service being conducted in her dining room? In the middle of the night?

"No home can shelter both love and fear," said the man called Venerable. "As this Nation is our home, it, too, cannot shelter both love and fear."

"But the fearful aren't ready," said a man merely called "Brother." "We need a strategy, a plan, to advance the multitude beyond the level of apprentice."

"My Dear Brother," said Worshipful conducting the meeting. "We must trust. The third millennium is upon us; we have no choice but to proceed. We are here in answer to the call of the Angel of Destiny. Although we cannot presently see how it will unfold and are not privy to the details, that is no different than when we began this New Order of the Ages. We at no time had anything more than trust to guide us, trust and signs at critical junctures to assure us our actions were consistent with the Ancient Wisdom."

Christi wrinkled her brow. "Destiny? What signs? What New Order of the Ages are they talking about?" she wondered. There was further discussion that she could not make out. Edging her way down the top three stairs, she leaned as far down the railing as she dared. Hanging on with both hands, one above and one below her stretched body, she hoped to peek into the dining room, but could not.

The meeting continued. Several men tried to speak at once when Worshipful indicated that Venerable had the floor.

"We can rest in knowing that what appears to be separated from its Divine Source has a complement that will appear to provide balance," he said.

The words were so clear, Christi was sure she had heard them correctly. And yet they made no sense.

He continued. "As our Dear Worshipful has stated, we have been given the sign that indicates the time is now. The table has at last been returned to our meeting place, here, where we so often came together as we developed our vision of a Nation under God."

Instantly, Christi lost her grip. She tumbled down several stairs making a terrible racket. Quickly picking herself up she stepped closer to the bottom of the stairs and again leaned over the banister, peering into the dining room. The room was empty, the voices were gone. She descended to the bottom of the stairs and walked into the dining room. The table sat in all its grandeur, undisturbed. George Washington peered down from his place above the mantel, seemingly quite content.

Christi was trembling. Was she going mad? Walking back upstairs, bits and pieces of the strange conversation fleeted through her mind. What did it mean? Had it even been real? She returned to bed, sorting through the words she had heard. Falling asleep, she began to dream of being an aide to a great general in a mighty army.

CHAPTER SEVEN

The small law office was ready for business. Christi had painted it herself. The walls were hung with her college degrees, court admissions, and Virginia and Washington, D.C. bar certifications.

She had grown fond of Hap and June. Down-to-Earth people, what her mother would call "salt of the Earth." Hap's integrity was impeccable and, if anything, he underbilled his clients. She also discovered he was an exceptionally well-educated man, apparently having spent years absorbing knowledge, instead of activity more physical in nature. He began introducing Christi to several new areas of law.

Sam Taylor had become a friend who graciously provided her with unlimited quantities of pure spring water. The first sprouts had begun to appear in her garden. She felt life would once again become routine when the plumbing was replaced and a bathroom installed upstairs in her house.

But Christi continued to be bothered by her "dream" about the meeting in her house. She called it a dream, for lack of a better term, even though it had seemed so real. She had shared its vivid details with no one, intimidated by what others might think if she revealed such a secret. But one day at lunch with Hap and June she ventured to ask Hap if he had ever heard of anything called a "New Order of the Ages."

"New Order of the Ages... New Order of the Ages...." Hap repeated thoughtfully. "That seems to ring a bell, but only if you translate it into Latin. I've heard of 'Novus Ordo Seclorum,' if that's any help."

"Nope. I've never heard of that, so that doesn't help," Christi said disheartened. The subject was dropped until it came time to pay for the meal.

"June, leave a Novus Ordo Seclorum for the waitress," Hap said jokingly as the three rose from the table in the small restaurant near the courthouse.

"What are you talking about?" asked June. "I don't know any waitress that needs one of those, whatever it is."

"A dollar bill," said Hap, as though everyone should know. "You're the one who reads for me. I must have you read a dollar bill."

"Oh, I forgot!" Turning to Christi, June explained. "I gave Hap a book in braille about the Great American Seal. It came complete with a clay relief of the Seal, and Hap fingers that thing constantly each time he reads the book. He's probably memorized it."

"I'll leave the tip," Christi offered. She pulled her wallet from her purse and slipped a worn dollar bill from its pocket. As she looked at it, her gaze was returned by a single eye enshrined in rays of light atop a pyramid. On a banner arched beneath the pyramid were inscribed the words "Novus Ordo Seclorum." New Order of the Ages.

Christi's mind began to search for a connection. Could this have anything to do with the dream she had had?

When the day finally arrived to commence renovation of the plumbing, Billy Waldrop and his helper arrived bright and early. First, they had to locate the old pipes and to determine where the new ones should be installed.

"Miss Daniel, I've checked all around. I think the best location for the pipes to the upstairs is behind one of these panels by the dining room fireplace." Waldrop diagramed the plans with his waving hands. "We'll put the bath in the small room next to your bedroom, bring the pipes across the floor, down through the wall here next to the chimney, and join them with the pipes in the kitchen directly below. That should work. Main hang-up is we have to take this panel off. It'll mess up your nice paint job. Might mess up the panel, too," he said regretfully.

"That's a small price to pay for a nice large bathroom. The panel is painted so any blemishes can be painted over. Let's begin," she directed.

"Then we may as well start here." Waldrop pointed to the narrow panel to the right of the fireplace. He left and returned with a hammer, chisel and screwdriver. He began by tapping the end of the chisel behind the trim around the panel just under the cornice. It easily sprang free. He continued down the side of the panel with no difficulty until he came to the area of the chair rail. Here it would not budge.

"Let me try it down here," he said moving to the area near the floor. It, too, easily came loose, but as he moved up toward the chair rail, it remained firmly in tact. "There must be something holding it here in the middle. I'll have to chip away some of the plaster around this area to see if I can figure out what's going on. Is that what you want me to do, Miss?" he asked looking distressed.

"Do whatever you have to do. We've come too far to stop now," she replied.

Waldrop placed the chisel just below the chair rail and pointed it upward. After a couple of taps there was a clinking sound.

"Sounds like there's a little metal casing in here, like a chamber for a lock," he said dubiously. "Maybe this panel used to open up and this is the lock. I'll have to pull this piece of chair rail off the panel to see what's under it."

Christi peered over his shoulder, watching as closely as she could without getting in his way. The wood trim squeaked as it was pried off the panel.

"Yes sir! Look at this, an old lock is hidden under here!" Waldrop exclaimed. "Someone sure went to a lot of trouble to hide this thing."

The exposed metal was rusty and weak. As Waldrop pried it open, the latch broke and the side of the panel sprung loose. But hinges hidden on the inside opposite the latch held tight. By rocking the panel back and forth they soon relinquished their hold.

Christi could see a niche in the wall behind the panel. A small pile of dirt fell out onto the floor. As Waldrop opened the panel, a bundle about a foot square and several inches deep lay at the bottom of the small compartment. On a shelf in the middle of the compartment were three candle holders, darkened with age.

"Well, Miss, I think you have yourself some buried treasure here," Waldrop said, matter-of-factly.

Christi knelt down to pick up the bundle. Dirt coated her hands and clothes. She brought a sheet to cover the top of the table where she placed the treasure. The outer layer was a large, heavy cloth. As she laid it open, she discerned a number of curious symbols painted on the inner side. They reminded her of the designs on the small apron hanging at Washington's waist in the engraving above the mantel. She compared the two. Some of the designs were similar.

The largest design was at the bottom center of the heavy cloth—a checkerboard with stairs ascending at the back of the board and columns on either side of the stairs. In each lower corner was some type of rectangular drawing. Toward the center of the cloth were three columns. To the left of the columns was a curious design that looked like a wide V with an inverted thin V on top of it. To the right was a picture of a key. Above the three columns was an open book with the same curious V design painted as though it were lying on top, and a ladder rising above the book. There were several other smaller designs, but the one that struck Christi was at the very top. A single eye surrounded by beams of light shining in all directions. She immediately recalled the eye atop the pyramid on the dollar bill.

Christi examined the objects that had been wrapped in the large cloth—a Bible, an L-shaped piece of metal and an instrument that was V-shaped. All appeared to be extremely old.

Waldrop picked up the dark L-shaped metal object and rubbed his hands over it. "I'll be darned. A carpenter's square! Look at this, it's so old you can barely see the marks where the inches are. This other thing must be a compass." He held the V-shaped instrument up for Christi to see as he demonstrated how one end could be used to circle around the other stationary point to draw a perfect circle. She recognized it from her high school geometry class.

"Why would this old Bible be with carpenter tools?" she asked, picking up the ancient tome. A small cloud of dust scattered about as she blew on the cover of the Bible. Inside the front cover were words written in elegant old script. Christi struggled to read the inscription.

To our V∴ D∴ Brother, Geo. Washington
On the occasion of his healing as an Antient Mason
Lodge of Social and Military Virtue, No. 227
Grand Lodge of Ireland
On the Festival of the Nativity of
St. John the Evangelist
This 27 day of December, 1756
In the City of Philadelphia
Colonies of America
Praise be to God.

Christi felt her body shiver. She glanced at the engraving of Washington above the mantel. He calmly looked down upon the scene.

Christi rubbed her fingers on her chin, thinking. "I have a friend at the Smithsonian," she said. "She specializes in American Indian arti-facts, but perhaps she can help determine if these things have any value. Maybe they need to be in a museum, if they have some importance."

She placed the items, including the three candlesticks, in a card-board box. The two plumbers continued with their work and Christi occupied herself in the kitchen where she baked a batch of cookies. Her mind dwelt on the meaning of the mysterious find.

CHAPTER EIGHT

T he new plumbing installation took days longer to complete than Christi expected. One difficulty after another had slowed the work. "Patience," admonished Billy Waldrop. "With an old structure like this, you just work with it 'til you convince it to cooperate." At last, clean hot water ran into the new upstairs bath.

With this project completed, a visit to Boston was in order. Friends were graduating from MIT and Christi and Tom were invited to the festivities. Christi welcomed the break from her new life and its accompanying mysteries.

Friday morning she packed her bag, including photos of the items found in the hidden compartment by the fireplace, and descended the stairs. As she headed toward the front door, she noticed a paper lying on the table in the dining room. She knew she hadn't left it there. It was a note written in elegant but difficult-to-read script, similar to that in the old Bible found behind the panel. "This must be a prank," Christi thought as she deciphered the message.

> *Dear Miss Christi:*
>
> *Please excuse my directness in informing you of my purpose.*
>
> *I have given much consideration to how we might best make the conscious acquaintance of one another. Since the circumstances are such that you will not find them ordinary, I choose to be most attentive to your possible discomfort in advance.*
>
> *Please consider how you might best accommodate experiencing the presence of a discarnate being, and indeed, even if such would be of interest to you.*

With kindest regards.
Your humble servant,
Geo. Washington

Christi read the note several times, each time picking out a different phrase to examine. Too late to make a copy, she folded it and tucked it in her baggage.

The afternoon flight to Boston was turbulent. Christi tried to study materials from a seminar on recent developments in trusts and estates law, but couldn't concentrate. The note left on the table was foremost in her thoughts.

She felt invaded. Obviously Waldrop had told everyone about the treasure they had found behind the panel in the dining room. She had become an easy target for pranksters. They just walk into her home, at will, and leave notes. Embarrassed and humiliated, she presumed they had heard the news about the color of her underwear, as well.

As Tom drove her to a restaurant to meet several friends for dinner, she discussed her distress. "Billy Waldrop, the plumber who installed the new bathroom upstairs, he must have told everyone in town about the Bible we found with George Washington's name in it. This morning someone left me a prank note from good ol' George. I must have become the village idiot."

"What does the note say?"

"Something about will I meet him," she said indignantly. She took the note from her pocket and read it in a deep voice, imitating a man. "Maybe he wants a date. What do you think?" she asked trying to make light of this development.

"That's pretty clever. How did they get into your house?"

"The door was unlocked. Hardly anyone locks their doors. I soon got out of the habit after moving there, so they just popped in and left the note," she explained confidently. "I'll have to start locking my door."

"You can read the note at dinner tonight. Everyone will get a kick out of it," Tom suggested.

"Don't you dare mention this note! I have no intention of telling anyone but you what a fool I've become in my new community," she protested.

After dinner, Tom, Christi and their friends continued their congenial chat while having dessert. The topic turned to physics, but this time with a new twist from Julie, the wife of one of the physics graduate students and a Ph.D. candidate in psychology. She noted that the discontinuity being discussed in relation to the release of atomic energy reminded her of the discontinuity experienced by people who have near-death experiences.

There was a silent pause as the others tried to follow this abrupt shift in thinking.

"Well, Tom just said the Newtonian principle that all change is continuous, that for every physical effect there must be a physical cause, has been disproved. He said it now appears some events occur with no measurable physical cause at all," Julie explained.

Antonio, Julie's handsome, dark-haired husband, flashed his eyes at her and smiled. "Julie! That's impressive. You should get a degree in physics."

"No thanks," Julie said. "I'm content with learning physics by osmosis, from you."

"Julie, tell us what you mean about near-death experiences," Christi requested.

"Tom said that mathematically they can compute a description of atomic behavior. But that description is as though the progression were occurring in linear time when in fact it isn't," Julie responded, obviously no novice to these concepts. "That's a perfect description of what I'm finding in a study I am conducting of people who have had near-death experiences. They all describe the experience in language that comports with our thinking in linear time, but they all insist they were outside of time when they had the experience. Everything occurs at once."

Christi and Tom exchanged glances. Another synchronicity between new physics and experiences that may relate to other dimensions?

Having captured everyone's attention, Julie continued. "Some people believe we are undergoing a rapid evolutionary change, evolving from Homo Sapiens to what some want to call 'Homo Universalis.' Some have used the term 'Homo Noeticus,' man with multiple senses. But whatever you call it, it's a human who has fully-developed multiple senses, not just the five senses with which Homo Sapiens have customarily operated."

"You know," Antonio said, hoping to be supportive of his wife's unconventional observation, "I have sometimes wondered how major steps in evolution have occurred. As some of the population developed new skills, did this cause conflict with those who lagged behind? Was there segregation or integration of the new breed? Did they turn on one another or did the more advanced exploit those who were regressive?"

"Perhaps we can find some clues in what is happening now," Julie suggested. "The new trend in evolution is believed to be toward a more visionary, intuitive being. How are such people treated in our society?"

"If your theory is right," Christi observed, "those moving into this advanced stage of evolution are probably more spiritual than religious. Traditional religious teaching is closely tied to the concept of linear time, just as Newtonian physics was. You sinned in the past, feel guilty and do penance now so you can receive the reward after you die—all along the progression of linear time."

"Yes," Julie replied. "But those who are spiritual often report experiencing angels now, and those who have had near-death experiences report they have already experienced what they believe to be God or Heaven. The point is, they do so outside of linear time. But when they return, our present vocabulary is so limited in this area it requires that they report their experience as though it occurred sequentially. Many claim the total experience was instantaneous, not sequential or related to time in any way. They apparently are using senses that are beyond the five we have traditionally relied upon."

"Julie," Tom interjected, "assume it were true that we are evolving toward a new stage in human development. You know, like when Neanderthal man made the transition toward Cro-Magnon man. And assume that our next stage of evolution will be a more spiritual, more psychic human being."

"This may be the hypothesis of the century," Antonio said laughing. "Buckle your seat belts for this one."

"No, seriously," Tom said. "If that's true, isn't it also true that major changes will necessarily occur in society, as well?"

"Yes!" Christi added excitedly. "For example, we would need new laws. We would have to govern this new genesis of humankind differently."

"An excellent point," noted Julie. "I hadn't even considered that aspect of such a major development in evolution."

The discussion was interrupted by dishes rattling noisily near by. Realizing they were the last customers in the restaurant and the waiters were anxious to hurry them along, Antonio picked up the tab. "That's a good point to end on," he said. "For the time being, at least."

Tom was intrigued by Christi's photos of the contents of the secret compartment and the inscription in the Bible about George Washington being "healed as an Antient Mason." He proposed that they stop by the library to see what they could find on the Masons. "The

MIT library probably isn't the best place to research the Masons, but maybe we can find something," he suggested.

They scanned the card index and found a small book written in Scotland in 1910 entitled *A Brief Description of Freemasonry History and Philosophy*. Appearing to be on point, they headed to the stacks to search for it and found themselves in a remote corner of the library.

"Here it is," Christi called softly to Tom. "Let's take it to that empty desk in the corner."

She opened the book and quickly perused the index. "Where shall we start, history or philosophy?"

"Oh, lets begin with philosophy. All I know about the Masons is that they're a secret order. Are they the ones who ride in parades, or are those the Shriners? See what it says about their philosophy, especially in the seventeen and eighteen hundreds, if it's there."

Christi began to read:

PHILOSOPHY.

It is the inherent nature of man to want explanations for his existence. Throughout history the pursuit of such knowledge has been accomplished through many modalities, but one of which is Freemasonry.

In the view of most ancient civilizations, the material world was but a small component of the whole. Spiritual realms beyond the reach of the multitudes were considered to be an essential ingredient in the composition of the Universe. The quest for knowledge of the non-material world, and the Natural Laws that governed this alternate realm, is an essential objective of Freemasonry.

As in the ancient world, Freemasonry employs diverse symbolism as a means of instruction to teach morality and build character as a candidate for Masonry advances through Degrees. Many of the symbols are drawn from the medieval stone masons' guilds that are the genesis of Freemasonry. However, latitude for personal interpretation of the meaning of each symbol is permitted, as it is the journey, the process of becoming a Mason, that is important in developing morality and character, not the particular form the ritual takes.

In order to be a Freemason, a basic belief in a supreme being is mandatory, but is not limited to the Christian image of God. Latitude is accorded to individual cultures with regard to what form the unified deity may take. Equality, tolerance, respect, morality and charity are essential premises to which a Freemason must subscribe.

In the ancient tradition, buildings, and cathedrals in particular, were often physical metaphors for the spiritual realm. Architects had knowledge of philosophical considerations as well as engineering skills. It is the wedding of these two realms, the spiritual and the physical, that is the foundation of Freemasonry. The physical world, the psyche, the spiritual and the divine are viewed as being the stages of the journey.

Drawing upon the tradition of masonry, the candidate progresses through three levels, symbolized as the three stories of a temple. The Ground Floor experienced by the Entered Apprentice represents the Earth; the Middle Chamber experienced by the intermediate Degree of Fellowcraft represents the Soul, and the top story, the Holy of Holies, experienced by the Master Mason represents the Spirit. The Fourth Level, Divinity, is represented by the Glory, a star emitting beams of light.

In each Lodge there must always be what are called the Three Great Lights, namely the Volume of the Sacred Law, the Square and the Compass.

"Tom! That's what was in the panel by the fireplace—a Bible, a carpenter's square and a compass!"

He looked over her shoulder at the small text as she continued to read aloud.

> One light, the square, is the perpendicular plumb combined with the level and united at right angles. With it the mason cuts rectangular stones for the building and lays them true and just. The square represents the Psyche. Upon progressing to the level of Master Mason, the square is closed with a third line to form the symbol of Pythagoras, or the great secret of the Universe.
>
> A second light, the compass, is the symbol of circles and of the celestial spheres. This represents the divine intermingled with the physical. It represents the Spirit.
>
> The third light, the Sacred Writings, represents the Divinity, the Divine Source from which all is derived.
>
> The ornaments of the Lodge are the chequered pavement which represents the Universe as it appears to those incarnate on the physical plane. The alternate black and white represents the easy and difficult, active and passive, forming a unified whole made of individual pieces.

"Tom!" Christi again exclaimed. "The heavy cloth that was wrapped around these things when I found them, it has a checkered black and white design at the bottom! That's on Washington's apron, too. Where was I?" she asked, turning again to the book.

> At the level of the Psyche, duality is represented by two columns, one Doric and one Corinthian.

"Oh, my god! That's on the cloth too. There are columns, Tom, just like it says." Her voice was quaking.

> The Principle of Duality holds that whenever the

perception of separation from Divine Source exists, its complement also must exist to assure balance. Symbols of duality are often repeated as a reminder that when a sense of separation from the Divinity occurs, polarization and opposition are inevitable.

"Tom, this is uncanny." Christi handed the small book to him. "Here, you read, please. I'm shaking too much to even hold the book."

"Let me find something on history. I feel like we're unveiling a secret that's been lost for generations." Tom began to read.

The earliest Masonic Lodges almost certainly developed in England in the seventeenth century. Early in the century there were many prominent and highly educated citizens knowledgeable of the Kabalah of the Hebrews and the Alchemists and Hermetic philosophers. The Mysteries that had their roots in ancient Egypt, Greece and Rome, had been rediscovered and became popular among the intelligentsia during the Renaissance. As the seventeenth century progressed, these mystical traditions became increasingly viewed with suspicion by the monarchy, possibly being associated with witchcraft or perceived as a source of personal spiritual power that could undermine allegiance to the king. The monarchy's hostility forced their observance to become more discreet.

By the middle of the seventeenth century many of the members of the London Company of Masons were speculative Masons, those accepted into the philosophical fraternity without being trained in masonry, which was a means of conducting the pursuit of mystical knowledge more safely. At the same time, the operative guild was in decline.

The open practice of Freemasonry did not begin until 1717 when four Lodges came together in London to form the Grand Lodge. The symbolism used by these speculative Masons was drawn from the Operative Mason's Craft and the mystical tradition of the earlier period. This enabled highly educated men, fearful of their pursuit of mystical interests in public, to do so within the secrecy of the Lodge.

Undoubtedly this was compatible with the spiritual needs of the time, as the establishment of Lodges quickly spread to other parts of Europe and the American colonies. Ireland had its first Grand Lodge around 1725, France probably had a Grand Lodge shortly thereafter, Scotland in 1736, Germany in 1737, Denmark in 1745, and so it grew.

"Hey, listen to this, Christi," Tom said, nudging her arm. "This part is about the American Colonies."

In the American Colonies, Lodges were established even prior to those established in many nations in Europe, the first being formed in Boston in 1733. The craft proved extremely popular among the Colonial educated and propertied classes in the eighteenth century. It gained importance in the Colonies even prior to the American Revolution, and indeed, a division between the Lodges may have expedited the severance of ties between the Colonies and the Mother Country.

"Tom, we must go," Christi said abruptly. "I've got to catch my plane."

"Christi, you're still shaking and pale. Are you okay?"

"The meeting... in *my* house. The note... addressed to me. I'm afraid, Tom. I don't understand what's happening."

Tom placed the book back on the shelf, noting its exact location so he could return. Then, caressing Christi's shoulders to steady her, they walked away from the dark corner toward the light.

CHAPTER NINE

Christi arrived at work early Monday morning, determined to see Hap before he began meeting with clients. After exchanging initial pleasantries, she got to the point.

"Hap, you've done so much for me. Shared your office space when you didn't even know me. Helped me in new areas of law. But I... I may not be cut out for this small town stuff. This might not work out."

"What are you talking about? Your new clients seem pleased with your work and you're doing well."

The knot in her throat tightened. "I know, but if I'm not respected in the community, if I'm viewed as an outsider and people ridicule me behind my back, I'm afraid I'll hurt your practice."

"Christi, I've sensed for some time that there were some under-currents brewing. Looks like they might be coming to a head. What's going on?" Hap prodded gingerly.

"That's the problem. There's too much going on. I thought I could find peace and quiet here, but my life is in more turmoil now than ever. Things keep happening that I don't understand. Everyone in town knows what I'm doing—not that I'm doing anything I want to hide." She was glad Hap couldn't see the tears gathering in her eyes.

"I knew when I met you that you were on a journey," Hap replied gently. "Anyone who had as much as you did in your practice in Washington, but wasn't satisfied, and would plunge toward the opposite extreme is clearly searching for answers. In your case, you're not only searching for answers, you're also looking for the part you are to play in finding those answers."

"True, I'm dissatisfied about many things. I worry about our legal system, the decline of society, the future of the world. But I can't change any of them," she said wringing her hands in her lap.

"When you first walked into my office you told me about your dissatisfaction with our legal system. I knew right then there was a problem. Not so much with the legal system, although that certainly exists. But your anger. As long as you project so much anger, your vision is distorted. You can neither see the problem nor your role in fixing it."

Hap's words stung Christi like riled-up hornets. "For a man who's blind you sure talk a lot about vision and seeing," she blurted out angrily. Then she gasped and covered her mouth. Her hand dropped to her heart. "Oh, Hap. I'm sorry. You know I didn't mean that. That just shows you how upset I am." She wiped a tear from her cheek with the back of her hand.

"Christi, I'm not offended. I've long since released any attachment I had to feeling sorry for myself because of my physical blindness. I wish I could share some of the insight... there I go again. It's difficult. So much of our vocabulary about understanding and knowledge is expressed in terms of physical sight, when in fact they're unrelated." Then Hap chuckled. "Long ago I discovered that some of the blindest people I know have 20-20 vision. In fact, I think being able to see the physical world must be an obstacle to experiencing what I experience."

"What do you mean... what you experience?"

"It seems that the clutter people see around them on the physical plane deludes them into thinking that's all there is, that there's nothing else. How wrong they are. If you're not stuck in a four-dimensional world, there are so many other dimensions to experience."

Other dimensions? Tom mentioned other dimensions in their discussion under the apple tree. And so did Julie, in Boston on Friday. As Christi reflected, her thoughts were interrupted by voices down the hall.

"Good morning," she heard June say. "Hap can see you in just a minute."

June poked her head in the door. "Mr. Martin is here, Hap. And Christi, there's a call on hold for you. It's a young man named Mark Reuben."

"Thanks." Christi darted out the door before June noticed her red eyes.

"Good morning, Mark," she said, picking up the receiver.

"Hello. Christi?"

"Yes. How are things at Harp, Harrison & Humphrey?"

"Not so good. I was terminated last week. But if I hadn't been, I would have quit. So I'm looking for a job. I thought it would be easy, but it's a tight market. My wife gave birth to our son just before I was fired. I'm a dad now. I've got to get a job."

"Congratulations, about your son, I mean."

"Thanks. He's a great little guy. I'm calling to see if you'd be willing to give me a recommendation. I can't get one at Harp, needless to say."

"What happened?" Christi asked, hoping it hadn't been too brutal.

"With all the political involvement at the firm, a lot of clients took their work elsewhere. Some were major clients who covered much of the overhead. When I was preparing a final bill for a client, I was instructed to bill for time I hadn't put in on the case. I refused."

"That's the only thing you could have done. That won't be a strike against you." Christi tried to sound upbeat.

"Yeah, but that wasn't the ostensible reason for firing me," Mark replied glumly. "Someone changed a tickler I had entered in the computer for filing an appeal. I know I put the correct date in the system. I always double check. And I found several outdated printouts with the correct date entered. But I didn't notice the change until it was too late. I missed the filing deadline."

"It wasn't Smith's appeal, was it?"

"No, I never worked on that. I knew they had been wanting to get rid of me for some time. Anyone perceived to have liberal leanings, or who wasn't a WASP, had become suspect. I was treated like an outsider after you left. And, God knows, I wanted to leave, but I had to find a job first. I put out some quiet inquiries, but hadn't found anything when this disaster happened. But then... we Jews are used to being uprooted."

"Mark, don't view this as an opportunity to be a victim. Of course I'll give you an excellent reference," Christi said. "You're one of the most competent and honest attorneys I know. Too good to work for Harp. I'm sorry about what has happened, but it'll turn out for the best."

"Thanks, Christi. You were the only person I felt I could turn to. I should have helped you when you needed me."

"Forget it, Mark. I'm the perfect example of how everything always turns out for the best. I'm much better off where I am. By the way, I'm curious about one of the new associates who joined the firm earlier this year. Do you know how Virginia Goode is doing?"

"Yeah, she's doing real well. Fits right in. She recently began working half-time on cases for the firm and half-time on Harp's political career. He had a survey done to see if he'd be more likely to win an election in Virginia, Maryland or D.C. Rumor is he's considering running for the Senate. I'm sure she'll end up with a top-level job in his campaign."

"How is the party doing? The R.R.s, I mean."

"So well it's scary. The firm had a cash flow problem, but not the

R.R.s. They're raising money like they had a money tree—an orchard, in fact. They might take over the government at the rate they're going. You're lucky you left when you did."

"You're right, I am lucky. You'll be better off somewhere else, too. Just send me a copy of your resume and I'll put together a recommendation for you right away. I'll do whatever I can to help."

When Christi hung up the receiver she felt relieved and the urgency to change her course had dissipated. Mark's call seemed to have affirmed that she was better off now than before.

+≡·≡+

When Tom called later in the week, he asked Christi if she had decided what she was going to do about the letter from George Washington.

"What do you mean, do about it?" she asked curtly.

"Well, are you going to answer it? What if it isn't a joke? Is that an opportunity you'd take a chance on missing?"

Christi folded her arm across her chest and frowned. "Why don't you answer it, if you think it's such an opportunity?"

"The invitation was to you, Christi." Tom paused then resumed, his voice sounding less urgent. "Maybe he wants to talk to an attorney and not a physicist. Even if it's a prank, how could it hurt? Wouldn't it be better to play along with the joke than look like you were sour grapes over it? You should give it some thought, at least."

"And how do I reply? Do you have Mr. Washington's address?"

"Just leave the answer on the table. That's where the note to you was left. Whoever left it would most likely look there for your response."

"And what do you suggest I say? 'Dear Mr. Washington. Charmed by your nice invitation.'"

71

"Why don't you ask him why he wants to meet with you? Tell him you want to know what the meeting is about before you decide," Tom persisted.

"It sounds like you're more interested in this meeting than I am," she protested.

"I just think you ought to give it some thought. But it's up to you."

Christi was determined to make no commitment he might hold her to.

That evening, as Christi worked at the table on a client's file before going to bed, she thought about the discussion with Tom. What if he was right? Perhaps it wouldn't hurt to leave a note. She could leave it here tonight and throw it away first thing in the morning. She was sure the prankster wouldn't come in during the night, and she'd lock the door to make certain. Then she could tell Tom he was wrong, she had left a note and nothing happened. End of discussion. Taking pen in hand, she began to write.

Dear Mr. Washington,

Thank you for your kind note. I believe it is the first I ever received from a discarnate person, . . .

Scratch "person." Too tangible. "Being" is better.

so I don't quite know what the options are for such a meeting. But before making any commitments, I would like to inquire regarding the purpose of the meeting you propose, if it is not too disrespectful to do so.

Your ever trusting subject,

C.D.

She was content with the experiment. What a good way to conclude the joke yet be a good sport about it. She left the note on the old table next to her stack of work papers.

When Christi descended the stairs in the morning the note was lying on the table, right where she left it. "Thank goodness!" she thought. After breakfast she went to the dining room to gather her papers for work. As she reached for the note to throw it away she noticed the writing was different.

> *Dear Miss Christi:*
>
> *It is difficult to express how appreciative I am that you have chosen to respond to my correspondence. I am most pleased to inform you of my purpose, as it is of the highest in nature.*
>
> *I wish to discuss with you the Seven Spiritual Principles for Governing a People.*
>
> *Please advise me at your earliest convenience if this is an undertaking in which you are willing to engage.*
>
> *Your humble servant,*
>
> *Geo. Washington*

Christi stood motionless with the note in hand. She could feel her heart pounding deep in her chest. Had someone broken into her home again last night? Or was she entangled in events far beyond her comprehension?

CHAPTER TEN

Washington's second message made Christi wonder if she was losing her rational mind. A month passed and Christi told no one, not even Tom. She immersed herself in her work wanting all thoughts of these strange events to disappear. But they didn't.

"Psychiatrist! Isn't that a little extreme?" Tom said on the other end of the line.

"Sometimes I feel out of touch with reality, like I'm losing my mind," Christi explained. "I have all these questions running through my mind about the American Colonies, the Masons, this house. And the picture of George Washington above the mantel—it's so strange. I feel like he's alive."

"You're definitely not crazy," Tom said decidedly. "You just need to keep centered and see what happens. Here's a suggestion. Is it as beautiful a June morning there as it is here in Boston?"

Christi glanced out the window. "It looks like a pretty day outside."

"Why don't you go buy the Sunday paper and sit under the apple tree. Take it easy. You work yourself too hard, even when you don't have to."

"Maybe you're right. I haven't taken any time off for about a month."

After they spoke, she drove into town to the small grocery store that carried most of the necessities of country life, even several copies of the Washington Post on Sundays. Christi picked up the last copy, feeling lucky she got there before it was gone.

At the cash register she took out her wallet. As she pulled out a dollar bill, the eye at the pinnacle of the pyramid stared at her. She glanced at the inscriptions beneath the pyramid. "Novus Ordo Seclorum." "The Great Seal."

"Hap studied the Great Seal," she thought, recalling her discussion with Hap and June at lunch some time ago. She paid the clerk and hurried to her car. She drove directly to the home of Hap and June.

No one was at home. Through the open kitchen window, Christi could smell the aroma of chicken baking in the oven. Assuming they were at church she sat on the porch, enjoying the yard in glorious bloom. She soaked in the beauty of the flowering plants and shrubs that were everywhere. Hap was reportedly the gardener. June told Christi the nature spirits tell him what to plant and where, a remark Christi had assumed was a joke. The yard being so alive with nature, she speculated this claim might be true.

Hap and June soon arrived. "Well, fancy seeing you here," June said gaily as she stepped out of the car. "Just in time for Sunday lunch. I have a chicken roasting in the oven."

"If you don't mind, I'd love to have lunch with the two of you. I realize I'm uninvited, but I need some company today."

As they sat at the small dining table covered with a crisp white cloth, Christi raised the issue of the Great Seal.

"Hap, do you remember a discussion we had some time ago about a New Order of the Ages, and June said you had studied some book about the Great Seal?"

"Sure. I'd loan it to you but it's in braille. But I can tell you most of what it says. It's so interesting, I get it out every now and then."

After lunch Christi followed Hap to the family room, a bright room with large windows and bookshelves lining two full walls. No shelf had empty space.

"Now let me think where that book might be," Hap said running his hand across the books on a particular shelf. "I try to keep the books I use the most right here. But I have so many, they sometimes stray away.... June," he hollered into the other room. "Please come help me find this book."

June entered the room and went directly to a book on a shelf below the one Hap had searched. "Here it is. Right where you left it." She smiled as she handed him the small blue book.

Hap sat in a large overstuffed chair. "You know the symbols in the Great Seal came from the Masons."

Christi raised her brow. "No, I didn't know that. Never studied that in school."

"Nor I," Hap said. "I think the Masons were perceived as a threat to organized religion. Freemasonry is a personal path to God, not dependent on the intercession of any church or religious leader. There was a concerted effort to discredit them in the eighteen hundreds. Quite successful I might add. Masons were attacked by the Pope. The Protestants had their hands in it, too. Maybe that's why the connection to the Masons that certainly existed when this country was founded isn't reported in the history books."

Christi hesitated. "Was George Washington... was he a Freemason?"

"Of course! Along with Benjamin Franklin, Patrick Henry, Paul Revere, John Hancock. Even Benedict Arnold was a Mason. Many of the signers of the Declaration of Independence were Freemasons or shared their philosophy. The gathering places of the Masons may have been where sedition was hatched in pre-revolutionary days. Certainly their principles had a profound impact on the founding of the Nation."

"Could a strong spiritual bond among Masons have played a role in the success of the Revolution?" Christi asked cautiously.

"Indeed. How else could the weak and poorly armed Colonists have conquered England, one of the most powerful nations at that time? Masonic lodges throughout the colonies were a ready-made network of kindred spirits. They could trust each other and their meetings were strictly secret."

"Do you know if a division among Masons contributed to the separation from England in some way?" she asked, vaguely recalling mention of this in the book she and Tom found at MIT.

"Sure. The British soldiers who were deployed to protect the colonies usually belonged to a branch of Freemasons called the 'Moderns,' although it was actually the older order of Masons. The Royal governors assigned to the colonies also patronized these lodges. But earlier, when Masonry had become elitist, a branch began that was called the 'Ancient Masons,' sometimes known as the Irish Grand Lodge, which was less exclusive. The division between the British loyalists and those who developed a loyalty to the Colonies fell closely along the lines of these two branches of Freemasonry."

"The Irish Grand Lodge.... Where have I heard that before?" pondered Christi aloud. "Hap, what I actually came to ask you about is the strange symbols on the dollar bill. I never paid any attention to them before, but now I must find out what they mean."

"You mean the Great Seal? Sure. Let me get my clay model of the Seal. Here, I'll show you." He handed Christi a reddish round object. "Look at the top of the obverse side, the one we usually think of as the Great Seal. It's the one that hangs in the President's office. At the top, above the eagle's head is what is called the 'Glory,' a circle enclosing stars and beams of light. This is a heraldic representation of the Deity.

This symbol of God, or some variation, is prevalent in Masonic imagery."

Christi studied the object.

"If God was so prevalent in Masonic tradition, why were the founders of this Nation so adamant it would be exclusively a secular nation?"

"Because they were forming a nation under *God*, in accordance with Natural Law, but not under the control of any church or organized religion. That distinction was critical," Hap emphasized. "The Colonies had been settled to escape religious persecution. Fear of governmental power being misused by religious leaders was well-justified. They knew all too well that religious tyranny is among the worst.

"The Eagle, beneath the Glory, is a symbol of the spirit," he continued, "a tradition that dates back to ancient Egypt and Greece where many Masonic traditions have their roots. An eagle was often released at the funeral pyre of important leaders to carry the ruler's soul to Heaven. The shield on the breast of the Eagle represents the 'form' of the Nation, like its coat of arms. In the Eagle's feet are the paired opposites, the Laurel of Peace and the Arrows of War. This represents balance, an important aspect of Masonic teaching."

"Balance is important in quantum physics, too," Christi said intrigued by the parallels. "What do the symbols on the other side mean?"

"On the reverse side of the Seal the levels are completed. The pyramid rises from a broad base, representing the People, to the single divine center, the all-seeing eye, the Creator, the Nation's source. Under the pyramid is the proclamation, 'Novus Ordo Seclorum,' which means 'New Order of the Ages.'"

"Curious, I don't recall reading about the Mason's part in the Revolution in any history books I ever read," Christi noted.

"Certainly not. History is in the eye of the beholder. Ben Franklin wrote in his *Poor Richard's Almanac* that 'Historians relate, not so much what is done, as what they would have believed.' As Freemasonry fell into disrepute, there was a desire to disassociate it from the Founding Fathers. The history writers no doubt believed their purity would somehow be tainted by the association."

"Seems a shame...."

"An important lesson was forgotten. It was the spiritual strength and insight that George Washington learned as he progressed through the levels of Freemasonry that no doubt sustained him at Valley Forge. Legend has it that an angel appeared to Washington at Valley Forge and informed him of a secret spiritual destiny of a new nation that was soon to be formed."

A chill ran through Christi's body. She touched Hap's arm. "Secret spiritual *destiny*, did you say?"

"Yes. There's another story told about Washington while he was at Valley Forge," Hap continued. "His headquarters were in the home of a Quaker ironmaster. One day his host was walking in the woods when he came upon Washington on his knees, crying. Like Christ at Gethsemane. Valley Forge was Washington's Garden of Gethsemane. He was undoubtedly a deeply spiritual man, more spiritual than he was religious, and he relied upon his inner spiritual strength to endure conditions that otherwise would have been intolerable. He was in charge of troops that were in deep despair. But they eventually prevailed, testimony to the power of spiritual strength."

"All I was taught about Valley Forge was that it was a bitter cold winter, no money to pay the soldiers or even buy supplies to feed and clothe them," Christi said, thinking back to her high school history class. "Many of the soldiers died and morale was at its lowest ebb. But no one mentioned it being like the Garden of Gethsemane for Washington."

"Of course it was," Hap asserted. "And we even had our own American Judas, Benedict Arnold, who turned traitor at the eleventh hour, plotting to surrender our critical fortress at West Point to the British. He believed this would be the final blow to the struggling Revolutionaries whom he betrayed for his own gain. Judas sold one man for thirty pieces of silver. Arnold got 6000 British pounds for his attempt to sell the Continental army. But in the end, neither was successful."

"You mean there are parallels between the story of Christ and the American Revolution?" Christi was puzzled by the potential link.

"A few. The greatest parallel between Judas and Arnold is that in both instances there was something much greater at stake than a mere conflict between mortals. Both involved a powerful idea, a truth that could not be denied." Hap's words were filled with inspiration as he spoke. "Just imagine the dream the Colonists shared. They had a vision of a Nation governed by spiritual truths, not by religious doctrine. It was a land of promise and untold opportunity. By seizing that moment in history, they had the opportunity to create a new secular Nation under the Divinity, but unfettered by the separation that divides religious denominations. Think about our Pledge of Allegiance. 'One nation, under God, indivisible, with liberty and justice for all.' Although 'under God' was added later, it reflected the original intent. Imagine being there, discussing this revolutionary concept, when all they had previously known was the excesses of a monarchy!"

"Are you sure your optimism is justified? If they knew how far we had strayed from their original vision they might be sorely disappointed."

"I don't think so," Hap reassured her. "I have no doubt they know that promise will be fulfilled. An ideal as powerful as theirs cannot fail, but the time must be right. It will be achieved, just as they envisioned."

Christi sat in deep reflection. "I've always wondered why our Constitution was so different from that of other nations I studied in college. Even state constitutions. Most constitutions are so long; every little detail has to be spelled out. You can just see the authors clutching to control each aspect of government. But there is so much trust expressed in the United States' Constitution. Its authors set out only the bare essentials. This must be a reflection of the faith by which they were guided. So much trust was placed in those of us who followed, but I'm not sure it was justified."

"Are conditions now any more desperate, any more hopeless, than they were at Valley Forge?" Hap asked.

"Are you trying to make me feel guilty?" Christi asked smiling. "Maybe I need to join the Masons to fortify my faith." They both laughed.

"There's much to be learned from the Masons," Hap said. "Just as the cathedrals of Medieval Europe were designed by the stone masons to reflect their understanding of the Natural Law, our Founding Fathers designed our government to do the same. This symbolism in turn was to provide instruction to individual citizens about their own nature."

"How could our form of government possibly teach us about Natural Law?"

"Symbolism. They used symbolism as their teaching tool. Even the form of our government is based on Masonic principles." Hap's enthusiasm continued as he spoke. "The three branches of government, for example, reflecting the aspects of the Divinity. And the pyramid organization, with the House of Representatives reflecting the broad base of the pyramid, elected by the People every two years.

The Senate, a much smaller body, serving six years, representing the soul. And the President at the pinnacle of the pyramid, a symbol of the spirit that is to guide this grand undertaking in its mission."

"Hap, you are a national treasure," Christi said laughing. "I feel like I have been in a history class, making up for what I wasn't taught before. Thanks for sharing a special Sunday with me."

"How about some dessert before you leave," June asked, having slipped in quietly in the midst of the conversation. "I have some brownies with fresh strawberries to go on top, one of Hap's favorite desserts."

"I'd love some. Can I help?" Christi hummed a few bars of "We Whistle While We Work" as she followed June to the kitchen. Her mind was clearer, like a fog was beginning to lift. With Hap's guidance and support, the strange events in her life seemed less intimidating.

When Christi returned home that afternoon, she went directly to the table. As she rubbed her hand across its grain, she considered the pros and cons of leaving a reply to Washington's note. She considered the possibility that even considering it confirmed she was slipping away from reality. But on the other hand, perhaps Tom was right. What if she were to miss an extraordinary opportunity, one that may never come again, just because of her fear? She looked up at the engraving of Washington above the mantel. Sensing encouragement, she began to draft her reply.

> *Dear Mr. Washington,*
>
> *While I feel most unworthy, I will not allow that to be an excuse. I will indeed help in any way you deem fit.*
>
> *Most respectfully yours,*
>
> *Christi Daniel*

The dining room ceiling danced with a myriad of rainbows as the afternoon sun slowly descended in the western sky. The invitation was accepted.

CHAPTER ELEVEN

In the morning Christi went directly to the table. A note lay where she had left hers the evening before.

> *Dear Miss Christi:*
>
> *My joy is immense upon your willingness to be of assistance. I acknowledge your courage in doing so.*
>
> *The first item to attend to is closure of a matter yet unresolved, on the physical plane, that is.*
>
> *May I kindly have the use of the table on the evening of June 24, for a special meeting on the Nativity of Saint John the Baptist?*
>
> *In your service,*
>
> *Geo. Washington*

Again Christi could feel her heart pounding in her breast. What now? She must talk to Hap. She drove straight to the office, unmindful even of the speed limit. Luckily she found him alone at his desk.

"Hap, have you ever been in a haunted house?" she asked without even so much as the usual pleasantries being exchanged.

Hap laughed. "I live in a haunted world, if you measure it by most people's standards."

"If I have some spirits or ghosts, some type of discarnate beings come to my house, would you be willing to be there with me?"

"Willing!" he exclaimed. "If that happened and I wasn't invited, I would be sorely disappointed."

Relief flowed through Christi's body. With Hap there, she believed she could muster the courage to grant Washington's uncanny request.

"Good morning, Christi," June said as she laid several papers on the desk. "Hap, this is Mr. Shield's will. He'll be here at 9:30 to sign."

"June," Hap said, paying little attention to the papers. "If Christi has a ghost party at her house, do you want to go? Christi, am I being presumptuous in extending your invitation to June?"

"No, of course not," she said reluctantly.

"Don't worry, Christi. He's teasing. He knows I wouldn't be there, even if George Washington himself were coming."

"What! Did June know Washington was in some way involved, even though he hadn't been mentioned?" she wondered but dared not ask. "Can I borrow Hap on the evening of June 24th, to come for dinner and a sort of 'seance' afterwards?" she asked tentatively.

"My guess is you couldn't keep him away with a team of horses. That's right up his alley. But not mine. I'd have a heart attack, a stroke at least, if someone from the past showed up at my door. I'll be content to just hear about it afterwards," June replied laughing as she returned to her work.

Christi crossed the hall to her office. She took stationery from the desk drawer, contemplated her response, then began to write.

Dear Mr. Washington,

Having agreed to assist you, I am at your service in whatever way you deem fit. My only request is that I be permitted to also have a guest present...

Christi hesitated, thought how best to describe Hap, then continued.

who is very knowledgeable and understanding, assuming, of course, I may be present.

Unless you indicate it is inappropriate, my guest and I will quietly observe from outside the dining room on

June 24.
Sincerely,
Christi Daniel

It was done. She would leave the note on the table tonight then wait to see what happened.

The awaited day soon arrived. Although it was an adventure she could not resist, she was undeniably fearful when she considered the prospect. She had decided not to tell Tom until she knew the outcome.

For dinner Christi prepared fresh corn from a neighbor and a vegetable casserole and salad using produce from her garden. She arranged two places at the end of the table on Wedgwood blue place-mats that matched the dining room walls. Hap was due at 7 p.m. Christi wanted to be sure he was there when the sun was low and the dining room was filled with rainbows. Even though she knew he couldn't see them, she felt on some level he would experience them, perhaps even more keenly than she.

When June and Hap drove up precisely at seven Christi was in the front yard to greet them. She opened the car door and took Hap by the arm.

"I can't stay," June said from behind the wheel. "I'm late for a church committee meeting. We're planning summer Bible school."

"Is it okay if I call you when it's over? I can drive Hap home," Christi offered. "I have no idea when that will be. I don't even know what 'it' is, or, indeed, if anything will happen."

"No problem. Hap's been so excited, I don't want him to miss even a minute of this adventure," June said, winking at Christi.

"Now, June, don't tell stories on me," Hap scolded.

As June drove away, Christi assisted Hap up the stairs and through the front door.

"Here to the left is where I believe something might happen," she said as they entered the dining room.

Hap approached the table and stood silently. He took a deep breath. "The energy in this room is overpowering."

"What do you mean? Do you feel something?"

He paused a moment in thought. "Have you ever been to Stonehenge or Avebury?"

"No, I've never been to Stonehenge. Where is Avebury?" Christi was perplexed by their association with her dining room.

"They are both Stone Age sites in England where megalithic stones are placed in certain patterns. They were sacred sites in ancient times," Hap explained, as he took a few steps around the room, running his hand along the edge of the table. "Near Avebury there is a ceremonial chamber. Great granite stones form several small rooms, and these rooms are covered with a huge mound of dirt. It's called East Kennet Long Barrow. The last time I felt energy this strong was about seven years ago when I visited that chamber."

Hap was again quiet, then turned toward Christi. "This is a very special place, like a vortex. Something is going to happen."

Christi stood motionless as she, herself, felt a sense of energy in the room. She breathed deeply and consciously tried to relax. "Hap, we must eat first for fortitude. After dinner I have some things I want to show you." She led Hap to his place at the table.

During dinner Christi recounted the unusual events that had occurred since she had moved to the old Tyler place. She described the "dream" as she called it, the meeting that had taken place in the dining room soon after she arrived. She recounted the discussion among the men who were at the meeting, about it being time to proceed with their work because the table had been returned to their meeting place. That this room was where they had often met to create the vision of a Nation under God. She told him about the first note left on the table and how she assumed it was a prank.

After dinner she read him each of the notes from Washington. "I didn't keep copies of my replies," she explained. "I wish I had but I never expected them to disappear." Then she carefully laid the bundle from the secret chamber on the table. She gently opened the old Bible and read the inscription.

To our V∴ D∴ Brother, Geo. Washington
On the occasion of his healing as an Antient Mason
Lodge of Social and Military Virtue, No. 227
Grand Lodge of Ireland

"That's where I saw it!" she exclaimed. "The Grand Lodge of Ireland. Remember when you were telling me about the history of the Masons? You said the Colonists were members of the Grand Lodge of Ireland. That must have been what George Washington belonged to."

"I'm sure it was. He would never have been associated with the Moderns. They were the Tories."

Christi continued.

On the Festival of the Nativity of
St. John the Evangelist
This 27 day of December, 1756

"Another nativity, Hap. Didn't the note say today was the Nativity of St. John the Baptist? Do you know the significance of those dates?"

"Your mystery is increasingly intriguing! Those were the two most important dates for the Masons. They were required to hold regular meetings on the Nativity of St. John the Baptist and St. John the Evangelist. Today, June 24th, is the approximate time of the summer solstice, the beginning of summer. December 27th is near the winter solstice, the commencement of winter. That relates to the idea of balance and parallel associations."

Christi spread the heavy cloth that had contained the other items on the table. She took the fingers of Hap's right hand between her hands and carefully began to trace each design painted on the cloth.

He immediately recognized what it was. "This is called a floor cloth. These designs used to be painted on the floor of the Masonic lodges, but that was expensive and difficult to maintain. So the designs were later painted on a heavy cloth, like this, that could be placed on the floor when they were holding a meeting."

"What on Earth was it used for?"

"Floor cloths were teaching tools, used to illustrate principles taught in each of the three degrees of Masonry."

"It looks like a checkered floor in the foreground, with stairs ascending at the rear," Christi said as she traced the design at the center bottom for Hap.

"That represents the ground floor, the physical world, composed of opposing or complimentary forces—light and darkness, mundane and fantastic, yin and yang, male, female, and such. The stairs, of course, lead to the higher realm."

She continued tracing. "Here, in the middle area there are three columns."

"They must be in the middle chamber of the soul. They were no doubt used to teach about the 'Rule of Three,'" Hap speculated. "The Masons taught that three was an extremely important element in construction, be it on the spiritual plane or the physical. And above that, I'll bet there's an open holy book, the entrance to the spirit. For Christians it would be the Bible, but any teaching of a unified deity was accepted. And above all, I'm sure you will find the Divinity itself, represented by the Glory at the top of the floor cloth. Am I right?"

"Yes. Here, I'll show you where they are." Christi guided Hap's hand over the designs.

Hap nodded as she drew. "These levels are also represented in the design of our government, in the local, state and federal levels of government, with God above all. This stands for one Nation, composed of divisions, but unified under God. A meticulously balanced design. Just like a carefully constructed medieval cathedral was meant to reflect the spiritual in physical form."

"What do these distinctly different cornices that adorn the top of each of the three columns in the middle mean? In the area of the soul." She described the details of each.

"They represent three different characteristics or agencies that are essential for balance, on both the physical and the spiritual levels. The Corinthian column represents the active, creative, expansive aspect of the psyche—or the Lodge, as the case may be. The physical is always a mere reflection of the spiritual. The Doric column represents the passive, reflective characteristic or agency. The Ionic column represents the agency of balance, the one that coordinates the other two and maintains equilibrium."[1]

"How do you remember all of these details?" Christi asked, amazed by the wealth of knowledge Hap repeatedly displayed.

Hap smiled. "It's not so hard. These were actually very effective tools for teaching. If you think of the three branches of our government and the purpose each was designed to serve, you have the functions represented in the three columns painted on this floor cloth."

She had to think for a minute. "The Corinthian represents the executive branch, the active, creative aspect of governmental power. The Doric represents the legislative branch, which is supposed to be reflective. So many people must reach consensus in a legislative body, I suppose that does assure a degree of reflection before action can be taken. And of course, the Ionic column represents the judiciary, the agency maintaining equilibrium between the other two. That's awesome! Are you saying these three aspects of the psyche were known from ancient teachings and our Founding Fathers incorporated them in the form of our government?"

"Exactly. To secure balance. They knew precisely what they were doing. That's why our democracy has been so enduring."

"Hap, you're incredible," Christi said, as she folded up the cloth. "While we wait for this mysterious event, would you like to take a walk around the house? There's time before nightfall."

"Yes, but don't put the floor cloth away. We must place it on the floor. I think the Masons are going to meet here."

Christi laughed at the idea of preparing for such an event, but immediately joined in the effort. "I'll put the Bible, the compass and the square in the center of the table. I'll put the three candle sticks on the mantel. I have a box of long candles in the kitchen cupboard," she said going to the kitchen.

Hap located the fireplace and carefully spread the floor cloth on the floor in front of it. When everything was in place, Christi guided Hap out the back door and down the steps to the open area adjacent to the woods. The early evening air was cool and fresh. The woods surrounding the house were filled with the melody of a cicadian orchestra, punctuated with the occasional cooing of a dove.

"We were so engrossed in our conversation I forgot to tell you how delicious dinner was," Hap said as they traversed the moist grass. "You're not only a good attorney, you're a good cook, too."

"Thanks. Cooking offsets the left-brain legal work," she said modestly.

Hap breathed deeply, relishing the fresh evening air. "We all instinctively gravitate toward balance. It's our nature. We either find balance or misery. I'm sure that's what concerned our Forefathers. Creating a government that would last required balance."

"If you think back, balance was certainly not a characteristic of the monarchy that existed in England at the time of the Revolution," Christi said as they strolled near the woods. "There was nothing to check its excesses. The destruction of its relationship with the Colonies, and eventually most of the British Empire was obviously the result." The moon rose behind the pine trees. "I knew one of the unique aspects of our government is the balance of power incorporated into its structure. But do you believe that our three branches of government and the Holy Trinity have a connection?"

"Indeed. The Rule of Three. They're both built on the strength of three. The Masons understood the importance of the triangle as a symbol of unity and balance."

"Hap, I'm bothered by the extent we have forgotten our past. We're like a village that has lost its storyteller, the remembrance and understanding of its history."

"That's not exactly correct. We haven't forgotten. Much of this ancient knowledge was never revealed to the masses. It was believed to be too powerful to be entrusted to any but a select few. It appears the time has come for this to change."

"But why now? Why us?"

"Of course we're at the commencement of the third millennium—passage into the twenty-first century. But more important, we're at the dawn of a new age, the Age of Aquarius. Christ was born at the commencement of the last age, the Age of Pisces. Did you know Pisces means fish? That's why the fish was the sign of the early Christians—it stood for the Piscean Age, an age that is now coming to a close," Hap explained.

"What is the symbol of this new age, the Aquarian Age?"

"It's Aquarius, the water bearer. Aqua is Latin for water. The Piscean Age was an age in which the masculine energy was predominate, but in the Aquarian Age, feminine energy will prevail."

"Balance!" Christi said laughing.

Hap gently squeezed her arm. "The pendulum can only swing so far in one direction, then it must swing in the other. Just think of the wide-spread implications of a shift in energy of this nature! Significant changes in law and government lie ahead. However, through all the ages humans have continued moving forward, progressing in our journey toward closing the gap between the physical plane and God. Or rather, our mistaken perception of a gap between us and God, because there is none."

"That's what Tom said. With quantum physics they have discovered that everything is connected."

"The Masons would not consider that a new discovery!" Hap retorted. They both laughed.

"Hap, it's gotten dark. I suggest we go inside. Don't want to miss anything." As they ascended the stairs to the house, Christi's fear began to reemerge. She pulled Hap's arm closer to her. "I'm so grateful that you're here. You know I could never do this without you."

"Nonsense! You mustn't entertain such limiting beliefs. When you believe you are limited, you no doubt believe others are limited, as well. Such beliefs are mere illusions."

When the candles were lit and all was in order, they positioned themselves on the stairs and began to wait.

Chapter Twelve

Intrigue and terror concurrently clutched Christi and she grabbed Hap's arm with both hands. The dining room had instantly come to life, full of men, some seated at the table and others standing. All were dressed in colonial attire. A meeting was being called to order with great formality.

A stout man stood at the head of the table near the fireplace. "I, John Blair of the Williamsburg Lodge," he said in a deep, booming voice, "Grand Master of Virginia, convene our Beloved Brethren of Ancient Free and Accepted Masons for a most sacred purpose. We return to the table where we so often met before our departure, to this place of physical nourishment, but above all, where our souls were so often nourished in Brotherhood and Love. We come to teach a sacred truth."

His voice became more reverent. "Just as Jesus gathered his disciples to break bread and promise a new covenant, we too are grateful for the past, but obediently and with great joy accept our role in the evolution of Spirit. Before we commence, Very Dear Brother Peyton Randolph, who in our time so ably served as Provincial Grand Master of Virginia, will you kindly lead us in prayer."

A man stood and came forward. "It is my honor, Venerable Master." There was a pause before he commenced. "Most Holy and Glorious Lord God, the Great Architect of the Universe, the giver of all good gifts and graces, Thou hast promised where two or three are gathered together in Thy name, Thou wilt be in the midst of them and bless them. In Thy name we assemble, most humbly beseeching Thee to bless us in our undertaking, that our actions on this occasion may tend to Thy glory and to the advancement of knowledge and virtue. And we beseech Thee, O Lord, to illuminate all minds with the divine precepts of the Ancient Wisdom, and direct them so they may walk in the light of Thy divine countenance. We are thankful that the trials of our probationary state are over, and we are now admitted into the Temple not made of hands, eternal in the Heavens, to continue our service to Thee. So be it. Amen!"[2]

"So be it!" Grand Master Blair added, then turned to those assembled. "Daily the Sun rises in the East, journeys by the South and sets in the West. Yearly, leaving the Equator at the Autumnal Equinox, he falls more and more to the South, on the ecliptic, until, at the Winter Solstice, the Feast of St. John the Evangelist, he reaches the Tropic of Capricorn. There, seeming to pause for three days, he again gradually ascends, crosses the Equator at the Vernal Equinox, continues northward, and pauses at the Tropic of Cancer at the Summer Solstice and Feast of St. John the Baptist. Today is an especially sacred Feast of St. John the Baptist; a special moment in the journey of the Son."

He raised his hands above his head and continued. "'I indeed,' said John the Baptist, 'baptize you with water unto repentance; but he that cometh after me shall baptize you with the Holy Spirit and with fire.' Nations, like men, to be free must first be virtuous. For them, too, the purification of fire and the Holy Spirit. In the end, all things are tested by the Square and Rule."

The room was silent as Grand Master Blair slowly surveyed those present. "In the past, the Mysteries were carried into every country in order that, without disturbing the absurd popular beliefs, Truth, the Arts and the Sciences might be known to those who were capable of understanding them, and to maintain the true and sacred doctrine incorrupt, which the masses, prone to superstition and idolatry, have in no prior age been able to do. It was so in past ages that the profoundest of truths were wisely covered from the Common People, as with a veil. It was so because everywhere, what was originally revered as the symbol of a higher Principle, became gradually confounded or identified with the object itself, and was worshiped, until this proneness to error led to the most degraded form of idolatry. And even in our own day on Earth, while they no longer worshiped idols and images made with the hands, they formed and fashioned ideas, images and idols in their minds, which are not the Deity or even like the Deity, and worshiped them. Still it continues literally true that many men worship Baal and not God," the Grand Master said, punctuating "Baal" and "God" with a wave of his hand.

Many present nodded silently. The Grand Master stood erect, motionless for a time before he again spoke. "But a New Age is upon us." There were murmurs of consent throughout the room. "Those who now comprehend the Ancient Wisdom are no longer so few in number that such secrecy is required. Indeed, within the Oneness, there are no secrets. And so it is that we gather on this occasion to remove the veil from a profound truth—to unveil Forgiveness of the Holy Spirit."

Voices in the room called out, "Amen." "So be it."

The Grand Master continued. "Forgiveness... not in the sense of a patronage dispensed to one deemed to be of lesser purity. Such is not forgiveness but rather a temporary dispensation so easily revoked when it serves the patron's purpose. No, my Brethren, it is not of such forgiveness that I speak. Forgiveness of the Holy Spirit is one with the recognition that there was never any deed to be forgiven... that what God created in Perfection can know not imperfection... that sin is but an illusion that cannot even exist in God's omnipotence, omniscience and omnipresence. Until each citizen of this great Nation under God learns Forgiveness of the Holy Spirit, and thus learns to recognize what many deem to be sin is in truth a call for love, the teaching must continue. The form the lesson takes is unimportant;

only its content matters. But my Brothers, in order to teach such Forgiveness, and indeed receive it for ourselves, we must give Forgiveness of the Holy Spirit to *all*, without exception. Even to those whom we perceive to have been our worst enemies... to have committed the most dastardly of deeds."

Those in the room expressed their concurrence with nods and murmurs. The Grand Master continued. "So long as Forgiveness of the Holy Spirit is not given, it cannot be received. What we give to others is a measure of what we are willing to receive unto ourselves. Indeed, what you believe you are worthy of giving, you shall receive through your own manifestation, as it is delivered through others who willingly co-create the reality you choose to experience. Yet many, having been taught the false scripture of judgment, do not understand," the Grand Master said waving his hand in the air as he spoke. "It is for the purpose of teaching this truth, for this most holy purpose, that we are grateful for the willing participation of our Beloved Brother, Benedict Arnold."

The room was silent. Anticipation hung in the air. The Grand Master again continued. "Brother Benedictus, Latin for 'blessed', was chosen long ago for the role he would play in teaching this ancient truth. Brother Arnold believed he deserved to be nothing more than a traitor to our cause. However, this Principle was also taught by Brother Washington, who, when called upon to do so, came to know he was worthy of leading our new Nation as its first President. Each received the exact measure his heart deemed him worthy to receive."

The Grand Master stood straight as though at attention. "But we are not here to judge Brother Arnold, or Brother Washington. The role of the student is to learn the lesson, not judge the teacher. Moreover, among equals, judgment has no place, and in God's Creation, all are equal...." He reached out his hand toward one of the men seated at the table. "Blessed Brother Arnold, please come forward."

A tall, handsome middle-aged man with dark hair and fiery eyes stepped forward shyly, despite his size and presence. At the same time a second man, slightly older, stood and also walked toward Grand Master Blair. He was even taller, surely over six foot. He had white tufts of hair at the temples, a high collar about his neck with a cascade of delicate lace at the neck. He wore a dark waist coat over a long cream-colored, buttoned vest, tight trousers and dark leather boots rising nearly to the knee. And from his waist hung a small apron decorated with symbols.

Electrified, Christi leaned toward Hap. She whispered, "George Washington! George Washington has gone to the front with Benedict Arnold!"

When both men stood at the head of the table beside Grand Master Blair, the Grand Master nodded toward them. "I now turn this proceeding over to our Most Beloved Brother Washington." The Grand Master then seated himself in a chair near the fireplace.

Standing before the assembly, Brother Washington and Brother Arnold embraced one another. Brother Washington then spoke respectfully and lovingly to the man who stood before him.

"Our Blessed Brother Arnold, I am pleased that we again meet on the physical plane and are here, together, to unveil this sacred truth. As this ceremony unfolds, the veil too unfolds, and the knowledge we impart thunders through the Universe.

"Brother Arnold, you chose a difficult path. Therein lies the value of your teaching. The illusions you created, then worshipped as your truth, is a failing of many. But freedom from illusion is one of God's many treasures that is ours, if we so choose. To dissolve illusion requires but a mere shift in belief, but it is a shift one must choose to make. To come to this choice one must accept that everything, *everything* one believes within, becomes manifest in the world without.

May your sacrifice of your honor, your family name, teach all generations to come that one cannot dispel the illusion of hate by making it real and then atoning for it through treason, or war, or any other act of destruction.

"We thank you for your role in teaching that hatred exists only in the mind—nothing more than a mental image that is then expressed in actions of the body, but those actions, too, are mere manifestations of what is in the mind. Hatred is an illusion that is made real only in a dream, a nightmare. It is now time to awaken from the dream by dispelling all hatred in order to perceive the world as it truly is.

"In truth, there are only two emotions to choose between—love and fear. Many choose fear and thereby construct their own guillotine. Each time they project fear upon the world in place of love, they mount one step closer to their own execution. Today we dismantle forever the trappings of fear. We scour away pain, suffering and grief that are the only gifts fear has to give.

"Blessed Brother Arnold, you were at all times just as God created you. Your journey on the other side so perfectly portrays mistakes, but not sin. It perfectly portrays the power of guilt, which manifests as hate, to destroy all we believe to be good, and yet in no way diminishes the perfection of God's Creation.

"We now see clearly your path away from the truth of who you are. When all but one of your siblings died in childhood, and especially your sister Mary, four years your junior, whom you loved and had nurtured as though you were her parent, your guilt became consuming. She was most precious to you. When the plague in your hometown of Norwich claimed Mary's life, you assumed responsibility for her death, although you were a mere lad of twelve and had been away at boarding school. But illusions may be created of any fabric. Because you were not at home when she died, you reasoned that if you had only been there she would not have died. Moreover, if you had been at home, you could have died instead, or at least died together, with her.

"And the greatest source of your guilt arose because she had been so perfect, so mindful of others and yet she died while you, whom you believed to be far less deserving, had lived. Perceiving this to be unjust, you concluded that God was cruel and deserving of the hatred you thereafter harbored in your heart toward our Creator.

"When your father's business failed due to his drunkenness, you suffered embarrassment by being taken from boarding school, further embittered that this misfortune had brought you home too late to save Mary or your other siblings from their untimely death. And you felt humiliated and degraded when you were thereafter reduced to an apprentice in your uncle's shop instead of being elevated through education to a higher status. Your garden of hatred and distrust of God flourished, nurtured by your misperceptions.

"When your father's drunkenness caused his ruin and ultimately his death, your fate was sealed, your belief in God's injustice solidified. By then there was only one source upon which you would thereafter rely—yourself. Having created the illusion that God was deserving of your attack, there was nothing that could escape your perception that attack was essential to survival, and in all circumstances, justified. Your life became a mirror of your mistaken belief that attack was grandeur. Your material success was, of course, assured, because the end of filling the black, godless pit you believed you had become would be achieved by any means.

"Your brilliance was unmatched, and yet, each measure we took to affirm your worth was rejected. Your belief in your lack of worth was so firmly established there was nothing we could do that would convince you to the contrary. In fact, each opportunity that came to you only increased your measure of guilt. There was always someone who, in your mind, had more, was worthier, was evidence of your lack of worth. We knew your trust in others had been lost.

"At many junctures we heard your cries for help. But all we did to affirm your value to our cause was for naught. Yes, Brother Arnold, the wounds you perceived in your past became your crown jewels, more precious to you than life itself. Their hues colored and distorted your view, tainting every aspect of your existence. Your belief in illusions was total, and belief is so powerful it can move mountains, or destroy heroes, with equal ease.

"You demonstrated your belief in your unworthiness on many occasions, in your heart desiring to be punished for being so unworthy. Each time you successfully lied your way out of trouble, it merely increased your determination to prove how undeserving you were of the love of those about you. In your insanity, above all, you wanted to hurt those whom you perceived were so foolish as to love you, one so undeserving.

"You requested command of West Point, one of our most critical fortresses at a most precarious point in the Revolution. It was at a time in our effort when our resources were nearly exhausted. The French were withdrawing their support, believing our cause against the English to be lost. Our troops had not been paid for months; we existed on faith alone.

"I knew this would be a turning point for you. It would be the opportunity for you to at last accept your value to our cause. Or, I knew, it would be yet another opportunity for you to affirm your lack of self-worth. But we needed your leadership, your courage, your intelligence. I believed we could not lose you, especially at that moment. It was a risk I felt we were compelled to take. Your request for this command was granted.

"But your course had been firmly set. You believed your redemption could only be gained through your crucifixion. Your plan to surrender West Point to the British was your plan to guarantee, at last, your own crucifixion. So you chose that moment to attack. You masked your real motivation of attacking yourself by the delusion you were attacking the Continental Congress for having treated you so shabbily, and the People for their weakened resolve for a war they had come to doubt could be won. The sacrifice you devised to purify yourself was the destruction of the very undertaking you insanely believed needed purification. You could never have believed this insanity had you not created it. You saw a meaningless world, but it was your own miscreation, hiding the light of the world inside you.

"Yet there is another way of looking at the world. Holiness envelops everything, including you. When the rubble and dust of your life on Earth is swept aside, the truth nonetheless shines through in its full glory. You are and always have been a blessed son of God, just as you were created—perfect and innocent. All was in Divine Order and there is nothing to forgive."

Brother Washington paused. The room was silent. He looked around at those present, then continued. "It has all turned out just as it was meant to be. Our effort was never truly threatened by Brother Arnold's acts, any more than it is truly threatened now by the seditious acts of others. Destiny cannot be diverted by cries for love."

Brother Washington turned to Brother Arnold. Standing proudly he continued.

"To judge a Brother apart from ourselves is pure arrogance. Everything being created in the image of God there is nothing which can be less than perfect. How arrogant to believe we can undo what God has done! We, too, would be misguided if we were to accept your errors as a true reflection of you. No, our perception must not focus on error, for what we perceive becomes our truth, despite how insane it truly is. Blessed Brother Arnold, we refuse to harbor any hatred in our hearts, knowing it is an illusion and not of God's making. You are blessed, Benedictus. We love you as we love ourselves."

The men again embraced and the entire room seemed to emanate light. Then Brother Arnold turned toward those present. "Most Venerable Grand Master, my Beloved Brother Washington, may I speak?" he asked. In reply, they nodded.

"I now understand what Brother Washington has said. First as a child, and then as a man, I hurt so deeply, I hated myself so much that the only vindication I could imagine was to make you and our other Brothers hurt just as much as I. Each act of love extended to me I twisted and defiled. Believing I was unworthy, I dismissed each offering of love as not enough to compensate for my unworthiness, and therefore yet another attack upon me which justified an attack in return. While it is not necessary, I ask your forgiveness, and the forgiveness of all who harbor hate in their hearts for my deceitful acts.

"Upon the instant of my death, death upon the physical plane, I understood all of this, and more. I saw the pain I had felt when I could have chosen to experience love, and the attacks I had so wrongfully justified in my warped mind. I saw those whom I had hurt. But I also understood the value of the lessons they had learned from the role each played in my learning. I understood on a level words do not express that we were co-creators of our shared lives. I saw that the many are one, mere reflections of the same Power being expressed as individuated aspects of God, the source of Creation. I knew Brother Washington, whom I had loved as a father, in all his goodness and honor—I knew that even he and I were one. I knew that I was loved—indeed that I am love, as is each and every aspect of God's Creation.

"The mistakes I made shall not be repeated again and again. I know it is so, for I see the soul of this Nation rising, as the Great Eagle, in holy flight. In the twenty-first century upon Earth, I see the fruition of our vision of a Nation under God, with liberty and justice, *free from judgment*, for all. My Brothers, so be it."

All eyes on Brother Arnold, he bowed before his Brethren.

"So be it!" exclaimed Brother Washington.

All of the voices in the room swelled in unison, "So be it! So be it!" There was a chorus of voices, far more in number than merely those present. It sounded as though voices from all parts of the Earth had joined in unison. Christi and Hap too were saying "So be it!" their hearts swollen with love. The vastness of the experience was indescribable.

Then just as suddenly as it began, only Christi's and Hap's voices echoed in the hallway. All else was silent. The table again sat empty and the three candles on the mantel flickered their last rays of light.

CHAPTER THIRTEEN

Following the events of June 24th, Christi anguished over their meaning. They forced her to examine her concept of reality, sometimes leaving her in serious doubt about what sanity meant to her. And a seemingly unanswerable question haunted her—why me? She saw herself slipping into an abyss of despondency. She welcomed the opportunity to discuss her inner turmoil with Hap one afternoon when June left work early and he was alone.

"Hap, I must talk to you about what happened the other evening."

"I shared every detail with June," he said enthusiastically. "It was unbelievable!"

"That's what bothers me—I don't know what to believe. I'm confused. I don't know whether to be angry or sad, or just conclude I've slipped over the brink into insanity."

"My friend," he said with empathy, "our view of reality dictates what we can see as possible or impossible. As one's view of reality is challenged by new discoveries, the perception of chaos results. The view that cause and effect are a tidy continuum in the dimension of time, that the Universe consists of separate parts with empty space in between, that guilt can be isolated and laid upon certain individuals to the exclusion of others—it's all being challenged. A new truth— that we are all one magnificent field of energy, that empty space does not exist, that our salvation depends upon the salvation of our brothers and sisters—this is creeping into our consciousness. Our world is shifting from one paradigm to another, from the belief in separation to the reality of unity."

"But how did I become involved in such bizarre events? I didn't ask for this."

"Are you sure, Christi? There appears to be only one explanation to me. It seems you have been chosen to play a role in facilitating this shift—an important role, I would say. Perhaps you've been chosen to participate in events so historic, so monumental, we cannot possibly fathom their meaning at this juncture."

"What are you talking about?" Christi demanded. "Are you mad, too? Why would this happen to me?" Her voice quivered. "I'm just an average person, an average American career woman, just like millions of other women in this country. I'm not a fallen woman like Mary Magdalene whom Christ memorialized by forgiving her sins to set an example for the world. I'm not a saint who was given extraordinary gifts at birth. I'm just an average woman going about an average life. Why would something like this happen to someone like me?"

"I understand your dismay. My guess is that a major commitment is being asked of you."

"Commitment!" Christi retorted. "Commitment is like chains binding my wrists, my ankles. I can't stand it. I've never married, Hap, or had children, because I'm terrified of commitment. What you're suggesting would require a commitment that is even more... irrevocable and eternal. I feel like I'm losing control of my life."

"The need for control is a master of many," Hap observed, "but the ransom it demands in return for its illusion of security is exorbitant."

"Is it just an illusion? When I started practicing law I was in ecstasy, because the lawyer is in control. She calls the shots; she gives the advice and directs events. I have to be in control of my life. What you're suggesting would require that I surrender completely to an unknown course of events. Why would I do that?"

"Haven't you answered your own question? Don't you see? You are being given the opportunity to face your inner demons... as we all must do. The only choice we have is when. You can delay facing your fears, but you must realize at what price. We are all one, Christi. As long as you are bound by the chains of fear, we are all in chains. As long as you choose to live in darkness, all of humanity is denied the light, because we are one. I understand your apprehension. All I can say is... I will do all within my power to love and support you on this journey, because it's *our* journey."

"Hap... you're special. How did I deserve to find you?" Christi asked, blinking away tears as she took a tissue from her pocket. "I want to be like you. How did you learn such compassion? Where... where did you come from?"

There was a pause before he answered. "Only June knows of my past. But I've never had a friend like you. Sharing it with you, as well, would be an honor." Hap leaned back in his chair. "I will tell you where I came from.... I was born into a prominent political family. A family of means and position. But I was born blind. My mother wasn't prepared to make the commitment it would take to raise a blind child. My father could not imagine putting a blind child on display when he appeared in public. So I was quickly put up for adoption. I believe they told everyone I was dead.

"As you can well imagine, the choice babies, those without serious handicaps, go to the choice families, those that are the most well off. So I was eventually adopted by a poor family, by parents who could have no children but who wanted a child to share their love. Now, *they* were special. I don't think the idea that I was tainted or devalued by being blind ever entered their minds. Because I was blind, my adoptive father worked two jobs so Mother could stay home and care for me. He spent so little time at home, I never knew him well. I know he loved me mainly by the sacrifices he made for me. I was raised by Mother."

Hap seemingly looked toward a distant place. "I never saw Mother's face, but her presence was the most beautiful experience one could imagine. We couldn't share the same visual experience, so she created worlds for us to share that didn't depend on physical sight. The thing I remember most was that she was always present in the moment. Her mind was never in another place when she was with me. There was never a word I spoke that she did not hear. If she taught me a game, she played it with me. When we were together she believed each moment was a treasure to be relished. I don't recall a time with Mother when I didn't feel loved."

Christi admired Hap's round, ruddy face. "That would explain why you are so extraordinary. Such love! What an exceptional experience for a child to have. Do you know what became of your birth family?"

"I never met them in person. But they sent money to my adoptive parents for my education. And my birth father arranged for me to be admitted to law school, after Mother contacted him and pleaded my case. They paid for me to go to law school and provided funds to hire an assistant to read the course material to me. That's how June and I met. She was a college student and applied for the job as my aide to pay her living expenses. We soon fell in love and wanted only to be together."

"Do you feel resentment toward your birth parents?"

Hap laughed. "Not at all. I had the best of both worlds—the material resources of my birth family and the love and support of my adoptive parents. Imagine what a miserable childhood I would have had if I had been raised by my birth family, even if I had not been blind! June reads me articles about them that appear in the paper every now and then. My birth parents died years ago, but the family name is well-known. The escapades of my brothers are reported from time to time. If I had to do it over, I wouldn't change a thing. It was a miracle, perfect in every way."

Hap smiled knowingly. He extended his arm across the desk. His open palm invited Christi to hold it. She placed her hand in his. He spoke softly. "The beautiful events that have come to you are miracles, Christi. They have come to you because you asked the Universe for them."

Christi felt energy flow from his hand into hers. Tears again filled her eyes. She knew the words he spoke were true. "What's so frightening, Hap, is that I know what I must do. I cannot turn back." Her eyelids dropped as she looked inward. "I must find the strength to go forward, even though I have no idea where I'm going. I feel like I'm standing on the edge of a cliff. I know I must jump, for my own good, but I'm afraid."

"If you are to make such a leap, you must surrender. You must place your trust in God."

"But how? How does one do this?"

Hap paused before he answered. "To begin, you must dissect your emotions to find the veils that hide God. Like a pathologist would dissect a body to find the source of disease. To do this, pay close attention to your intuition. Note how the emotions associated with events in your life make you *feel*, deep inside. Whether it's a thought, a conversation, a person in your presence, even the feeling of a room. Begin to develop your awareness of the energy about you, the emotional response it evokes in you. Observe how your emotions affect others. To practice these skills, perhaps this will help.... Close your eyes and imagine you are blind to the outward world."

CHAPTER FOURTEEN

Christi felt a sense of urgency about taking the Masonic artifacts to the Smithsonian, to seek Shenan's advice. Perhaps Shenan could direct her to someone with related expertise. She called her friend, described the objects and gave a vague description of the events of June 24th. Shenan said it sounded like a good mystery and agreed to meet on Friday.

When Christi arrived at the Smithsonian she carried the large briefcase with its precious contents to Shenan's small office. She carefully laid the Bible, compass, square and three candlesticks on her desk and spread the floor cloth on the floor. She told Shenan what she had learned from Hap about each item, but Shenan said she could be of little assistance.

A knock on Shenan's door interrupted their discourse and a tall thin man with a toupee entered the room uninvited. "Ms. Adkins, here's the draft of the memorandum you prepared with my comments about. . ." He stopped in mid-sentence with a shocked look on his face.

Shenan looked alarmed. "Mr. Betnoir, this is a friend of mine, Christi Daniel," she said nervously.

He immediately began to inspect the artifacts laying on Shenan's desk and the floor cloth. "Where did these come from?" He spoke sharply. "Who do they belong to?"

"They're family heirlooms of Ms. Daniel's," Shenan replied, looking at Christi in a way that alerted Christi to a danger she did not understand.

"These are Masonic artifacts. Did you know that?" He looked suspiciously at Christi. "How long have these been in your family?"

"Oh... as long as I can remember. There's a long tradition of Masons in my family. Probably going back to the Revolution," she blurted out then grimaced with regret.

"It's not safe to have such things," Betnoir advised ominously. "These are from a cult that should have been destroyed long ago. These things are of the devil."

Christi immediately began to place the items in her briefcase. As she knelt down to fold the floor cloth, Betnoir demanded, "Where do you work, Ms. Daniel?"

"I just have a small law practice. Not anywhere near here."

"Is this your friend that left Win Harp's firm some time ago?" he asked, looking at Shenan.

"Mr. Betnoir is an ardent follower of the R.R.s," Shenan explained to Christi. "I think I mentioned him to you before. He's a strong supporter of Mr. Harp and I told him I had a friend working at Harp's firm. When you left I mentioned that to him, as well."

"You didn't tell me that she had any connection to the Masons," Betnoir said curtly. "Ms. Daniel, what are you going to do with these things?"

"I'm taking them back to my family, where they're appreciated. Last I heard this was still a free country."

"Christi has a wonderful sense of humor," Shenan interjected, grasping to ease the tension. "Please excuse us, Mr. Betnoir, we have a luncheon engagement and we're already late." She took her purse from the drawer and headed toward the door.

Christi locked the briefcase and followed Shenan as Betnoir watched them depart.

Over lunch Shenan told Christi it was rumored that there had been a display of Masonic artifacts planned at the Smithsonian in conjunction with the Bicentennial. But word of the project had gotten out and resulted in a near religious revolt. Reportedly there had even been a threat to bomb the Smithsonian if the project proceeded. It was politically too explosive and potentially dangerous to the public, so it had quietly been killed.

But she also knew there were occasional inquiries received by the Smithsonian regarding such matters. She had recently seen such a letter in which the author requested information about the Masonic connection to the founding of the Nation and its "secret destiny." She didn't understand what this referred to, but had gotten the impression open discussion of the topic was discouraged. She had been told that some Masonic materials had even been destroyed for fear they would reveal information about the founding of the Nation that would be detrimental to the "national interest." At the time Shenan had considered it to be of little interest to her. She never dreamed there was a connection between those events and Christi.

Reluctantly, Christi described in detail what had taken place on June 24th, fearing even her good friend would consider it absurd. But she didn't. Shenan said it reminded her of stories about visits from mystical beings told to her by her grandfather when she was a child, stories that were common among Native Americans. She had loved these tales and used to imagine what it would be like. She said she wished she had been there with Christi and Hap.

"What a relief!" Christi thought. "I must meet your grandfather," she said. "Can I do that sometime?"

"Of course. I'll take you with me the next time I go to see him. You'll love him," Shenan said, admiration for her elder glowing in her eyes.

As they finished their meal, Shenan looked intently at Christi. "Do you remember that time in our dorm room when you were really upset when I returned from class?"

Christi laughed. "Which time?"

"There was only one time that happened. Remember? You had heard a voice?"

"Oh, sure. . . . I'll never forget *that* time," Christi said, thinking back to events she had long since put out of her mind. "That was years ago. The voice said, 'Prepare yourself well, you will be called upon to lead.' It was weird and scared me to death. And all you wanted to know was whether it was a man or a woman who had spoken to me!"

"Yes, and you said neither, it was your own voice, and that's why you were so frightened," Shenan said laughing.

"Right, but it wasn't funny at the time. I decided I must have fallen asleep while I was studying, but I knew I hadn't. It's a shame how we immediately invalidate such events in our lives, instead of examining their possible importance, merely because we're afraid of being judged and considered crazy."

"Christi, do you think these events happening in your house with George Washington may be related to the prediction made by that voice many years ago?"

Exactly one week after Christi's encounter with Betnoir at the Smithsonian, Tom called early in the evening. He was agitated and uncertain about telling her what had happened for fear that would serve the very purpose intended by his visitor.

"I don't want you to be alarmed," he said as calmly as possible. "This afternoon a private investigator asked to meet with me. At first I thought it related to some MIT graduate or professor who was looking for a government job and needed a security clearance. So I told him to come on over. I was astonished when he began to ask questions about you."

"About me? What on Earth did he want?"

"He started out telling me that he understood you and I were close friends, in fact we were involved in a 'relationship', as he called it. I had the distinct feeling he was trying to make it sound immoral. I told him we were acquainted and asked what he wanted. He said he was investigating some antireligious group with Masonic ties and he understood you were involved with this organization."

"What! This must have come from Betnoir at the Smithsonian reporting back to Harp. It's something they concocted. This is ridiculous."

"That's all the further he got before I told him to get out," Tom said angrily. "I don't think you need to worry about your safety, but I just wanted you to know that someone may be trying to discredit you for some reason."

"I can't imagine what they think I'm doing that would cause such fear! Sending an investigator to Cambridge? What was his name?"

"He said it was Ralph Waldo. I wouldn't bet on it."

"Ralph Waldo... I'll have to remember that name."

When Christi arrived at the office the next morning, she immediately told Hap about Tom's call.

"That's interesting," he said with reticence, not wanting to alarm Christi further. "That must have been the same investigator who visited me, just a few days before he saw Tom."

"How could this be, Hap? You encouraged me to follow my intuition. My intuition told me to take the Masonic artifacts to the Smithsonian to consult Shenan. If I hadn't done that, none of this would have happened."

"Christi, I also told you to trust," he replied with characteristic calmness. "You must trust that all is in Divine Order at all times—that, for whatever reason, this was meant to be. You must accept everything that has ever happened to you as being for your highest good. Otherwise, you become consumed with guilt and shame, regret and blame, none of which is justified."

"How can being spied on by such reprehensible people be for my highest good?" she asked indignantly.

"If you judge them to be reprehensible, does that make them so?"

"Well... anyway, what did the investigator want?"

"He wanted to know if you were in some kind of antireligious group. I think he mentioned the Masons. I told him you were one of the finest attorneys with whom I had ever been associated. That you were involved in nothing *I* considered to be out of the ordinary."

Christi smiled at Hap's ingenuity.

"You mustn't let them take your power," admonished Hap. "If you allow them to instill fear in you, you surrender to their control. You must surrender, Christi, but only to God."

CHAPTER FIFTEEN

By early August, life had, for the most part, once again become mostly mundane. Nothing more had been heard of the investigator, Ralph Waldo, and Christi's fear for her safety had begun to wane. Hap and Christi often discussed the extraordinary events of June 24th, having shared them only with June, Tom and Shenan who were sworn to secrecy. But even those discussions had become less frequent.

And yet, for Christi, the questions were endless. Why me? What does it all mean? Was the "Forgiveness of Arnold Meeting," as they now called it, the end or was there more to come? As she worked in her garden on this beautiful summer afternoon, she pondered these riddles. Growing tired, she returned to the house for a cool drink and to rest.

She found her favorite place to curl up and read, a small couch in the dining room that had belonged to her grandmother. With her drink in one hand and a book in the other, she kicked off her shoes and made herself comfortable. As she read, her mind began to wander and she felt drowsy. She soon fell asleep.

While asleep, a voice spoke softly, "Miss Christi. Miss Christi.... Please don't be alarmed."

She stirred, but drifted back to sleep.

"Miss Christi," the voice said again. "If you don't mind, I'll just wait here until you awaken."

She blinked several times, then squinted at the tall imposing man who stood by the table, one hand resting on the table, the other tucked in his waistcoat at the chest. His white hair was pulled back and tied at the nape of his neck. He wore knickers atop white stockings and high black boots. She recognized him from the Forgiveness of Arnold Meeting.

"Mr. Washington, is that you?" Christi was still mostly asleep.

"Yes, Miss."

"Mr. Washington, I'm not dressed for this occasion," she protested, still half asleep.

He laughed. "I have not come to judge imperfections, Miss Christi. I have come to experience your total perfection."

There was a silent pause. "Did you... did you bring the laws, the spiritual laws you mentioned?" She remained curled up on the couch, uncertain what to do or say.

"Now, you must not think you are a second Moses, about to go to the top of the mountain to collect stone tablets," he said smiling broadly. "We will discuss the spiritual laws as you are ready."

Christi decided she must get up. She stood, looked up directly into his eyes, then held out her hand, which she quickly withdrew. "Did women shake hands in your time?" She fumbled for words. "I mean... I don't have on a skirt, or whatever, so I can't curtsy. I'm sorry, I'm at a loss for what is proper." They both laughed.

"Please forgive me, Mr. Washington," Christi said, struggling to regain her composure. "May I offer you some tea and cookies?" She clapped her hand over her mouth. "I can't believe I asked you if you'd like tea and cookies!"

"Yes, indeed, I would. You are so kind," he replied, himself emitting a kindness that was palpable. "I would be most grateful for a light repast. May we just enjoy it here at the table while we visit?"

"Of course." Christi darted to the kitchen where she quickly put the tea kettle on the stove and took cookies from the cookie jar.

Mr. Washington waited by the large bay window as the afternoon sun hung low in the western sky. The ceiling danced with shimmering rainbows as the sun's rays were refracted through the cut-glass window pane.

Christi soon returned with a pot of hot tea, two cups and saucers, and a plate of homemade drop cookies on a silver tray. "I hope you like these cookies." She set the tray at the end of the table. "It's a recipe I have developed over the last six months or so. Living here in the country I have time to do that sort of thing."

She invited him to sit at the head of the table, where she placed a cup and saucer in front of him. She poured tea into his cup. "Do you like milk or sugar in your tea, Mr. Washington?"

"Thank you, a little sugar, please."

Christi fetched a small bowl of sugar. "Please help yourself," she said, placing a spoon next to the sugar bowl and offering him the plate of cookies.

"May I ask what sort of tea is this?" he asked politely after taking a sip.

"Lipton tea." She watched for his response.

"Hmmm. Lipton tea.... The cookies are delicious. Very unusual. What do you have in them?" he asked as he finished one cookie and reached for another.

"Well, I'm not sure you would recognize everything in them. They have chocolate chips."

"I know of chocolate, of course. And I see you have raisins in them. What are chocolate chips? And what type of nuts are these?"

Christi giggled. Was it true she was discussing her cookie recipe with the first President? She was certain this was not a dream. She tried to explain chocolate chips, and told him that the nuts were actually sunflower seeds, and some pecans, and there were also sesame seeds in the cookies. That seemed to satisfy his curiosity about the cookies.

"Well, Miss Christi. How shall I commence? I am immensely grateful for your assistance. Occasionally one is presented with a unique moment in history and one must choose. Not everyone would demonstrate your courage."

"Mr. Washington, there are so many things I don't understand. I have hundreds of questions and so few answers."

"Where would you like to begin?"

"First, would you please tell me... are we presently in the dimension you exist in or the dimension I exist in?" she asked timidly.

"That is a good question," he replied, trying to conceal his amusement. "But it has an inherent flaw—it presupposes that the two are separate and distinct. It will be easier if you just relinquish that belief."

"But Mr. Washington, who sent you? Why have you come?"

"You asked me to!" he replied emphatically. "Not the singular you, of course, but the collective YOU. There are presently a large number of correlating interactions taking place on a global scale. By your intent you connected with a global consciousness seeking a better way and a global determination to find it. When the student is ready, the teacher will always be there, having patiently waited for that precious moment to share the glory of the student's enlightenment."

"I remember asking that engraving of you to help guide me," she said motioning to the picture over the mantel, "but I didn't expect this. I'm honored to be a participant, I think, but how did this come to pass?"

"Perhaps I can explain it this way." Mr. Washington's eyes sparkled. "What you see when we meet is a visual experience. That is why most people could not see me, although you can. Simply put, they have not chosen to dismantle their defenses to such vision, as you have. They choose instead to believe that a physical presence is a condition precedent to their seeing, which of course is nonsense; a tragic limitation to which most humans unwittingly and needlessly submit. But most don't know that expanded new skills are now accessible to them, skills they have not yet learned to use."

"But I still don't understand. How can a person have such a visual experience?"

"In your case, you simply chose, not consciously of course, but you nonetheless chose to dismantle the mechanisms that would normally filter out my higher level of vibration."

"I see..." She rubbed her chin pensively.

"The primary ingredient is correlation," he continued. "There must be a correlation between the desire and intent of the human in physical form and the desire and intent of the... the... well, ghost, shall we say, for lack of a better term. And the correlation must occur simultaneously, although you will most often not be conscious that it has occurred at all. One soul communicates with another, so to speak, having agreed upon the need to do so. You are simply using senses that others are not yet aware they possess. So, Miss Christi, here we are. Your role in this and mine are of equal importance, you understand."

"So, you are not really a physical body, although you are sitting here with me drinking tea and eating cookies?"

"Even you merely *appear* to be a physical body!" he exclaimed. "Indeed, even the core of the Universe is not physical matter. The Universe is pure energy, energy that is capable of being formed into any physical reality. It is from one's intent with regard to this energy that one's physical reality manifests. This is how everything, even political systems, are produced. This is the true nature of reality."

"Such a notion of reality is difficult to comprehend. Although... I have a friend, a physicist. Well, actually, he's more than just a friend.

He's been trying to explain this type of thing to me. But I must admit, I'm not picking it up as quickly as I would like."

"Miss Christi, it's not important that you understand the physics of this phenomenon. Application, not theory, is what you are to learn. You need only understand the practical application of what I am saying."

"I have tried to understand the significance of the meeting when Benedict Arnold was forgiven, here at the table." Christi spoke hesitantly, reluctant to acknowledge the extent of her ignorance about the process in which she now found herself. "Perhaps you can help me."

"It will take time for many, not only yourself, to recognize the process the Earth is presently in, and beyond that, the significance the Earth's present evolution plays in the Cosmic Plan. But it is critical for all Americans to reflect upon their past learning about Brother Arnold, and all others whom each has judged, and to understand that those images are nothing more than projections of themselves. The judged, be it Brother Arnold or any other, are convenient tools that many use to reinforce their mistaken beliefs about truth and justice, sin and punishment. In truth, Brother Arnold and all the others are just as God created them—perfect and unblemished."

"Yes, I heard that at the Meeting, that it's foolish to think we can create Brother Arnold in an image different from the image God created. I have thought about that. It's obvious that no human possesses the power to undo what God has done. And yet our legal system. . . . "

Mr. Washington interrupted. "Indeed, to believe otherwise is to believe that illusion is real and that truth is unreal. I recognize this is contrary to what so many have been carefully taught, and threatens that in which they have much invested. It will require much unlearning. And for some, it is so foreign that they will be unable to accept it at this time. But timing is the only choice they have, for ultimately the truth shall be known by all."

Christi gazed intently at her guest. "But what am I to do in all this?"

"Miss Christi, when we fought to found this Nation, these United States of America, we had a dream of a new type of government, one governed by spiritual principles, by the Natural Law. That dream is at risk unless a new genre of leadership emerges, leaders who understand the role of the dream in creation and are prepared to lead the People in its manifestation. Our dream must manifest in the twenty-first century or this opportunity will be lost and dark forces may prevail far longer than necessary."

"So you have come to tell us what needs to be done?"

"I have come to impart certain knowledge to you, with your consent, of course. It is knowledge that is essential for governing the People in the next age. Your role is to hold the dream, the vision, until it manifests." Mr. Washington spoke with such gentleness it did not sound threatening. "When enough people share the dream, it will come into being. Not instantly, but on the most etheric level at first, moving slowly into more and more concrete form until it at last manifests on the physical plane. That's why the choosing of a leader is so important. The leader of a People plays a major role in creating the dream, then holding the vision and leading the People to the collective manifestation of that dream on the physical plane. The process began long ago. Your role is to assist its progress at this critical juncture."

"Leaders are responsible for creating the dream and holding the vision? I don't understand what you mean."

"All that exists on the physical plane had its beginning at the point of infinite possibilities. Anything can become manifest. For example, whether a political system is a dictatorship or a democracy is a choice.

It is a collective choice, but the leadership that exists is critical in affecting the choices that are made and what ultimately becomes manifest."

"But how do leaders create dreams and hold visions?"

Mr. Washington thought for a moment. "Have you ever heard of 'healers'?"

"Yes. When I was a child there was an elderly African American woman who could stop bleeding by holding her hand over a wound. I saw her do this once when a child had been badly injured in a bicycle accident," she replied, confused by the question.

"Good. This is done... such healing is done by removing oneself from the situation, by becoming a mere instrument of God, by being a presence through which God's energy can flow, but at the same time being totally unattached to the outcome. And so it is with the enlightened leader. He serves only the greater good and has no personal attachment to the outcome, as it is not for himself that he acts. He is clear and focused in the eye of the storm, but a mere instrument, the voice for God, speaking to all and for all, in a purely non-self-serving manner." Mr. Washington drank the last of his tea and Christi refilled his cup.

"How does one develop this ability?" she asked, spellbound.

"In order to be an enlightened leader, one must have evolved beyond the level of the ego. Perhaps this will help. Imagine a fetus in the womb. As it manifests in the physical, it slowly develops awareness, but without any concept of relationship. It knows of nothing but its own existence and it has nothing with which to compare itself.

"After birth and in early childhood the child begins to differentiate between himself and the world about him. The child experiences events that begin to collect in his memory, and his desires begin to evolve. Eventually, as the child develops, ideas can be formulated and a sense of self-awareness begins, an understanding of one's self in relation to others.

"Eventually he perceives himself, the world around him, and he has the ability to reflect on the relationship between the two. At this point, he has developed a sense of self-perception, and has the ability to reflect upon his effect on others and his place in the world. He has a certain sense of history, one might say. Many people journey no further than this. A leader who has evolved only to this level may be self-serving and can cause great harm.

"To be enlightened, one must have evolved beyond this point. He must have experienced a spiritual awakening. It is through this experience that he... or she, as the case may be, is able to serve on a higher level." Mr. Washington looked directly into Christi's eyes, as though looking into her soul. "She has undergone a process of purification resulting in an understanding that what is important is far greater than self. She recognizes her importance, not as an individual, but as a symbol of the collective dream and the power she possesses to direct the dream toward manifestation."

"These concepts are all so new," Christi said shaking her head. "How does someone achieve such a spiritual awakening and such purity?"

Mr. Washington sipped his tea. He took another cookie. "There is no particular set of rules," he patiently explained. "It can happen in the Garden of Gethsemane. Or at Valley Forge. Or it may simply happen one day, as though a veil that has concealed the knowing of which I speak has been lifted, but most often it is not this easy. How much effort must be exerted to access this type of knowing depends on one's level of resistance. It is available to all, but it requires a detachment from the physical that yet remains beyond the reach of many."

"It is still very much beyond me, as well," Christi confessed.

"This perception is transitory," Mr. Washington said, with a gentleness that seemed uniquely his. "As it is your intent to master this information, you will do so. Intent, when all is said and done, is actually all that matters. There is no good or bad outcome independent of intent, because it is intent that determines the outcome. The greater the power of one's intent, the greater is one's power to manifest change in the physical world."

Christi gazed at her guest. "This is all so different from what I have been taught. I don't know what to say."

"Nothing need be said, Miss Christi. Trust that what you have been taught will yet serve you well. A leader must not only be spiritually enlightened. She must possess analytical ability as well. She must be able to communicate her vision with pragmatism and reason. You will find your training in the law most useful in this regard."

Mr. Washington smiled and touched her hand. "We have done quite enough for this encounter. I must let you absorb what we have discussed. I believe I will walk over to that hill." He gestured to the west, toward a distant hillside visible through the large bay window. "A walk in the early evening air will be refreshing. You know, you can see Mount Vernon from the top of that hill," he said nostalgically.

They rose from the table and walked toward the door. Then he stopped and turned toward Christi. "Before I depart, there is something I must explain." A gentle breeze blew through the doorway. "Perhaps you believe that I have come from the past, but I come from the future. I have come to assist in the propagation of certain choices backward in time, from the future to the present. By doing so, you see, I can lend guidance in directing the present and determining the outcome. Certainly, the choice remains a free one. But through my intervention, its probability of materializing is enhanced."

Christi looked at him, silently pondering the meaning of his message.

"Now, Miss Christi..." he said cheerily. "Despite all this discussion about one's personal desires being of no importance, may I ask a small indulgence of you? It would be such a great pleasure to have some fine English tea. Do you believe that would be possible when we meet again?'

"Of course," replied Christi before even considering where she could find fine English tea. They shook hands and Mr. Washington, with long strides, walked into the sunset toward the distant hill while she watched. When he was out of sight, she went to the telephone.

"Tom," she said when he answered. "Do you think you could find me some good English tea in Boston? Mr. Washington would like some."

"Yes!" Tom's excitement was like that of a child on Christmas morning. "He came, didn't he? I knew it, George Washington came back!"

"Yes, he has come again."

CHAPTER SIXTEEN

Christi began reading a number of books Tom sent on quantum physics, the new physics that has replaced many of Isaac Newton's theories about the Universe. It wasn't yet clear how this material was relevant, but she was drawn to it in her efforts to make sense of the unusual events transpiring in her life.

There was a common theme in all that Christi read, and in Hap's philosophy, as well—the interconnectedness of all Creation. She was slowly embracing a view of reality that no longer included the concept of separation of one part from another. Instead, she was beginning to see an unbroken web within space that was rich with the flow of process, as well as matter. In this context, she began to realize that an event in any part of the whole had an instantaneous impact upon the whole.

It became increasingly difficult for Christi to view law in the classical sense, as the whole being nothing more than an interaction of the parts. She was coming to the conclusion that the behavior of the parts is actually orchestrated by the whole. In fact, at some level, the parts do not even exist.

In a late afternoon discussion with Hap, Christi asked, "If one accepts the theory that we're all one, if nothing is separate, then how can a criminal act be viewed as something separate and not in relationship to the whole?"

"It can't," he replied. "Nor can punishment be viewed as merely a consequence imposed by 'society' upon those who commit certain acts. It, too, must be seen in a much broader context. Our history of ignoring the interconnectedness of all things is responsible for many of our problems. An illness in one part of the body can't be treated without considering its connection to the whole person. Using parts of the Earth with no regard for the impact upon the totality has caused many of our environmental problems. By the same token, we can't deal with problems in our society—crime, poverty, drug abuse or any other issue—without looking at the totality of the system and the impact each part has on the whole."

"The physicists have already had to adjust their theories," Christi observed. "They say the quantum potential that permeates all of space results in all particles being nonlocally interconnected. They call it 'nonlocality.' I'm certain nonlocality is just as applicable to law and social order as it is to physics. You know that old adage 'all politics are local'? That's based on the belief in separation when, in truth, no politics can be local because of the impact each part has on the whole. It's the same with many of our laws. They're mistakenly based on our belief in separation.

"The more I study the principles of new physics," she continued, "the more I'm led to the conclusion that simple assumptions that have undergirded fundamental principles of law and social order for centuries, perhaps millennia, are inherently flawed. For example, when we hold someone who causes an injury to another liable for the resulting injury, that's based on the assumption the injury would not have occurred but for their wrongful act, as though it's an isolated event."

"You mean like the 'last clear chance doctrine'?" Hap asked.

"Yes. Like when two people are involved in an automobile accident. If the party who was injured had a clear opportunity to avoid the accident, by turning away or stopping before the accident occurred, but didn't take advantage of that last clear chance, then we don't hold the other party liable. But this view of causality is much too narrow. It ignores the vast sequence of events, each one of which is an essential element in the intricate web that results in the ultimate outcome, and focuses instead on just one event immediately preceding the injury. I no longer think a single cause-and-effect relationship can actually be separated from the Universe as a whole. In quantum physics, chance hasn't been proven. It's more likely that every event occurs as the result of choice on some level. In other words, for an automobile accident to occur, both parties, on some level, must choose to participate. Applying this theory to our legal system, everyone has a last clear chance."

"Haven't the physicists also suggested that disorder doesn't exist?" Hap asked. "I always figured when things appear disordered it's merely because their order is hidden. Perhaps apparent disorder is a necessary condition precedent to change. A period of chaos or crisis may be the precursor of restructuring that will ultimately result in a new order that's more functional than the old order had become."

"Yes. We'll have to revise our notions of order and disorder in law and society, just as the physicists have had to do," Christi declared.

Hap tapped his fingers on his mouth as he thought. "You know, I think many of the basic legal principles we continue to apply were devised to bring order to an entirely different society," he said. "The way we now practice law is still reminiscent of the Code of Hammurabi that was developed by a king of Babylonia over 1700 years before Christ. It was best known for the principle 'an eye for an eye and a tooth for a tooth,' which was a progressive idea at the time. It at least imposed some restraint on vengeance, requiring that it be in proportion to the wrong for which vengeance was sought. But Jesus rejected the concept of an eye for a eye, and admonished instead that you must do good to those who harm you, an admonition still honored mostly in the breach.

"The old legal system, based on the notion of an eye for an eye, is becoming progressively out of balance with what many people now believe to be just," Hap said, holding his hands palm up, like a pair of scales. "All is in Divine Order, in perfect balance. We merely believe we experience chaos because transformation has the appearance of disorder. There are major global forces at work, causing a new social order to be expressed in both action and structure throughout all levels of social organization. I think that's what we're experiencing now."

"Hap, I've thought a lot about your statement that the Piscean Age was dominated by the masculine energy, but with the Aquarian Age, the feminine energy must emerge predominate," Christi said, leaning forward, her elbows on the edge of Hap's desk. "That's beginning to make sense. Assume the Code of Hammurabi was compatible with the dynamic of the Piscean Age which, as I understand it, had to do with domination of the strong over the weak. This seems to be reflected in old English Common Law time and time again. You know, all those doctrines governing relationships between master and servant, parent and child, husband and wife, all having to do with the dominion of one over the other. In the past, that was the dynamic expressed in both action and structure throughout all levels of social organization.

"But if you look for evidence that the feminine energy is emerging, it's all around," she said, gesturing excitedly. "We're undoubtedly reordering society in the direction of partnership, team-work, balance... equality. Think of the success of the American Revo-lution; the abolition of slavery; the Civil Rights Movement and Women's Liberation; property and inheritance laws being revised to reflect partnership, instead of subservience; marital rape now being defined as a crime, instead of a virtual right accorded to husbands; children are no longer property as they were under English Common Law and are not to be brutally beaten or abused as a matter of right; and growing equality in the workplace and even in tenant's rights."

"And change has just begun," Hap said nodding in agreement. "If the very thoughts that we create generate frequency patterns that become manifest in some form, and our thoughts are constantly affecting the subtle energetic levels of the Universe, we'll even have to find ways to be held accountable to one another in this regard. It seems remote, but I'm confident it will occur as the new order of social and legal organization continues to unfold."

When Christi arrived home that evening, she immediately called Tom. "Your theories in quantum physics are going to revolutionize law," she teased.

"Of course they will," Tom replied. "All those laws based on the assumption the Universe is composed of distinct particles of matter separated by empty space are going to have to go. You'll have to figure out what to do with Bohm's theory that the Universe is composed of a seamless fabric, just like the physicists are doing. Reality is not just the 'explicate order,' the physical world in which we believe we exist. It's also made up of the 'implicate order,' even though that's not consciously accessible to us through our five senses. One is enfolded in the other. What appears to be concrete matter is actually a vast ocean of waves and frequencies from which our brains create the illusion of matter. We think of ourselves as physical bodies moving through space, but we are also an interference pattern enfolded within the cosmic hologram."

"Are you saying we are an energy field, as well as a physical body?"

"Certainly. Each of us is an interference pattern that contains comprehensive information about our physical, emotional, mental and spiritual evolutionary history," he explained. "And, just as drops of water form an ocean, the history of each of us is intricately related to the interference pattern of other beings. Together it all forms the Universe."

"All these revolutionary new ideas!" Christi remarked. "I appreciate your instruction. I'm beginning to understand that viewing the Universe as composed of parts, as the law does, is meaningless and counterproductive. What's troubling is that I'm no longer sure what reality is. I'm beginning to wonder if the objective world exists, at least in the way I've been taught."

"It doesn't," Tom replied.

"There's so much to learn. I'm still grappling with the idea of the hologram— not on a credit card, but on a universal scale. Your books say each portion of the hologram contains an image of the whole, and that every part of the Universe has the whole enfolded within it, as well. I'm having trouble with the concept that, in principle, all of the past and all of the future are enfolded in each small region of time and space. And the ensuing principle that even every cell of my body has the entire cosmos enfolded within it. It's a radical new way of looking at reality!"

"Perhaps the most radical theory postulated in some of the new physics materials is the assertion that every action begins from an intention created at the level of the implicate order," Tom said. "Within the intention are the seeds of all the movements necessary to carry out the intention. The process of creation moves through the subtle levels of the implicate order, and ultimately manifests in the explicate order, the material world as we know it."

"Tom! That must be what Mr. Washington was referring to when he said all that exists on the physical plane had its beginning at the point of infinite possibilities, including dictatorships and democracies. This has to be what he meant by creating the dream and holding the vision. That's why the leadership that exists is critical in affecting the choices that are made and what ultimately becomes manifest!"

"That must be it!" he agreed. "If Julie was right, Christi, that we're in a new stage in evolution of the human species, a new system of laws must be formulated, comparable to the revolutionary changes taking place in physics. It'll be interesting to see what this new system looks like... and the part you are to play in its development."

CHAPTER SEVENTEEN

Heaps of books and papers cluttered one end of the table. It was late afternoon as Christi sat reviewing her materials on physics and law. When she looked up she realized she was not alone. Mr. Washington sat at the opposite end of the table, his silhouette outlined by the sun shining though the bay window.

"Good afternoon, Miss Christi. I hope I did not startle you."

"Hello," she said, pleased to have her guest return. "No, in fact, I was wondering when you would come again. It seemed like it was time."

"I see you have done much preparation since we last met. We are now ready to begin our study of the Seven Spiritual Principles for Governing a People." He rose and moved to the end of the table near Christi.

"I have some tea for you, I mean good English tea," she said smiling. "I hope it's good; it came from Boston. The man in the shop said in Colonial times each home had its own formula for mixing varieties of tea to create a distinctive flavor. He said he likes the mix that I have. May I fix you some?"

"Please. Do you have some of those nice cookies, too?"

"I made a batch yesterday. It must be a coincidence," she said as she rose to go to the kitchen.

"No, indeed. There are no coincidences."

Christi laughed. "I think you previously mentioned the need for much unlearning to take place. I'm beginning to understand."

Returning quickly with tea and cookies, she placed the silver tray on the table. "I've been studying quantum physics," she said as she began to serve the tea.

"You are determined to understand not only the application, but the theory as well, aren't you?" Mr. Washington sipped his tea. "Oh, my! This is delicious. You know, we had to sacrifice our custom of serving fine English tea before the Boston Tea Party."

"Of course," she said, especially pleased that she had provided something that brought her guest such pleasure. "I never thought I would have the opportunity to tell you in person how grateful we are for the many sacrifices you made."

"Well, this is your opportunity to do something in return." He returned his tea cup to its saucer. "As you have chosen to participate in this special undertaking, let us begin forthwith with the first of the Seven Spiritual Principles."

Christi could feel her heart leap to her throat. Her hand held her teacup tightly. She had waited for this moment with such anticipation, but upon its arrival she was filled with fear.

"The first principle has to do with fear," Mr. Washington began. "Fear is a powerful emotion, the very opposite of love. In fact, there are only two emotions, love and fear. All other emotions are mere descriptions of aspects of these two."

"What does fear have to do with spiritual principles for governing people?" Christi managed to ask, embarrassed that her response to commencing this study had been so inappropriate.

"The first Spiritual Principle has to do with the misuse of fear by those who govern. This is quite common." Mr. Washington took a second cookie. "Fear is based upon the concept of separation. It divides a People, one group against the other, instead of promoting harmony and peace within a Nation. Its misuse by those who govern will destroy a Nation, lead to war within, and eventually without. It promotes hatred, which is but an aspect of fear. Its use to manipulate the very people who are to be governed is the greatest offense a leader of people can commit—sedition of the worst nature. Anyone willing to use fear to promote one's own agenda at the expense of the public good must not be entrusted with the power of the People," he stated emphatically. "**FEAR SHALL NEVER BE USED TO MANIPULATE THE PEOPLE.** That is the First Spiritual Principle for Governing a People."

Christi poured herself more tea and took another cookie while she listened silently.

"This principle is very sound, but perhaps not for the reasons you presently understand" he continued in a gentler voice. "Those who must use fear to achieve their objectives are, in fact, exhibiting a profound sense of vulnerability. They feel vulnerable because they believe in separation, upon which fear depends. They are unable to recognize when it is love, not fear, that threatens their way of thought, and that love can heal their fear. They are incapable of judgment except in terms of attack. The only choice they see is whether to attack now or withdraw and attack later."

"I know fear is powerful, but it's hard to understand *why* it's such an effective tool to manipulate the People," Christi lamented.

"Fear derives its power from the underlying belief that God's love is conditional. For many, this instruction begins at birth when their parents withhold love as a form of punishment—manipulation it could be called. Unfortunately, the conditional nature of God's love is also a lesson often taught by organized religions when those who minister are themselves seeking to manipulate. Having been taught that love is conditional, the People believe it can be withheld, that it does not exist in certain places, or is not associated with certain groups or persons. This is the root of all fear, the fear you will be excluded from those loved by God. You surrender your power to those who hold out the promise of victory over the imagined source of your fear. Having surrendered your power, you believe you are nothing, and willingly submit to the will even of tyrants, thinking you deserve no better."

Mr. Washington paused and chose another cookie. "Contrary to what many believe, access to God does not depend upon the intercession of others. Peace can be found only at the altar of God and that altar is within you. It is here that freedom from fear is assured. To experience the truth of what I say, you must love without attack, if only for an instant."

"But Mr. Washington, is this realistic? How can such concepts be learned?"

"Do you remember when you were learning to read? At first you just saw lines and circles, but then you began to connect them to see new meaning. Once this skill had been learned, a new world lay before you and you could go anywhere in your mind through the pages of a book. You are at just that point with this new learning. Once you have grasped the basic principles, you will have a new understanding of yourself and all that is about you."

Leaning back in his chair Mr. Washington smiled. "You will understand in time. But we must stop, for now," he said as he rose to depart.

"Mr. Washington," Christi said urgently as she stood. "I have moments of serious doubt about my role in all of this."

He paused, examining her anxious face. "You have come too far to turn back. To know you could change a world so bitterly bereft, but to step back now because you are afraid, would that not be your condemnation?"

She lowered her head in acquiescence as he continued. "As you heal, your healing will extend and be brought to problems that you thought were not your own. For many different problems will be solved as any one of them has been resolved."

"But... well... How do I begin? Where do I start? It's all so much larger than I am."

"It's very simple," Mr. Washington replied as they walked toward the door. "Do not believe it is your responsibility to change the world. You are responsible only for change within yourself. Begin by reclaiming your power. When someone tries to manipulate you through fear, remember that God's love is not conditional. Return only love. This act alone will change the world."

CHAPTER EIGHTEEN

Dulles Airport was crowded with summer travelers. Christi watched the passengers pass until she saw a stout, gray-haired woman carrying a small package carefully wrapped with heavy string. Only treasures such as homemade jams and jellies would be given such special treatment by her mother, tipping Christi off to the fact she would soon be the benefactor of such bounty.

As she watched her mother approach, she wondered how much information she should reveal about the unusual events in her life. Christi wanted more than anything to share every detail, but was concerned about her mother's reaction. After all, she was expecting to see Christi's new house, not to hear of events that a "rational" person would consider delusional.

They greeted one another with hugs, then gathered Mrs. Daniel's luggage and set out for the old Tyler place. As they drove, Christi directed the conversation toward small talk, catching up on the activities of family and hometown friends. They discussed various attributes of the season's weather and how the farmers in southern Colorado had been affected.

"Are you sure you should live so far in the country?" Mrs. Daniel asked after they had driven for some time.

Christi smiled. "I don't live any farther out than we did when I was growing up."

As they turned into the long drive to her house Mrs. Daniel exclaimed, "Oh, my! It's such a large house. Are you sure you need such a large place? Who takes care of all this yard for you?"

"It was the best investment I could find. I hadn't planned to get such a large house, but it was a better buy than anything else I looked at. I do most of the yard work, although sometimes a neighbor helps me out. I actually enjoy it."

"Wonders never cease," her mother said, as they stopped at the end of the drive. "When you were a child you thought you were Cinderella when we asked you to work in the garden or do yard work. But this is beautiful."

They got out of the car and walked around the house. Mrs. Daniel looked it over carefully. "Seems to be in good repair... for such an old house." Then she remarked on the size of Christi's garden and asked, "You spaded this all by yourself?"

"Indeed I did! I had my share of backaches, but it felt great to work with the soil. I guess a lot of things change when a child grows up and leaves home."

Christi invited her mother through the front door and, as they stepped inside, directed her to the dining room.

"Oh, my," her mother said. "Why such a large dining table?"

Christi couldn't help but laugh. "I don't need such a large dining table, but I love it. The table and I have a special relationship."

"A special relationship?" her mother asked. "How can you have a relationship with a table?"

"Let me show you the rest of the house. Then I'll try to explain."

Their grand tour ended with the guest room, newly decorated in honor of Mrs. Daniel's visit. It was a spacious corner room on the front of the house with cross ventilation that she knew her mother would enjoy.

"I'm overwhelmed," her mother said as Christi sat her luggage on the floor. "My little girl with such a beautiful home. It's a far cry from that little basement apartment you had when you were with the Justice Department."

"I'll let you get settled in. Then we can have tea and cookies at my special table."

Christi went to the kitchen. She put the tea pot on the stove and arranged homemade cookies on a plate, just as she did when Mr. Washington visited. She tried to imagine herself telling her mother about her visits with the first President.

"It is a beautiful place," Mrs. Daniel said as she came into the kitchen to watch Christi's preparations. "Such a beautiful view. Are you sure you are safe here all by yourself?"

"Mom, I'm thirty-seven. I'm not a little girl anymore. Of course I'm safe here." She carried the silver tray into the dining room and placed it on the table. "Rainbows will dance on the ceiling as soon as the afternoon sun gets low in the western sky. The light comes through those cut glass panels in the window. This is my favorite place this time of day."

"This does seem to be a special room. What an unusual decoration on the marble around the fireplace," Mrs. Daniel observed as Christi poured tea. "I like your picture of George Washington. He was such a good man. What's that little apron he's wearing?"

"Washington was a Mason. That's an apron decorated with Masonic symbols. I think the star and key carved in the fireplace are Masonic symbols, too."

"Well, what do you know! Of course your father was never a Mason. He was Catholic." She sipped her tea. "This tea is delicious. What type is it?"

"Should I tell her?" Christi wondered. "Oh..." she said. "I buy it for a friend who comes to visit me every so often. He likes good English tea. Tom found this for me at a tea shop in Boston. It's actually a blend of teas, because that's the way they used to do in the American Colonies. Each house had its own distinctive blend of tea."

"Now you not only garden but are a connoisseur of fine English tea!" Mrs. Daniel remarked with a tone of wonder. "Who is your friend that comes to visit?"

Christi swallowed hard. "You would never guess who it is. Not in a million years. You see... he comes from the future."

"What does that mean?"

"Well, most people would think he comes from the past but he doesn't. It's difficult to explain. Mom..." Christi placed her hand on her mother's. She looked at her mother's aging face. "I want very much to share something with you. It's something very unusual. I don't know anyone who has ever had anything like this happen to them. And maybe it isn't really happening, but I think it is. You see, shortly after I moved into this house, I heard voices here in this room, one night when I was in bed."

"You heard voices? Were you afraid?"

"I was terrified, at first. But the voices didn't seem to be interested in me. They were just having a meeting."

"A meeting? What sort of meeting?" her mother asked nervously.

"A Masonic meeting."

"Who was having a Masonic meeting? In your house?"

"Here, at this table. That's where the intrigue and mystery begins. It was some of the Founding Fathers."

"Founding Fathers of what?"

"Of this Nation. Some of them used to meet here, in this room, at this table, when they were creating this Nation. When I returned the table to its former location, that was a sign that they were to meet again."

"Oh, Christi. Is this a story that you are writing? I'll bet you are not only into gardening and fine teas, but you have begun to write fiction, too. How wonderful that this old house has inspired you to do so many new things."

"Well, Mom," said Christi reluctantly. "It may be fiction, but I don't think so. It seems so real, I think it's really happening."

"What is really happening?"

"That George Washington comes to visit me. When he comes to visit, we always have these cookies and this tea. And then we talk."

Mrs. Daniel's eyes narrowed as she examined her daughter intensely. "Christi, you are serious, aren't you?"

"Yes, Mom, I'm serious. It's so real. I know it sounds crazy, but I really believe Mr. Washington comes to visit me."

"Why, what do you believe is the purpose of these visits?" her mother asked skeptically.

"I only know what he's told me. He says he must deliver Seven Spiritual Principles for Governing a People. But he has only delivered one so far."

Her mother looked worried. "Has anyone else seen George Washington on these visits?"

"Well, my partner, Hap... he was here during one of the meetings."

Her mother thought for a moment. "Didn't you tell me he was blind?"

"Yes, so he didn't actually see anything, but he heard it. And I saw it. I saw the whole thing, and I'm *sure* it was real. I know it sounds bizarre, Mom, but it's a wonderful adventure, and I want to share it with you, more than anyone else, as it unfolds."

Mrs. Daniel was silent. She sipped her tea. "These are delicious cookies. Where did you get the recipe?"

"I concocted it myself, since I've been living here."

Mrs. Daniel reached over and gently put her hand on the side of Christi's face. "How could so many things change in a child's life so quickly? These meetings… they must be a dream. Are you on medication or something?"

"Mom, please trust me," Christi pleaded. "Even if it's a dream it's a wonderful dream and I want you to know all about it. But I don't believe it's a dream."

"Darling, I want to believe you. You are the most honest child that ever was, but this is so out of the ordinary. Don't you think you should, well… perhaps check to see if it might be something else? Have you seen anyone, you know, like a doctor, to see if you have any problems?"

"I've thought about it. But the people closest to me, Tom and Hap, don't think I'm crazy. They think I'm involved in some extraordinary event. That I've been chosen for this."

"If that's true, wouldn't you like to have it confirmed? Shouldn't you see someone, just to be sure? I don't want to sound alarmed, but it would be good to see if someone can tell you what this is."

"I admit I've considered it. I don't deny, in these circumstances, it might be a good idea. I'd like to know myself if it's as unusual as I think it is. I know several people who don't think it's all that strange," she said, stretching the truth just a little.

Mrs. Daniel set her tea cup aside. "So you will promise me you'll see someone… a psychiatrist maybe?"

"I promise, Mom. Like you said, it won't hurt. And anyway, I had thought about doing that myself."

Christi was uneasy as she perused the directory of the tall office building looking for the name of Dr. Lester Lumpkin. Her only knowledge of this particular psychiatrist was what she had read in a newspaper article. It reported some honor he had received from peers in his profession—evidence, she assumed, that he was qualified and competent. Room 444, Christi noted when she found the name.

Intuitively Christi knew that she was not crazy, but intellectually she had to admit it was a distinct possibility. Within a week of her mother's visit she had made the necessary arrangements to make good on her promise and to satisfy her own qualms about her mental condition. She had told neither Tom nor Hap that she was seeing a psychiatrist. The only person she had confided in was Shenan who had objected vigorously to the idea. She told Christi if they locked her up, she would hire a lawyer and come get her out.

Christi entered the meticulously decorated office with its carefully coordinated turquoise and mauve rugs, chairs, walls and paintings. She informed the receptionist she was here for her 11:00 a.m. appointment. She had waited only a few minutes when a middle-aged woman entered the reception area, apparently having just completed her session with the doctor. She looked sad as she paid her bill and made her next appointment.

"Please step this way," the receptionist said, as she directed Christi through the door toward the doctor's inner office. Dr. Lumpkin met Christi at the door to his office, a middle-aged man with a salt and pepper goatee and bifocals.

"Good morning, Miss Daniel. I'm Dr. Lumpkin."

"Good morning," she said as they shook hands. "Did you receive the forms I filled out and mailed to you?"

"Yes." He motioned for Christi to sit in a large chair in front of his glass-top desk. "I have a few questions that we'll go over. But first, please tell me why you are here."

"I don't quite know where to begin. Some unusual things have been happening in my life." She chuckled nervously. "So I thought I should check with someone to see if I'm okay."

"Had you been under any sort of stress before these events began?"

"Well, actually, I had. I had been at a large law firm in Washington, and I hated it. I saw so much dishonesty. That bothered me a lot."

Dr. Lumpkin began to make notes on the pad that lay before him.

"And then the senior partner assaulted me," Christi added.

"Were there any witnesses to this assault?"

"No. It happened in a motel room and we were alone."

"What were you doing with the senior partner in a motel room alone?" the doctor asked, peering at her over the top of his bifocals.

"We had gone there for lunch." She hesitated. "At least that's what I thought, but he had other ideas. He was interested in me, not lunch."

"Did you know he was interested in you before this happened, before you went to the motel room to have lunch with him?"

"Yes, he had been coming on to me for some time."

"I see. He had been coming on to you, but you went to a motel room with him for lunch... alone. Who is the gentleman whom you allege assaulted you?"

"You might know who he is. He's pretty high profile. It's Winston Harp."

"The organizer of the R.R.s! Doesn't he have a wife and two lovely daughters? He has a reputation for being a fine family man. But you say he took you to a motel room for lunch and assaulted you after coming on to you for a period of time?"

"Yes." She folded her arms across her chest and straightened her shoulders. "His public image and what he's like in person are not at all the same."

"Have you ever been married, Ms. Daniel?"

"No."

"Are you in a serious relationship at this time?"

"I have a close friend, but it's not all that serious."

"How long since you last had sex... I mean, with a man?"

"Dr. Lumpkin," Christi stated firmly. "I came here to see about these unusual events in my life, not my sex life."

He wrote more notes. "I see.... Please tell me what happened after you experienced the stress at the law firm."

"I left the firm and moved to a small town in northern Virginia. I bought an old house and began to fix it up. And I started a small law practice in different areas of law from what I was practicing in D.C."

"So, you had several major changes in your life. The stress of the move, a new job that was different, and you were renovating an old house, as well. Any one of those could be a major source of stress."

"Yes," she agreed, "but I liked my new house and my new job so much, it didn't seem all that stressful."

"Well, then, what did seem stressful?"

"The problem began one night when I heard voices in my dining room in the middle of the night. At first I was afraid, but they didn't seem to be bothering anything. They were just having a meeting."

"What sort of a meeting?"

"I later determined it was some sort of Masonic meeting."

He peered at her over the rim of his glasses. "Who was in attendance at this Masonic meeting?"

"I know it sounds weird, but it was some of the men who founded this Nation. Some of the Founding Fathers, but I'm not sure exactly who was at that meeting. At the next meeting they said some of their names, but not at the first one."

"I see." Dr. Lumpkin frantically wrote notes on his pad. "Why do you believe they chose your home as their meeting place?"

"Because of my dining room table," Christi reported reticently.

"Tell me about this dining room table," the doctor directed.

"Well, it's a big old walnut table, about eleven feet long that had been at the D.C. law firm when I was there. When I would get upset I would sit at the table and it made me feel much better."

Dr. Lumpkin looked at her skeptically and wrote more notes.

"So after Mr. Harp assaulted me, in our settlement he gave me the table. I moved it to my old house in Virginia, which apparently was where it had been to begin with. When it was returned to its original place, that was a sign that these Masons were to meet there again."

"And how long have these meetings been going on?"

"Oh, there were only two meetings of the Masons."

"Have any other unusual events occurred since then?"

"Well, that's actually what brings me here. You see, now I have begun to meet with George Washington. That was why I thought perhaps I should see someone. It's all so strange, but when it happens it seems so real," she explained meekly.

"Sometimes we encounter these types of symptoms in patients who have been under severe stress, the way you have," he reassured her.

"Patients!" Christi thought. She was offended at being lumped into such a general category. He was ignoring her particular circumstances.

"What is the purpose of these visits with George Washington?" Dr. Lumpkin continued.

Christi hesitated, but she had already told him so much. "He's delivering Seven Spiritual Principles for Governing a People," she answered with as much confidence as she could muster.

"Where do these meetings occur?"

"At the table. Oh! I forgot something important. There's more evidence that this really happens," she blurted out. "Mr. Washington has written me some notes. When the first note was left on the table I assumed it was a prank by a neighbor."

"What did the note say?"

"He wanted to know if I would meet with him, even though he was 'discarnate.' That was the term he used. I decided to play along with what I thought was a joke, just to see what would happen. So I wrote a note saying I would agree to meet with him. Then I received another note from him. He asked if he could use the table in my dining room. So I said 'yes,' providing a friend could be there with me."

"Who was the friend you wanted to be there with you?"

"My law partner," she said with increased confidence. "So I'm not the only one who was there."

"And does your law partner see Mr. Washington, too?"

"Actually. . . he's blind. But he was at the second meeting with me. We both remember it being just the same."

"What happened at this second meeting?"

"Benedict Arnold was forgiven. I mean by George Washington and the other Founding Fathers. I know it's hard to imagine, but it was actually a beautiful experience."

Dr. Lumpkin opened the file lying next to his writing pad. "You indicated in the papers you completed that you have no history of psychological or psychiatric disorders."

"That's correct. I'm quite healthy, as far as I know."

"Have you experienced any headaches during the period of time you have been having these episodes?"

"No."

"And no history of any emotional disorders in your family, is that correct?"

"None that I know of. My family members are mostly farmers in Colorado. Some were a little eccentric..."

"In what way were they eccentric?" Dr. Lumpkin asked. "Did any of them hear voices or see ghosts?"

"No, not that I know of." Christi looked down at her watch to see how much longer before her session would end.

"Miss Daniel, you have symptoms that fall within a couple of possibilities described in the DSM IV, the bible of mental health disorders. You are clearly experiencing a brief psychotic disorder with marked stressors." He picked up a thick blue book on his desk enti-tled *Diagnostic and Statistical Manual of Mental Disorders*. "I believe that's identified as 298.8. Yes, here it is. These unusual perceptual experiences and seeing the presence of George Washington could indi-cate schizotypal personality disorder. However, you don't seem to be exhibiting unusual mannerisms or eccentric behavior. But then again, with the notes that you find lying around, you may have what we now call dissociative identity disorder. It's what we used to call multiple personality disorder."

"What! Are you suggesting that I'm leaving these notes to myself? But what about the fact that Hap, my law partner, was at one of the meetings, too. He doesn't think I'm writing notes to myself," she argued.

"That happens sometimes," replied Dr. Lumpkin coolly. "You and he may have a shared psychotic disorder. I believe that's designated as 297.3." He again picked up the thick blue book to confirm his recollection. "It appears you are experiencing a psychotic break triggered by the recent stress in your life. But, of course, I can't rule out the possibility of brain lesions until some further tests have been done. You know, you could also be suffering from a case of delusional disorder of the grandiose type, 297.1. Have you ever heard voices in the past?"

Christi remembered the incident she and Shenan had discussed, the voice telling her she'd be called upon to lead, but remained silent, glaring at Dr. Lumpkin as he opened the drawer in his desk and took out a prescription pad.

"I'm going to start you on Haldol immediately. It's an anti-psychotic medication that should stop these episodes. But if you experience any more visits from George Washington or these Masonic meetings, I want you to call me immediately. In the meantime, I'll make arrangements for you to have a brain scan done as soon as possible. Get this prescription filled in the pharmacy in the lobby downstairs," he directed as he stood up and handed her the prescription.

Christi silently accepted the written prescription and solemnly left his office. After paying her bill for the visit, she went directly to the pay phones in the lobby and placed a credit card call.

"Tom, I've just been to see a psychiatrist," she said, her voice trembling. "He says I have a delusional disorder, that I hear voices and hallucinate. He says it's some sort of psychotic break triggered by the stress in my life, or it may be a brain lesion."

"Oh, Christi, why did you do that?" Tom asked in disbelief. "The therapeutic community is still living in the days of Freud. They're still operating on the Newtonian assumptions about reality—the belief in separation, that we're just physical bodies that can be programmed, or fixed by masking over a few symptoms with medication. Many of them don't even acknowledge that their patients have a soul that needs healing, along with the body. They haven't accepted the oneness of all life, or that there are more dimensions than those we knew about a century ago."

"He wasn't even interested in the information that's being conveyed in these 'episodes', as he calls them, nor the potential significance it may have for the future of the Nation or the human race," Christi added. "I knew I should have talked to you about this before I went. But I promised Mom I would see someone, just to be sure I was okay. According to Dr. Lumpkin, I'm really sick."

"Christi, you're not sick. We're moving into a new paradigm. You're facilitating a transition from one level of understanding to another. Of course it seems strange, it's all very new," Tom asserted. "Don't let him medicate you or treat you like you're sick. Hap isn't sick, and he shared one of these experiences with you."

"Oh, Dr. Lumpkin says Hap may be sick, too," she retorted. "We might have a 'shared psychotic disorder.' And the notes I'm getting from Mr. Washington might be written by an alternate personality of mine."

"Listen to me, Christi," Tom demanded. "You don't have split personalities. You and Hap are not psychos. Don't let this man get you off track, just because he's living in the past and is unaware of the major shifts in evolution that are occurring. Please, Chris, don't listen to him."

"I hope you're right. What you're saying feels right. I don't feel sick. In fact, I'm more alive than ever."

"Just continue to be open," he advised. "Don't lose your connection with the physical world, but don't deny the reality of these new experiences, either. You're a pioneer and we need you to do this work."

"Tom.... If you ever suspect I'm out of touch with reality, please, will you promise to tell me?" pleaded Christi.

"I will. I promise."

Christi hung up the receiver and began to walk away. She stopped, pivoted toward the pay phone and dialed her mother's number.

"Hi, Mom. I've just seen a psychiatrist. Everything's fine. I don't have any unusual mannerisms or eccentric behavior, so I can't be schizoid."

"Oh, good. I'm so relieved. Did he give you any idea about what was going on?"

"He said this sometimes happens when a person is evolving rapidly on a spiritual level. Nothing to worry about."

"Now, aren't you glad you took my advice? This puts our minds at ease."

"Yes, Mom. I love you. I'll keep you posted on any new developments."

CHAPTER NINETEEN

The prospect of Mr. Washington's next visit troubled Christi. While she was eager to see him again, she was nonetheless experiencing the strain of living in two worlds. How much easier it would be to simply walk away from the world of Mr. Washington and return to "normal." But it was in his world that she felt surrounded by peace and love.

"Perhaps it was just a dream," she thought after nearly a month had passed since their last meeting. Maybe her visit to Dr. Lumpkin had caused the dream to end. But she hoped it was her exceptionally busy schedule with her growing law practice that had caused the delay.

As she descended the stairs on her way to work one morning she noticed a piece of paper lying on the table. She hurried to read its message.

Dear Miss Christi:

*Before we meet again, I ask that you consider the Second Spiritual Principle for Governing a People. It is as follows: **JUSTICE SHALL BE DELIVERED WITHOUT JUDGMENT.** As this may seem quite foreign to your present mode of thinking, especially as one trained in the law, it will be beneficial to our discussion if you contemplate this principle before we meet.*

Your faithful servant,

Geo. Washington

Christi breathed a sigh of relief and tucked the note in her pocket. When she arrived at the office, she went directly to Hap's office where she found him at his desk.

"Hap, let me read the note that was on the table this morning," she said as she sat in the chair before his desk. She read the note twice. "Justice without judgment. Does that make any sense to you?" she asked.

"I don't think he's going to cut you any slack. That goes to the very heart of our present legal system."

"What do you mean?" she asked anxiously. "How can there be justice without judgment? Those at the pinnacle of our profession are called judges because it's their job to judge. That's what we pay them to do for us, impose judgment on wrongdoers."

"True, that's what we claim we are doing. But is that what really happens? Perhaps being blind gives me an unusual perspective on what happens in the courtroom. When I sit in the courtroom I have to listen within myself to see beyond myself. When I say 'see' I don't mean seeing with physical eyes, of course. I mean seeing with an inner vision that illuminates people's souls. I feel their presence. On occasion, I even hear their thoughts, in my mind." He chuckled. "Needless to say, this gives me a very different view of what's going on in the courtroom."

"Tell me what you see," Christi urged, moving to the edge of her chair.

"When I'm in the courtroom I see this intricate web of laws we have created, but they're actually abstract concepts—often unconnected to the truth. Our law books are full of them, like whether the evidence is proven by a preponderance of the evidence, or by clear and convincing evidence, or beyond a reasonable doubt. What do these rules actually mean and how do they relate to our search for the truth? Our myriad of laws have little to do with loving one another. Oh, they preserve an appearance of law and order, so we don't have to examine the truth. But they promote vengeance, not justice, and come from a place of fear, not love.

"Then we insulate ourselves from responsibility for our mistakes by seeing only separate parts—pieces of the whole. The judge measures out the requisite degree of vengeance then pretends that he sends his victims to a place of redemption. He escapes personal responsibility for his acts by seeing himself as a mere agent of the 'system,' which means no one in particular. The 'system' then absolves the judge of responsibility for the pain he levies upon the accused. The warden or executioner, too, is free of blame, because he had no part in laying judgment upon his victims. We construct this mythical wall between the judge and those who carry out his sentence, to keep the whole out of sight.

"It's as though everyone is in a dream, but it's a dream they have made to save themselves from what they, themselves, have created. They're like people living in a cave where the light cannot shine. They don't know they live in darkness because they've never seen the light. And if they did, it would be terrifying. Because of their fear, they actually prefer to live in the darkness of the nightmare they have created than search for the light."

Christi listened intently. "But Hap, what are you suggesting? Do you mean that those who commit crimes should not be punished? How would you explain this to a mother whose child has been senselessly murdered?"

"How is that mother helped to heal by a system that desires only vengeance and denies the need for forgiveness?" Hap retorted. "Indeed, not only is the victim denied healing, but the offender as well. In being made the object of vengeance, the offender responds by denying his guilt and minimizing the harm he has caused. The opportunity for confession and repentance, both essential elements in accepting true responsibility for the wrongs committed, is lost. We've made confession unsafe because retribution is the reward—not love. And reconciliation between the victim and the offender, whose lives have become inextricably intertwined, is not even given a passing thought. How does any of this help the mother of a murdered child heal?

"Perhaps we fail to understand life," he continued. "Why do we believe what God has created can die? What is the opposite of life? Life may appear to change its form, yet is not the opposite of life yet another form of life? In whatever form, must not life be reconciled with its Creator and reflect God's attributes? Nothing that God has created can be the opposite of God, and to die would be just that."

"You know..." Christi said as she thought aloud, "I remember reading about an American woman who went on a walk with Australian aborigines for several months in the arid outback. The members of the tribe each took a turn being the leader and using their intuitive abilities to find food and water for the tribe. After a time, they told the American woman it was her turn to lead the group. She protested that she didn't have the ability, but they gave her no choice. So, they began to walk, on and on, while she tried to think where food and water could be found. Days passed and she found nothing. When she asked to be relieved of this responsibility, they refused, even when their tongues were parched from lack of water. They told her this was a lesson they were all to share. If she found no water they chose to perish with her. That was just part of the journey they had chosen to experience together.[3]

"They felt no animosity because of her ineptitude or the danger of death she placed them in. They were willing to share this experience, knowing there were lessons for them to learn, as well. Regardless of the outcome, there was no blame, no guilt, no judgment. What struck me most was their willingness to sacrifice even their lives for her to learn who she truly was. That's a concept we can't even imagine. It seems we're so attached to the material aspects of life that we are blind, I mean inwardly blind, to the truth of our spiritual nature. We see all of this chaos and disorder around us because we fail to see the patterns that exist beyond physical matter."

"But we're paying such a high price!" Hap declared. "Remember the Forgiveness of Arnold Meeting, when the perfection of Benedict Arnold was acknowledged? I now understand those who commit crime believe themselves to be so despicable they desire their own crucifixion. And the State blindly participates in their plan! So in the end, it's the criminal's plan, not the State's, that is actually being achieved. It's insane and the People are not made safe by the money spent building endless prisons to lock up thousands upon thousands of citizens. It merely confirms for others who believe themselves to be despicable that if they, too, commit crimes, the State will affirm their lack of self-worth… in the name of the People. What a waste! Because of our fear, we lack resources to build schools where children could be taught love. In the end, the one who judges cannot escape the penalty he imposes upon another."

Christi nodded in agreement. "At times I've felt what was happening in the courtroom made no sense, that everything was upside down. But I never understood why. Hap, you may have found the key. The power of the State is like a toy used by children, and everything the toy appears to be exists only in their minds."

"Indeed," replied Hap. "They exert their power with the tiny wisdom of a child. So what is good is destroyed and what is bad is perpetuated. And then they're surprised when their policies don't work or achieve results that are the opposite of what they had expected. Somehow we must awaken from this nightmare and see that we not only mirror God, but that we are one with God. Only then can we know our perfection and that all is in Divine Order, at all times, without exception."

"The question now," Christi said, "is how to consciously awaken the legal system and our public-policy-making process from the nightmare. How do we promote a system built on the concepts of equality, balance, teamwork and partnership? What will it look like, Hap?" she asked eagerly.

"I want to share a dream I recently had. Not a nightmare, a dream," Hap said laughing. "I think it may have been prompted by an article June recently read to me about a woman using holistic techniques at a correctional center near here. My dream may have been a glimpse of a better way," he said with a sense of intrigue.

"I dreamed I was in a place where everyone was dressed in uniforms that were the same. They all had assigned tasks that they were required to do daily. They were isolated from the outside world. At first, I thought it was a cloistered religious order, but then I realized it was a prison, but a different sort of prison. It was a prison that was no longer considered a warehouse for the scourge of the Earth. It had been transformed into a place of extraordinary healing.

"I dreamed that the inmates were being taught new techniques for healing using the body's energy field. They were first encouraged to focus their energy and attention on healing themselves, then they were taught to heal others. Some became so proficient they, themselves, became teachers. The skills spread exponentially as they were taught to larger and larger numbers of prisoners. Upon their release, they carried their ability to do healing work back to their families and neighbors, to help them heal. It was a partnership, teamwork among equals, not domination of one over the other."

"Wow, Hap, that's a long way from those who want to deprive prisoners of exercise equipment for fear they'll be physically stronger to attack us when they're released," Christi said, thinking of an ongoing debate about the lives of inmates being too comfortable.

"Yes," Hap said, "but fear can only breed fear. So our attack upon those prisoners by deeming them unworthy, even of exercise equipment, actually promotes their attack upon us when they are released, not their repentance. When we see justice as harming one who has harmed another, all we achieve is more harm in the world. We destroy what is good and perpetuate what is bad."

"But the argument about depriving prisoners of exercise sounds sort of logical when the politicians make it," Christi noted. "I guess when you are in a place of fear, as Mr. Washington said about the First Principle, that fear can then be used against you by the politicians to achieve their own objectives, not to serve yours. This must be an example of the First Principle at work."

"Logic and insanity are not always mutually exclusive," Hap observed. "Many people make logical arguments, based upon fear, about the effectiveness of punishment. But the belief that punishment produces correction is insane. It produces further hate and fear, not correction. Only love can produce a win-win situation. Consider this, Christi. If attorneys knew their clients charged with crimes would be sent to a prison where they would be given the opportunity to heal, wouldn't that destroy the incentive to have clients lie or to conceal evidence, which undermines justice? Now, mind you, the attorneys might not make as much money," he said laughing. "Perhaps they could take up healing, as well."

"Oh, sure!" Christi said, joining in the laughter. "But you know, Hap... perhaps justice without judgment will show us how to awaken from the nightmare."

CHAPTER TWENTY

Christi was consumed with restless anticipation as she awaited her next meeting with Mr. Washington. It had been nearly a week since she received the note requesting that she consider the Second Principle. Driving home from work, her sense of expectation was magnified. As she opened the front door, she felt a presence in the dining room. "At last," she thought. Mr. Washington was waiting at the table.

"Good afternoon," she said. "I had begun to wonder if you were going to return."

"Now, Miss Christi," Mr. Washington replied smiling, "you surely knew I would come back for your fine tea and cookies."

Christi laughed and headed for the kitchen. It wasn't long before she had set the silver tray upon the table and their discussion had begun.

"You were right when you said it might be difficult for me to understand the concept of justice being delivered without judgment," Christi confessed as she poured tea.

"Only because it is so foreign to what you have been taught," Mr. Washington said as he accepted her offer of cookies. "Once you grasp the basic precepts, it becomes easy. In God's law there are no inconsistencies, no exceptions to the rule."

She took a cookie, too. "But at first, the very idea of justice without judgment was inconceivable."

"Only to those who fail to understand the difference between justice and vengeance," he replied. "The desire for vengeance arises from the belief in sin. Those who believe in sin will find the justice of which I speak difficult to understand, even fearful. When you believe in sin, you must then create a world that is consistent with the notion that there are wrongs that cannot be undone, except through punishment. But the infliction of punishment only affirms that someone was a sinner to begin with—otherwise the punishment would not be justified. So the ideas of sin and punishment become integrally linked. Because sin is believed to be a violation of God's law, when you believe in sin, you cannot trust God for fear you will be struck with bolts of lightning or burn in the fires of hell, as God seeks vengeance for your trespasses."

"I suppose this is why we have come to believe that if God can be both just and vengeful, it is also just for us to be vengeful toward those who violate the laws created by man," Christi speculated. "In our minds, the desire for vengeance is seen as good, because we believe it is just. Is this what happens?"

"Precisely," he replied. "When a wrong is committed, unfortunately you believe you must seek vengeance in order for justice to be served."

Christi sipped her tea as she pondered this concept. "Perhaps this is why those who believe in sin have come to believe it was just for Jesus to have been murdered for our sins. Could it be they see the crucifixion of Jesus as a sacrifice made to appease God's wrath, and thus secure our salvation in exchange?"

Mr. Washington nodded. "The error, indeed the insanity, in all of this is that God has no wrath and cannot possibly be vengeful. God is love. God's love is unconditional, even for those who believe they are sinners, although it is a false belief. But those who believe in sin cannot understand love, because they mistakenly believe that love and justice are separate. They associate justice only with vengeance. They thus perceive love as weak and a threat to their safety. They see strength and power only in vengeance."

Christi thought for a moment. "But to tell those who believe in sin that sin does not exist would turn their world upside down. What they have defined as good and just would have to be seen as bad and unjust. Perhaps that's why, at first, the idea of justice without judgment was so shocking. It was contrary to all I had been taught."

"Exactly," Mr. Washington said. "All laws are set up to protect the continuity of the system in which the lawmakers believe. When those who believe in sin are told they have never sinned, that miracles can easily resolve all errors they have made, they cannot understand. When a wrong is committed, they believe they must seek vengeance in order for justice to be served. When it is understood that God seeks no vengeance because all are innocent, those who believe in sin lose their authority to seek vengeance. But when they have so much invested in vengeance, the investment in it cannot easily be withdrawn. Resistance must be anticipated."

"These concepts are so far removed from what we have traditionally been taught," Christi said as she gazed pensively out the window. "Why has it taken so long for us to understand that the old ways don't work?"

"The answer is simple," he replied. "The whole is seen as separated bits and pieces with empty space in between and truth is avoided by directing concern only at little bits of the whole. In this context, it is literally true that justice is blind."

Christi thought of Hap's description of the imaginary wall the legal system constructs between judge and executioner, and how each is thus relieved of responsibility because the role each plays is viewed as separate from the whole.

"Justice must be impartial, but not blind," Mr. Washington continued. "For there to be justice, men and women must see as God sees. To be a witness to the power of love and justice you must understand that no child of God deserves vengeance. When another acts insanely, he is offering you an opportunity to bless him. His need for love is yours, but you can attain it only by giving it."

"So if it's not just to attack the innocent, and all are innocent in the eyes of God, that means we don't need judges, or, for that matter, even lawyers!" Christi suggested, smiling at the idea.

"Indeed, their roles will change. When one commits a wrong, it is a cry for love. To recognize a cry for love in another is different from judging him," explained Mr. Washington. "The judgment one must exercise is only with regard to what one will choose for oneself. In your own mind you will be judgmental for a time, but only so that you can select and reject what is necessary for you to perceive without judgment. Undoing is necessary in your own mind, but you cannot undo what is in the mind of another by judging him other than innocent."

Christi sighed as she refilled their tea cups. "Is there any hope we will ever learn this distinction and that things will be better?"

Mr. Washington laughed. "Indeed! Fortunately, tolerance for pain may be high, but it is not without limit. Eventually everyone begins to recognize, however dimly, that there must be a better way. As the energy associated with this belief and the determination to find a better way grows, a turning point is reached."

The chemistry created by Christi's disillusion with the legal process, her outrage at Harp's attack, and her compelling desire to find a better way flashed through her mind. "I think I have some idea of how that works," she said tentatively. "You told me when we first met that you had come to help affect the choices that are to be made.... How can I help?"

"Ah, how I appreciate your question," he said. "The only reason the light cannot enter is because of the belief in darkness. You are needed as a leader, one who shares my aim of healing minds by changing beliefs. But as an enlightened leader, which you shall become, you must never attack. Know that the hearts of those, even those who attack you, are pure. All beliefs are real to the believer, and they believe what they do is just. You must see your fellow citizens in their perfect sinlessness. Only in this way can you fulfill your role in creating the dream and its manifestation. Only by becoming an enlightened leader can you help us to overcome dark forces that seek to prevail in our stead."

Christi sat motionless, her eyes fixed on Mr. Washington's gentle face. "But how can I achieve such a goal?" she asked timidly. "I have no idea where to begin."

"All you need do is be in the present moment. By that I mean, when a friend, or a client, or even an adversary is before you, that is where your awareness must be. Do not project your past, or his, upon him. Be totally in the present. In this light, from a place of love, consider what you find to be just for that person. As you do this, remember that what you give you will receive in equal measure. If you give love, love shall be returned."

Christi bowed her head and cast her eyes down at the table. "I will pray to attain this goal."

Mr. Washington placed his hand on her head. "You shall. . . in time. Don't think that you, or the entire system, can change overnight. People must have time to adjust to the light before being immersed in it."

Rainbows from the late afternoon sun danced on the ceiling. Mr. Washington sighed. "We have done quite enough. It is late and we have eaten all your cookies," he said motioning toward the empty plate. "But before I go, there is a question I must ask."

"Of course," she said without hesitation. "Please ask anything at all."

He paused, then inquired, "Are you willing to be released from the effects of sin, Miss Christi?"

She looked blankly at her guest. "What do you mean?"

"You are not a body. You are a soul that is eternal. Only when you are prepared to forego the values of this world and forgive, can you deliver justice. Indeed, where forgiveness exists, justice *must* exist. And so it is through Forgiveness of the Holy Spirit—by acknowledging there is no sin to forgive—that justice shall be delivered without judgment."

CHAPTER TWENTY-ONE

Christi hadn't been in the office long when her phone rang. The caller identified himself as Winston Harp.

"Mr. Harp, I didn't expect to hear from you!"

"I'm sure you didn't," he replied gruffly. "I just thought I'd let you know you're being sued before the Sheriff serves the papers on you."

"What are you talking about?" Christi asked, alarmed.

"You've been sued. I just received a copy of the pleadings that were filed yesterday in the Circuit Court in Winchester."

"Winchester?" she thought. That was where she tried the molestation case and lost.

"Willard Smith has sued you for malpractice," Harp continued. "The Virginia Supreme Court denied Smith's petition for an appeal on the grounds you failed to preserve necessary objections. Remember the mother who testified at length to statements her daughter had made about the abuse? You didn't make a single objection to any of that. I thought you were better than that when we hired you, but I should have known."

Christi felt the beat of her heart throbbing in her chest as she recalled the testimony to which he referred. "But I was certain the comments came within the excited utterances exception to the hearsay rule," she protested. "The mother said they were all made soon after Smith had had access to the little girl. That was why I didn't note an objection. And even if that testimony had been excluded, we still would have lost. The evidence against Smith was overwhelming."

"Tell that to the jury," Harp said gloating. "This time you're the defendant."

"But I was an employee of the firm and covered by your malpractice policy when I tried that case."

"Oh, it's covered by insurance," Harp replied sarcastically.

"Who is representing Smith?"

"My good friend, Jim Marshall."

"Harp is behind this," Christi thought. Marshall and Harp live in the same neighborhood and belong to the same clubs. "Why did you get the pleadings before I did?" she asked.

"Jim gave me a courtesy copy. You'll be served by the Sheriff in a few days. As a favor, I'll fax you a copy."

"Please do," Christi said in a bitter tone.

"Smith has made an offer to settle," Harp stated smugly.

"To whom? I didn't even know I had been sued. How can settlement negotiations already be underway?"

"It's my malpractice policy that covered you at the time you committed the malpractice. Since it's my policy, *I* talked to them."

"What's the offer?" she asked dubiously.

"Five hundred thousand dollars," Harp said.

"Five hundred thousand dollars!" Christi exclaimed. "For what? He can't get that kind of money for being denied an appeal of a lawsuit he would have lost anyway, even if the mother had never testified. He was guilty, it was irrefutable. And to win a malpractice suit against me, he has to prove he would have won in the trial court, plus prove what damages he sustained. How can he do that?" she argued desperately.

"His reputation was ruined," Harp retorted. "Imagine being found guilty of molesting a child. He had to leave his church."

Christi recalled the verdict—it was for $500,000. "Has he paid the judgment, now that the appeal has been dismissed?" she asked.

"Of course not! That bitch will have to collect it, and I suspect that'll take some doing."

"Willard Smith has millions. He can pay it and never notice it's gone. And why has he sued me? He certainly doesn't need the money."

"He has a good use for it," Harp replied curtly. "He's pledged all that he collects in the suit against you to the R.R.s."

Christi was speechless. Harp had devised this suit against her to collect money for his new political party from his own insurance policy. What a scheme! "I'll look forward to reading the pleadings," she said cynically. "And please refer the insurance representative to me. I prefer to speak to him myself."

"I own the policy—I'll talk to him. After you read the pleadings get back with me about how much you'll pay toward the settlement. But make it quick."

Christi heard the receiver as Harp slammed it down. She sat numb looking into space, her shoulders slumped forward. What now?

Christi leaned forward, elbows on her desk, palms together, her forehead resting on her finger tips. Her last discussion with Mr. Washington began to play in her mind. "You must never attack. Know that the hearts of those, even those who attack you, are pure...."

"I must return love, but how is that possible?" she asked herself. "How can I forego the values of this world and forgive?" She took a deep breath and headed for Hap's office.

Hap and June were in his office drafting a trust document. They invited her in as June set the document aside and Hap leaned back in his chair.

"I think I have just been given an opportunity to practice the Principles," Christi said with a quiver in her voice.

"You don't sound especially happy about it," Hap noted.

"That's an understatement," she replied, then somberly described Harp's scheme.

June put her arm around Christi's shoulders. "How are you going to respond?" she asked.

"That's what I want to discuss with both of you. I know what I must do... but I don't know how.... I must do what Christ would have done in these circumstances. Does that sound crazy?"

"It's pretty extreme," June said. "The Bible reports exactly what Christ advised when a person is taken to court. Hap and I have discussed that passage on several occasions. It's diametrically opposed to what is taught in law school." June stepped toward the shelves that lined one wall of Hap's office and pulled out the Bible. "I think it's in Matthew. Here it is, in Chapter 5, beginning at verse 38." June read as Christi listened intently.

> The law of Moses says, 'If a man gouges out another's eye, he must pay with his own eye. If a tooth gets knocked out, knock out the tooth of the one who did it.' But I say: Don't resist violence! If you are slapped on the cheek, turn the other too. If you are ordered to court, and your shirt is taken from you, give your coat too. If the military demand that you carry their gear for a mile, carry it two. Give to those who ask, and don't turn away from those who want to borrow.
>
> There is a saying, 'Love your friends and hate your enemies.' But I say: Love your enemies! Pray for those who persecute you! In that way you will be acting as true sons of your Father in Heaven. For he gives his sunlight to both the evil and the good, and sends rain on the just and on the unjust too. If you love only

those who love you, what good is that? Even scoundrels do that much. If you are friendly only to your friends, how are you different from anyone else? Even the heathen do that. But you are to be perfect, even as your Father in Heaven is perfect.[4]

June closed the Bible and looked at Christi for a response.

"There it is... the Code of Hammurabi versus the Seven Principles," Christi stated with a wave of her hand. "Christ called upon us two thousand years ago to leave behind the law of an eye for an eye and a tooth for a tooth, and here I am today, considering whether or not I can do that. If this is the message that's been taught in our churches for the last two millennia, why has so little changed?" she asked, looking first at June and then at Hap. "We've already been shown a better way—we just didn't listen."

"So, Christi," Hap said softly, "what are you going to do? It's a frivolous suit, one they can never win. Will you file defensive pleadings as you are trained to do and do so well, or will you turn the other cheek? Can you resolve this without a counterattack?"

Christi rested her chin on her clenched fist. She thought of her years of training as a lawyer, years invested in developing skills as an adversary, the status she had acquired in her profession for vigorously defending the interests of her clients—by attacking. She felt like a four-star General about to declare herself a pacifist, turning her back on everything she had been trained to do and been rewarded for doing. Her stomach felt queasy.

Christi heard the fax machine signaling the receipt of a transmittal. "I'll have to think about it," she said as she hurried out the door. She picked up the copy of the pleadings and went to her office. As she read its contents, she thought of the many times she had served legal claims on others. This was the first time she had ever seen pleadings with her name as the defendant.

She laid the papers aside and began to roll a pencil between her fingers. Could it be true she had manifested these events in her life? Were she and Harp co-creators, meant to teach one another, to create opportunities for one another to learn who they truly are? Only one thing seemed certain—she had to trust that the Principles would work.

Christi picked up the phone and dialed the number for Harp, Harrison & Humphrey. She asked to speak to Mr. Harp who soon answered.

"Mr. Harp. . ." she began hesitantly, "I don't want to fight you or Mr. Smith in this malpractice suit. You work it out with the insurance company. All that I ask is this. . . that you do what you. . . what you feel is fair to everyone. . . in your heart," she said making a gesture near her heart. "I'll do the same."

There was silence on the other end of the phone.

"Mr. Harp? Are you there?"

"I'm here. . ." he said sounding confused. "Why would you give up so easily?"

"It's like this," Christi said calmly. "I perceived your assault in the motel room as an attack on me—that I was your victim and you should pay for what you did. When I confronted you about that, you saw it as an attack on you, that I wrongly accused you and was victimizing you. So you came up with this attack on me, to seek vengeance by embarrassing me and harming me in my profession. Now it's my turn to attack you, to fight you in court, or report your scheme to the authorities. And with that you would again seek vengeance for what you perceive as yet another attack by me on you. When will it end? When will we find a better way?"

"Are you mad?" Harp asked angrily. "What kind of world would this be if every defendant just called up and said I surrender? Let's just settle? What would become of the practice of law? I suppose you would have had us surrender to the Communists, or... or the Republicans surrender to the Democrats. That would be the end of all of us. The tyrants would take over the world and there would be no one to stop them. How is that a better way? We have to *fight* for what's right."

"Could the end result be worse than what we now have?" Christi asked. "To solve the problem, we must see that we created it—that the chaotic world we see is the world we have created—that we are the image-maker. Don't you see? This is why we have the power to change our world."

"That's gibberish," Harp snapped. "I don't know what you're talking about. I'll call you and let you know how much you have to pay to settle this thing. Don't bother answering the pleadings. I'll get back to you within the next couple of days."

As Christi hung the phone up she was proud she had had the courage to take such a bold step. And yet, there were still reservations. "How much will he ask for?" she wondered. Where would she get the money to pay him anything? Her house and her car are all she owned. Would Harp demand everything? She began to feel agitated.

Christi dwelled on Harp's possible demand the entire day. That night she couldn't sleep as she played out different scenarios in her mind. In one, Harp was suddenly repentant and called to apologize for having been so cruel. But in another, he drove up to her house in the firm limousine to inspect what she had and select what he wanted to settle Smith's claim and fund the R.R.s. What a terrible injustice that would be! He deserved nothing that she had. But Mr. Washington had admonished her not to attack and Christ said to give him more than he asks. By morning she was exhausted.

To resolve her torment, Christi vowed to sleep on it one last night, then make her decision when she awoke. That night she again tossed and turned, thinking of all the work she had put into her house. She thought of the inheritance from her grandmother that she used as the down payment, funds she could never replace. The possibility that money might end up supporting the ideology of the R.R.s was maddening. Christi pounded her fist on her pillow. "What am I to do?" she cried.

When she rose the next morning the decision was made. The prospect of giving up anything she had worked so hard to gain was a greater sacrifice than she was prepared to make. She would write Harp immediately to tell him that her offer was withdrawn. She would fight him in court.

When Christi arrived at the office a fax on Harp, Humphrey & Harrison letterhead lay on her desk. Her heart sank as she grabbed it, recognizing Harp's signature at the end. "We met with the insurance agent late yesterday," it read. "Smith has decided to non-suit the case and will not be pursuing his claim immediately. You will be informed of subsequent developments."

The fax slipped from Christi's hand and fluttered to the floor. Tears filled her eyes. Could it be that fear could not achieve its end in the face of love? Her body dropped to her chair. Despite Mr. Washington's efforts to teach her, she had been unable to trust that love was safe, or that giving and receiving were one. She had not had the will to change herself. Detachment from her physical world was still beyond her.

She reached down for the fax, crumbled it and threw it in the trash. "I'm sorry, Mr. Washington," she whispered, wiping tears from her face with her hand. "I will learn a better way. I promise I will."

CHAPTER TWENTY-TWO

Following her most recent encounter with Harp, the Book of Judges recurrently occupied Christi's mind. It was not a familiar scripture, yet she felt compelled to examine it. She took her Bible from the bookcase and searched for what it was that beckoned her. Chapter 19 leaped from the page.

It told of a man who had taken a wife who then ran away, back to her father's home. Her husband had gone for her and upon their return journey, although they were strangers, they were offered shelter by an old man in the village of Gibe-ah.

> Just as they were beginning to warm to the occasion, a gang of sex perverts gathered around the house and began beating at the door and yelling at the old man to bring out the man who was staying with him, so they could rape him. The old man stepped outside to talk to them.
>
> "No my brothers, don't do such a dastardly act," he begged, "for he is my guest. Here, take my virgin daughter and this man's wife. I'll bring them out and you can do whatever you like to them—but don't do such a thing to this man."[5]

As Christi read that the perverts were then given the stranger's wife whom they raped repeatedly throughout the night, she felt her jaw clench. How could females have been so defiled, so worthless as to be less valuable than a man who was a total stranger? Were not the virgin daughter and the reluctant wife created equally in the image of God, as was the man? The passage ignited her anger.

When she realized how quickly her emotions had taken control of her mind she took a deep breath and focused on being in the present moment. But her thoughts soon returned to the passage. How could women be subjected to such barbarism without revolting? She felt adrenaline again creeping into her veins. She filled her lungs with air and exhaled slowly. "Is there another way of looking at this? Is that why I see only chaos?" she wondered.

She desperately wanted to seek advice from Mr. Washington. "Why doesn't he come when I want?" she asked herself with a tinge of resentment. Her thoughts were interrupted by a phone call from Shenan.

"I'm going to see Grandfather the first weekend in November. Can you come?" she asked excitedly.

"*Can* I? I can hardly wait!" Christi squealed like a child. "I'm putting it on my calendar now."

"It'll be great to see you again. How are things going?"

"Not so well. Turmoil is a good description of my life right now," Christi replied with a meek laugh. "I need to talk to Mr. Washington, but I never know when he's going to come."

"Why don't you ask him to come at a time you designate? If it's your intent that he come, he surely will."

"I never thought of that. Maybe I can leave a note on the table inviting him to meet me in the morning. Good idea. I'll try it."

When she hung up the phone Christi considered the cookies. She had none on hand. In an abundance of caution, she decided to bake a batch as an additional assurance Mr. Washington would join her. Perhaps this was unnecessary, but she decided not to take a chance.

That evening she poured more love than ever into baking the cookies and they were her best ever. She was confident that if her cookies had anything to do with Mr. Washington's visits, he would surely come. When the cookies were safely in the jar, she left the note on the table and went to bed.

That night Christi had a vivid dream. She was witnessing a raging battle between huge armies when she was given a machine that enabled her to see the action simultaneously on the spiritual and physical levels. When she viewed the battle through this device, she saw that everyone on the battlefield was cooperating on the spiritual plane, even while they fought savagely on the physical. The soldiers on both sides were helping one another achieve their objectives.

When Christi awoke the next morning she dressed quickly and hurried down the stairs. She was not disappointed. Mr. Washington was sitting at the table looking out the large bay window. He turned to her as she entered the room.

"Good morning. I thought you might never rise. I have been enjoying the aroma of freshly baked cookies for some time now," he said jokingly. "And your fine tea will be especially enjoyable on this beautiful fall morning."

"Good morning," Christi replied with relief. "I'm so glad you have come."

She quickly prepared tea and arranged cookies on a pretty plate which she carried to the table on her silver tray. She served her guest with immense pleasure. Mr. Washington had become such a treasured friend, and to discover that he would come upon her invitation made the relationship seem more equal.

"I've had a difficult time since we last met. I need your help," she said as she sat at the table facing her mentor. "Justice without judgment... forgiveness... being in the present moment... seeing everyone as innocent.... It all seems impossible. I'm afraid I'm not up to fulfilling the role you envision."

"When you question your value, remember, without you God would be incomplete. Your part is essential. What is it that causes your doubt?"

Christi explained the troubling passage in the Book of Judges. She understood, on some level, all were supposed to be innocent. But she couldn't understand how the host's virgin daughter could have been offered to sexual perverts, to save a man who was a mere stranger from being raped. Nor could she understand why the women had not banded together and demanded better treatment. "Why hadn't *they* figured out that there was a better way?" she asked.

"Now, you were reading from the Old Testament," Mr. Washington first pointed out, "before the time of Jesus who taught that you must love even those who harm you. And you know it is the nature of mankind to suffer, while evils are sufferable, rather than seek to abolish the injustices to which people are accustomed."

"I understand what you are saying," she said, "but I still don't see how everyone can be innocent while this evolution is taking place and horrible deeds continue to be done, often with impunity."

"Perhaps the Third Spiritual Principle for Governing a People will help you to understand," Mr. Washington said in his usual gentle manner. "Its lesson is simple. Let us begin by first considering the crucifixion of Christ, for it teaches much that has been obscured.

"Please consider this. What was the intent of his persecutors when they placed a crown of thorns upon Christ's head?" Mr. Washington asked. "Why did they flagellate his body in public with whips made of leather thongs tipped with pieces of lead? What did they desire to accomplish when they forced him to carry his own cross to Calvary Hill, through the crowds who had come to witness the spectacle?" He looked at Christi with both intensity and patience.

"To humiliate him. To make him feel ashamed of what he had done," she said softly. "To make him feel guilty."

"Precisely. But did they achieve their purpose?"

"No, Christ knew he had done no wrong, that there was nothing for him to be ashamed of."

"Exactly. Who had control over how Christ responded? Who had the power to decide if he would feel humiliated, ashamed, or if this experience would destroy him?"

"It was Christ, of course," Christi said, concentrating on his course of reasoning. "He alone held that power, and he didn't give his power to his persecutors by responding as they desired."

Mr. Washington smiled approvingly. "Therein lies the foundation of the Third Spiritual Principle," he announced. "When someone attacks you, *you alone* have the power to decide whether it shall be an attack or an opportunity. It may be the desire of your enemy to destroy you, but if you choose not to be destroyed, if instead it is your intent that the experience be an opportunity that will lead to your resurrection, it shall. And each of you is *equal* in your power and your freedom to elect what your intent shall be. Thus you each choose the outcome of every experience you encounter."

"Mr. Washington, when we discussed the Second Principle I realized Jesus did not die to appease God's vengeance. But do you mean that the true significance of his crucifixion was to demonstrate our absolute power, even in the face of our worst enemies?" Christi asked with surprise.

"Confusion arising from the belief in vengeance as justice has obscured the meaning of this event for too long," he replied with a note of sadness. "To believe that God so loved the world that the murder of Jesus was required to atone for wrongs, even those not yet committed, is a misunderstanding. It arises from the belief that sin can only be resolved through punishment; from the misguided belief that the sacrifice of a living body would appease a vengeful God and atone for the sins of God's children. But how can this be when all are innocent—from the beginning of time? No, God is not vengeful. Therefore, Christ's death could not have been designed to spare you from such vengeance."

Christi sat quietly, reflecting, then said, "That may answer a question I've had since I was a child. It always seemed curious to me that Jesus was only dead for three days when he was atoning for the sins of everyone for all time. This made me think that our sins must not be too serious. Now I see why it made little sense—we have missed the point."

"Indeed," Mr. Washington said. "When you consider these events further it becomes even more apparent. What happened after Christ was resurrected? He then ascended into Heaven, his soul *and* his body. Through the attack of his enemies came the opportunity to sit at the right hand of God, forever. Christ chose his path, and thus demonstrated that you, too, are equally free to choose."

"Of course… I see," Christi said, her voice growing more animated. "I have had friends and family members who suffered much longer, terrible suffering, before dying of cancer or AIDS. Some rose above the physical experience to become an inspiration to those of us who attended them. I remember one friend who in the midst of terrible pain and suffering actually exhibited joy. She said she had seen a vision that was so beautiful that she didn't mind the pain if it was her path to such a place. But for some, it was a period of intense anger, of hatred and bitterness toward God. I see now that the same painful experience affected these people differently because of the choice each of them made."

Mr. Washington focused his kind gaze upon Christi. "The Third Spiritual Principle for Governing a People rests upon just that principle. **THE EQUALITY OF EVERY CITIZEN SHALL BE HONORED.**"

Christi thought a moment about what equality meant in this context. "You must not be speaking of equality in terms of money, power and sex—gauges many people use to determine who is equal and who is not," she said smiling.

Mr. Washington chuckled. "Correct, you are not all equal in those respects, but they are of little significance compared to the equality of which I speak. You are all equal in your ability to be in complete control of your life, equal in your opportunity to enjoy life, enjoyment that is not determined by the grandeur in which one is born. The right to be blessed with what is truly good in life—joy, peace, the experience and knowledge of God—these belong equally to all, irrespective of social rank."

Christi laughed. "What a paradox," she said. "The mystics chose poverty because they believed that physical objects were an obstacle to knowing God, that this journey was easier to make if one were free of physical possessions. And what could be of greater value than the knowledge of God? Nonetheless, in our society we accord physical possessions such value that we believe our worth in God's eyes is measured by our material wealth."

"But you must not judge," Mr. Washington warned. "Material wealth is not inherently bad, just as poverty is not inherently good. It all depends on how one responds to such circumstances. Irrespective of your position in life, your essential nature is that of pure poten-tiality. When you hold the intent to experience only love and joy, to live in peace and harmony, no one can take these from you. They may be experienced in a prison, indeed, even in a dungeon. Or they may be totally unknown, never experienced, even in a castle. It is a matter of choice. You are each equal in your power to determine the measure to which you shall know fear or love."

"This must be God's justice," Christi said recalling the Second Principle. "Are we each equally endowed with the tools to experience God's justice?"

"Would God make a promise that could not be kept?" Mr. Washington asked in reply. "If you truly want a problem solved, all that need be done is to give it to the Holy Spirit who mediates between the density of the physical plane and the highest vibration of all, Heaven. As the Holy Spirit is equally available to all, you live in a world filled with injustice and attack only if you so choose. No one can be unjust to you unless you have decided first to be unjust to yourself."

Mr. Washington sipped the last of his tea. Christi refilled his cup as he continued.

"Each Spiritual Principle, of course, brings us back to a basic principle that undergirds them all, that giving and receiving are one. The measure of what you give is the exact measure of what you shall receive. Accordingly, unless you believe that all other citizens are equal to you in the eyes of God, you cannot recognize your right to God's justice, because you have been unjust to one with equal rights. Under God's law, no one can lose, and *everyone* must win."

"Is this the equality you referred to in the Declaration of Independence, when you, our Founding Fathers, said 'all men are created equal'?" she asked as she looked upon her friend with admiration.

"Yes," he replied. "Every citizen is equally free to receive what belongs to God, and this equality must be honored by the State. Indeed, it must be nurtured by every agency and every program established by those who govern on behalf of the People."

"But how does the State carry out such a mandate?" she asked. "I'm sure it's not being done."

"It is difficult so long as you believe in separation. The law and those who enforce it must recognize that differences among citizens are but illusions; that all, in truth, are equal, and only equals can be at peace. Those within government must be non-judgmental, and understand that the eternal dance of consciousness is expressed in many ways. Each citizen is the result of past choices, but God has given free will to all so that each citizen can choose differently at any moment. By extending love, those in government can help transform the choices each citizen is free to make."

Christi thought for a moment. "Because all are equal, is it the duty of those who govern to extend love equally to all? Is that what the Third Spiritual Principle means?"

"Exactly. The power of the People must be employed only for this purpose. Condemn not a single citizen by sharing his mistaken belief that he rots within the prison of the illusions he has created. Affirm only his perfection as a child of God."

"But how can those in government do this?"

"It is through enlightened leadership that this shall be done," Mr. Washington stated succinctly. "It is the role of such leaders to ensure that the gift of love is given on behalf of the People to those who believe they are condemned. In this way shall the equality of all citizens be honored. The reward is that their light will shine back on the Nation a thousand times and more."

"I see," Christi said. "I am beginning to understand this Principle, but how does it answer my question about what happened in the Book of Judges? How were all innocent in that terrible event?"

"Perhaps you are too attached to the physical wrong to see the spiritual exchange," Mr. Washington suggested. "The story in Judges occurred at a time when male domination of the female was an energy through which it was necessary to evolve. There were lessons to be learned from such inequality, and it was from the resulting will to change that the intent to evolve toward equality and balance was born. You must not become lost in your personal drama of anger and revenge. In the larger design, a single tragedy may change the choices made thereafter, and thus serve a far higher purpose than if this cup had passed one by."

Christi became conscious of her hand resting on the beautiful old table. Her thoughts returned to the pain she had experienced at the firm of Harp, Harrison, & Humphrey, and especially from Harp's assault upon her. Those events affected the choices she had made. They had set her upon this journey. As her fingers traced the fine walnut grain she said softly, "I am grateful for everything that has led me to this present moment."

"Gratitude is a blessing, an expression of love," Mr. Washington said, nodding in appreciation. "Now you must ask, 'Am I willing to forgive?'"

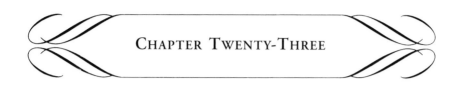

CHAPTER TWENTY-THREE

A summery breeze rustled through the red and yellow fall foliage as Christi ate breakfast at the table, enjoying a relaxed Saturday morning. She pondered the many positive changes that had taken place in her life in such a short time. The telephone rang.

"Hi, Christi. Remember the cookies you brought us a couple of weeks ago?" June asked. "Would you mind bringing the recipe with you when you come to work on Monday?"

"Sure will."

"Hap says they're good for enticing George Washington to visit you," June said laughing.

"Well, I don't know about that," Christi said, laughing as well. "I'll only share the recipe with the understanding it comes with no promises of magical powers."

"That's okay. I don't want to entice Washington. I just need a new recipe to take to a church meeting. But I also called to give you a message," June said in a more serious tone. "Hap and I stopped by the office to pick up some papers when a young woman happened to call. She seemed desperate to get in touch with you. Her name is Virginia Goode. Do you want her phone number now?"

"Yes, please," Christi said jotting down the number. "I'll call her right away, then copy my recipe so I don't forget."

Christi dialed the number and immediately recognized Virginia's voice when she answered. "Hello, Virginia. This is Christi Daniel."

"Thank you for calling," said the young woman, sounding

distressed. "Do you remember me? We met on my first day at Harp, Harrison & Humphrey when I began there as a new associate."

"I recall. I heard you were doing well at the firm."

"I was doing well, but things have changed. I'm calling to ask for your help."

"How can I help?" Christi asked.

"I don't even know where to begin. It's embarrassing.... I feel so ashamed." Virginia choked back tears. "I was so entrenched in my beliefs... so certain everyone else was wrong. I think I told you when we met that I was an admirer of Win Harp, that I wanted to become active in the R.R.s even more than I wanted to practice law. When Win was considering a run for the Senate, I offered to take half pay for the opportunity to have a position on his campaign staff. That was the exciting part. It's what happened after that that is so humiliating. I must have been blind to what was actually happening. As soon as I began working on the campaign staff, it became clear Win was attracted to me," Virginia said as her voice faltered.

The muscles in Christi's chest tightened. Images of Harp's attack on her began to appear in her mind.

Virginia continued. "I was flattered that a man of such power and ambition would even notice me. It began with flattering remarks. Then he started making sexual comments, discussing sex like we were just close friends. Next the touching began, especially when we were alone."

As Christi listened, her mind's eye focused on her own experiences with Harp—the touch of his hand, the smell of his breath, the weight of his body, the slap on her face—all returning in painfully vivid detail. Her breathing quickened.

"I quickly acquired so much power in the campaign, I was afraid to offend Win, for fear I would lose the dream that was coming true,"

Virginia confessed. "I wanted to keep it under control and go on as though nothing was wrong, but it became increasingly difficult. When I began to protest, he just ignored me. It was as though it made it more exciting, a greater conquest to overpower a woman who resisted. When it got to the point I told him his acts were offensive, he threatened to fire me from the firm and the campaign. I was in his power. Soon after that, we began having sex. As long as I was accommodating, everything went along smoothly."

Virginia began to cry. "And then..." she said between sobs, "and then I got pregnant and he demanded I have an abortion. I knew I had to have the abortion to protect him, or he could never run for the Senate."

Christi instantly reflected on the way she had handled Harp's sexual advances. Why had she not banded together with others and demanded better treatment? Why had she not taken action that may have spared Virginia this agony? Her anger at Harp intensified.

Virginia continued, sobbing: "I had the abortion last week and yesterday Win fired me."

Christi gripped the phone tighter and clenched her teeth. She recalled the subsequent events described in the Book of Judges. After the stranger's wife was offered to the sex perverts who had repeatedly raped her, the following dawn her mutilated body was left on the host's doorstep in Gibe-ah. Christi swallowed hard and searched her mind for appropriate words to say. "Now... Virginia... what are you going to do now?" she asked.

"I don't know," Virginia said, gaining some control. "He's not going to stop using his power in this way unless I do something, but I don't know how to handle it. That's why I'm calling you. You seemed so strong. Win didn't have control over you the way he did me."

"Virginia, you're not alone," Christi said bitterly. "He made the same type of advances toward me. What caused me to finally leave the firm was when he assaulted me in a motel room where I thought we had gone for a meeting. But I quietly settled with him and moved on, leaving him free to do the same thing to others like yourself."

"You too?" Virginia asked with disbelief. "I never dreamed this could happen to me, and certainly not to you. He was only able to do this to me because I have an illness I can't control."

"What do you mean, an illness you can't control?"

"You must promise never to tell anyone.... I have multiple personality disorder, but virtually no one knows," confided Virginia. "Now it's called dissociative identity disorder, just another fancy label for hell. I was sexually abused by an uncle when I was a small child. I was sent to live with him while my mother recovered from a serious car accident. He was in this group that took good principles, beautiful principles, and perverted them to use in these terrible rituals they created. I was sexually abused in their rituals, and I shattered into all these alters. My abusers were sick, truly sick."

Christi felt her stomach knotting. "What lofty principles did they pervert?" she asked breathlessly.

"Some sort of Masonic stuff, although they weren't actually Masons themselves," Virginia recounted. "I never knew much about it. They just got hold of this material and turned it into something terrible. A couple of them were eventually tried and convicted. One is still in prison for some of the things that went on, but they were caught long after I had been abused and returned to my mother. My uncle is dead now, but I still bear the scars from what he did."

"These are the worshippers of Baal and not God," Christi thought. "These are the men who fashion images and idols in their minds, which are not the Deity or even like the Deity, and worship them. They must pay for this," she pledged to herself.

Virginia continued, her anger emerging as she spoke. "Win discovered how to trigger one of my personalities. He brought her out whenever he wanted sex by calling her name. All I want now is to hurt Win as much as he has hurt me. I want vengeance."

"He deserves whatever you can do to him," Christi said, her adrenaline pumping. "I should never have let him off as easily as I did."

"What do I do now?" Virginia asked.

Christi slipped into her professional role. "A sexual violation has two primary facets," she calmly explained. "One is the emotional impact on you. The other is whether the fact pattern would make a viable lawsuit. I'm not qualified to advise you about how to put the emotional components in perspective. I suggest you go back to your therapist for that, someone who understands your particular circumstances, a therapist you trust. As for a lawsuit... this is one I'd give anything to win—but as a former attorney in the firm, I couldn't handle it. I can call around and ask who might be good to represent you in the suit."

"Thanks," Virginia said. "I feel better just knowing you believe me and are supportive. My greatest fear is that people won't understand, or worse yet, won't believe me if I report what Win has done."

"I'd sound foolish advising you to have more courage than I did, but I hope you'll find a better way to resolve your situation than I did mine," Christi replied.

Instantly her words echoed in her ears. "A better way?" she thought. Was she advising Virginia of a better way? Hadn't she concluded that her situation with Harp had been resolved in a way that served her highest good? How could she so quickly cast judgment? How could her desire to forgive be so easily forgotten? Her head fell to her chest, realizing she must tell Virginia there is a way to see this differently.

"Virginia... what Win has done to you is a terrible wrong," Christi began meekly. "I understand more than I want to admit the sense of violation that you feel. But there is a third consideration... you might call it a spiritual aspect of the case. Perhaps vengeance won't bring you the healing you desire." She hesitated before continuing. "I don't mean to minimize the depth of your pain. And yet, while it may seem impossible, perhaps this can be an opportunity for you to grow and heal in ways you never dreamed possible. I know it's difficult to imagine such an outcome. It was a long time before I could recognize hidden facets deep within Harp's wrongful acts toward me. In time perhaps you will see what I mean. Maybe this is how I can help... helping you to see this aspect of what has happened. When you and I are ready. We must keep in touch. Please call me again soon and know I want to help. I just don't know how—yet."

Virginia was silent. Christi waited a moment, then asked softly, "Virginia... can you answer a question for me? Do you know why Harp and Willard Smith dropped Smith's suit against me?"

"Oh, yeah.... The insurer threatened to report Harp to the Bar. Something to do with defrauding the insurer. Harp was furious but he couldn't risk it when he was planning to run for the Senate."

"Thanks," Christi whispered. "That provides a missing piece."

They said goodbye and as Christi hung up the receiver, she recalled her promise to June. She went to the cupboard and took out the hand-written card on which she had noted the ingredients of her recipe. The amounts of several ingredients had been crossed through and changes were penned in as she had perfected the mixture. Trial and error—a seemingly necessary ingredient in many aspects of her life.

As she held the recipe, she reflected on its association with Mr.

Washington's visits. Her hand trembled. It was as though each of her feet was planted in a different world and she was being ripped apart. She struggled to remain centered. She desperately wanted to understand Harp's role in her life and Virginia's, and how to respond in a way that was true to her evolving beliefs about justice. But how? She understood vengeance—her desire that Harp suffer for what he had done. But now, she also understood that her own peace was destroyed when she surrendered to a vengeful state of mind. What must she do to leave one world and enter another?

She threw on her coat and headed west toward the hill from which she could see Mount Vernon. As she left the house the wind grew stronger. She ran through her yard, past the garden, and into the adjoining field, leaning into the wind. As she plodded through the dry cornstalks, tears began to fall down her face.

She reflected on Virginia's earlier idealism. She realized what Virginia had believed when she joined the firm was consistent with the life experiences that had brought her to that point in time. Her harsh judgment of Virginia had not been warranted. The differences she had seen between them did not exist. As she pushed her way through the underbrush, hearing only the wind, she thought of many occasions when she, too, had been similarly blinded by her faith in false idols.

"Was it my own blindness or selfishness that led to Harp's abuse of Virginia?" Christi wondered. If she had publicly forced Harp to face his actions, could she have saved Virginia from this experience? She cringed at the thought of her own role in perpetuating the cycle of victimization of women through the ages. She hated the men who perpetrated such acts. Another layer of guilt emerged.

She stumbled into a patch of burrs that clung to her coat. "How beautiful the Principles are in the abstract, but how difficult they are to apply in practice," she sobbed as she tore at the burrs. She and Virginia must fit somewhere into a larger scheme of things. What lessons had they chosen to learn though such tragic experiences? How could Divine Order be reflected in such pain and chaos?

"What advice should I give Virginia?" she asked herself as she stumbled in the tangled brush. She felt like a child learning to walk. Virginia's anger seemed so reasonable under the circumstances. And yet a counterattack would hurt Virginia as much as Harp. How could she explain to Virginia that they were not victims—that both of them had chosen on some level to participate in Harp's schemes; that they were co-creators, each learning necessary lessons so they could more passionately articulate the importance of partnership and equality? How could she share the concept of Forgiveness of the Holy Spirit with Virginia, convince her that knowing there is nothing to forgive is the real source of one's power when one is attacked, when she herself had failed so miserably? A primordial scream was trapped in her throat, unable to release the torment of being torn between two worlds, in neither of which she now had a place.

As Christi reached the crest of the hill, the wind blew at gale force. She stood with her face to the wind, praying it would clear her confusion and purge the anger at her own ineptitude—she could not apply the Principles she knew were inherently true.

In the distance, Mount Vernon was gleaming white and serene. She knew she could not live in two worlds and be at peace. As tears washed over her face, she screamed, "I cannot both hate and love at once!"

On her knees, she cried, "It is impossible to see two worlds. I want to see differently." Her body fell forward, her head on the Earth. She prayed aloud, "Let me accept the strength God offers me. May I see this world I have invented has no value, so I may be free to experience transformation."

Christi recalled the transformation Mr. Washington described as necessary—learning to remove oneself from the situation, becoming an instrument of God, a presence through which God's energy can flow, yet unattached to the outcome. "To be an instrument for God, I must be clear and focused in the eye of this storm," she affirmed, then closed her eyes and struggled to visualize herself as a channel of white light.

"The only reason the light cannot enter is because of my belief in darkness," she wept. "God knows, I want to change. I want to share Mr. Washington's aim of healing minds by changing beliefs, but to do so I must never attack. That is where I fail."

She could hear Mr. Washington's voice in her mind, "Know that the hearts of those, even those who attack you, are pure. All beliefs are real to the believer, and they believe what they do is just."

"God, deliver me from this hell. Help me to see that all are innocent... even myself. Just grant me peace."

With the utterance of these words, a sense of peace enfolded her. Christi raised her head. Was it true—in her pain, God would be there for her? She had called upon the great unfailing Power. Could it be that God *will* take this giant step with her—in gratitude?

As quickly as it arose, the wind became calm. Christi stood up. A gentle rain began to fall and a rainbow formed a bridge over the Earth. She looked up to the sky and let the rain wash her face. An eagle soared high overhead. She stretched her arms toward the sky. "Yes!" she called out to the eagle... the rainbow... the sky. "All is in Divine Order. Once we see the problem as it truly is, our prayers will be answered! God, please help me to forgive, that I may know only love."

CHAPTER TWENTY-FOUR

Christi rose Sunday morning with a feeling that her life was beginning anew. As she opened the window to smell the fresh fall air a man walking briskly toward the house caught her eye. He was coming from the hill that lay to the west. "Mr. Washington... the Fourth Principle," she thought. She raced to the kitchen and put tea water on the stove, then stood in the door watching her special friend approach.

"Hello," Mr. Washington called out when he got within ear shot.

"Good morning," Christi loudly answered. "It's a beautiful day for a walk."

"This was one of my favorite times of the year," he said as he came nearer. "The hard work of summer is done and the fruits of your labor are returned to you. I especially enjoyed gathering with neighbors to celebrate and express gratitude for God's bounty."

Christi agreed as she invited him in. They were soon sitting at the table sharing tea and cookies.

"When we began this work, I didn't realize how agonizing it would be," Christi admitted with a smile. "If I had known how many tears would be shed along the way, I may not have agreed to travel this path with you."

"Imagine all you would have missed, and I, as well," he said also smiling. "You are an excellent student—progressing well toward an understanding of the new order. We have now come to the Fourth Spiritual Principle for Governing a People. Perhaps it will be easier. It has to do with the power of a People and we need only focus on the distinction between power and control which are distinctively different, but nonetheless often mistaken."

He sipped his tea thoughtfully. "What is often not understood is that the power of a People lies not in its physical might or the bombs contained in its arsenal—it springs from the spirit. You see, a Nation is a gathering of individual souls which, together, form the collective consciousness of a People. Each citizen is an integral part and an equally important reflection of Nationhood. When unified, there is nothing that a People cannot do. Its power is beyond the limitations of time, space or distance. It can feed the hungry or defeat dark forces with equal ease, because the power of God lies within it. Power abolishes all fear. It needs superiority over no one, for power emanates from understanding the equality of all. The desire to control others vanishes.

"Needless to say, only a spiritually enlightened leader can recognize this dynamic and work in harmony with it. She stirs the consciousness of the People into unified action so that their power may become manifest. The spiritually enlightened leader understands that when collective consciousness is aligned with infinite potentiality and love is the intent, policies that serve the highest good will be manifest.

"On the other hand," he said gesturing with his hand, "a leader who believes the power of the People rests in the physical domain has an intense need to control all that surrounds him. He manifests fear by building armies to impose control over everyone he deems a threat, including the People themselves. But such control must be distinguished from power. Power is constant, permanent, and is exercised by extending love, while control is temporary, fleeting, and depends upon instilling fear in others. One with power has the support of God's law. One with control has only the laws he has made."

Christi sat deep in thought. "When the Berlin Wall fell... it happened so quickly, it appeared effortless," she said. "And soon thereafter, the entire Soviet Bloc fell. Was this due to the consciousness of the citizens undermining the tyranny of the Communists? Was that, in essence, also what occurred when you founded this Nation and declared our independence from the King of England?"

"Yes," Mr. Washington replied. "When large numbers of people feel separated and live in fear, servitude can be imposed upon them. But no People can be subjugated without consent on some level. In time, unity in consciousness is achieved, and when it is, the power of the People is boundless. Where government is involved, ultimately the only source of power is the People. And **THE POWER OF THE PEOPLE SHALL BE INVIOLATE**. This is the Fourth Spiritual Principle for governing a People."

"The power of the People... inviolate," Christi reflected. "But how do the People achieve such unity of consciousness and thus such power?" she asked, taking another cookie from the plate.

"On the physical level, it manifests through the process of consensus-building, which can occur openly in a democracy, or in secret, and at great risk, in a dictatorship. But it nonetheless occurs. It is a process by which all citizens are heard, and thus, their equality acknowledged. Consensus does not mean that all are happy with the outcome," Mr. Washington said smiling. "It means that all have an opportunity to participate in the decision-making process before decisions are made, and they have a course of redress if they are displeased. With masses of people, this is done through freely elected representatives acting on behalf of their constituency. Democracy is the form of government based on this consensus-building process."

"Some would argue this process works more slowly than imposing control through force," she suggested.

"A mere illusion," he replied. "When force is used to decide an issue, the issue has not been resolved and must continually be revisited. Consensus-building is the path of least resistance. Democracy is not expedient, but it is enduring."

"Force only strengthens resistance," Christi added. "My mother says anyone who has children can attest to that!" They both laughed.

"This is because when force is used to decide an issue, someone always wins and someone always loses. But until all win, balance is not achieved and the conflict will continue, so no one has won."

"But Mr. Washington... something bothers me. When the People entrust their power to those who govern, how can they know which leaders are using it to impose control? Take Joseph McCarthy, for example, who led a crusade against the Communists in the 1950s. A lot of good people believed and supported him. How can we know who to follow?"

"It is very simple. In God's law, there are no secrets because all are one. Remember when I said that whatever you intend will be created? If one intends to promote love and peace, only love and peace can result. If one intends to promote fear, which can then be used to control people, only fear can result. Now, ask yourself, 'What did Mr. McCarthy create?' and you will know his intent."

"His intent to promote fear was soon evident. But perhaps that example is too easy. May I ask you about one that is more difficult?"

"More difficult situations do not exist," Mr. Washington replied with never-ending patience. "The same simple rule always applies, but please, ask your question."

"Take our national policy regarding guns, for example," she said cautiously, not wanting to offend her teacher. "Is it possible the Second Amendment was adopted to guarantee the People could have unlimited access to guns?"

"The Second Amendment.... Let me think.... 'A well-regulated militia being necessary to the security of a free State, the right of the people to keep and bear arms shall not be infringed.' Well… when it was adopted, freedom from England had just been secured but some doubted that it could be maintained. The militia had been important and supporters of the Mother Land were still about. The United States was such a vast, largely unsettled land. Under those conditions, it was no doubt perceived to be a prudent provision. But being based on fear, those who live in fear may seek to use it unwisely."

"The argument offered by the gun advocates is that people feel unsafe because there are so many criminals around, and the criminals manage to get guns," Christi explained. "So, they argue, people who are not criminals need unlimited access to guns in order to feel safe."

Mr. Washington winced. "The argument that guns can make people feel safe assumes the more anger you extend outside yourself the safer you will be. Attack is the purpose for which guns are designed, but all attack is self attack. When you attack it is a sign you have forgotten who you are—your identification is lost. God is there for you, but you do not see. If you realized how much havoc this makes of your peace, you would not make such an insane decision. You believe attack will get you something you want, but it is not peace of mind that you want. The outcome of this decision is clear—it is God against whom you are vigilant."

"But it's not easy," Christi contended. "When leaders support their proposals with arguments that sound logical, how can the People determine what the real intent is?"

"You need only examine the outcome. There are no secrets in the Oneness. The intent behind the policy will be revealed in its implementation."

Christi thought for a moment. "So, in order to determine if increasing a sense of safety is the real intent of those who want to increase the public's access to guns, all we do is examine the consequences when this policy is implemented? Is that correct?"

"It is just that simple," he replied. "If a greater sense of safety among the People is not promoted, then that is not the real intent of those who endorse the policy. There may be some citizens who *believe* they will feel safer if they can just have more guns. But material possessions gathered on the physical level can never cure fear which is experienced on the mental level. So after you buy one gun and still feel unsafe, you believe the solution must lie in owning two guns. When this does not end your fear, then it must be ten guns, more destructive guns, longer prison sentences, atomic bombs.... The search for a cure to fear is endless because the real solution, love, is seen as weakness and therefore is not even considered. When you live in fear, you are prey to leaders who promote solutions based on fear."

"We have no greater sense of safety now than when I was a child and far fewer guns were around," Christi said sadly. "When I was a child, my circle of safety included all of the small community where I grew up. But now we fear even strangers on the street who may be carrying a gun. Our sense of safety is being destroyed."

"It is your unity that is being destroyed by the distrust of one another brought about by such proliferation of weapons of attack," Mr. Washington pointed out. "How can the collective consciousness act in unison when you are separated by such fear? Attack is never discrete, for the many are one."

"And yet, many gun advocates become angry when you disagree with them," Christi complained.

Mr. Washington shook his head understandingly. "When people believe in separation, the only response they know is to attack. They identify themselves with their belief and recognize when you do not share it, you are weakening it. This is perceived as an attack upon them as individuals. Because it is not a physical response, love is perceived as a weak response, so it cannot be seen as a solution to their fear. They are thus unable to love those who disagree with them when, in truth, love is the only solution to their fear. There is no fear where there is love."

"It seems the gun manufacturers and dealers benefit the most from the proliferation of guns," Christi said, thinking of Willard Smith's gun shops and the wealth he had accrued from them. "If the real intent is to profit from the sale of guns, then in order to sell more guns, the level of fear must continually increase, which is the real result of the policy promoting unlimited access to guns. It's endless!"

"It demonstrates the power of intent—not what you *say* you intend, but what you intend on the soul level. It is this level that connects with infinite potentiality."

"We must be careful about what we intend!" she stated emphatically.

"Well put. The whole Universe is available to you. You have but to recognize your power. To do so, however, you must understand that this power exists in the Oneness. If you were in fact separate, such power could not be yours," explained Mr. Washington. "This is why the power of the People is inviolate. In coming together, the whole is greater than the sum of all the parts."

"This means when a People work together in harmony, their power cannot be chained or thwarted. They are inviolate," Christi said, affirming her growing understanding of this Principle.

"Good.... Very good," Mr. Washington said, pausing to look out the bay window toward the hill to the west. He turned to Christi smiling. "You have learned well and we have again achieved our goal. It is time for me to travel on." He rose from the table and walked toward the door as Christi followed. Before stepping outside, he looked at her. "All is not yet just.... But what is out of balance gives rise to the energy that creates change and maintains Divine Order. Rest peacefully—the power of the People shall be inviolate."

CHAPTER TWENTY-FIVE

"A man has been calling for you since a quarter to eight," June said as Christi arrived at work Monday morning. "He says it's urgent. I put the message on your desk. Oh, did you bring the recipe?"

"Indeed I did. I'll get it for you as soon as I return this call." Christi hurried to her desk. "Custody case—kids abducted. Call immediately," read June's note. She picked up the receiver and dialed. A deep male voice answered, "Hello."

"Hello. This is Christi Daniel, returning your call."

"Oh, thank you for calling back so quickly. My name is Richard Selander. I'm in a terrible situation. Last night my wife and her boyfriend ran off with my kids. I'm afraid they'll be harmed," he said sounding distraught. "The boyfriend is a detective and knows the ropes—I don't. I need a good lawyer. I heard you're the best, a real fighter. Can you see me?"

"What is your wife's name? I need to be sure there's no conflict."

"Her name is Susan, Susan Selander. Jones was her maiden name. I'd like to see you this morning, if possible."

"What is the boyfriend's name?"

Richard paused. "Uh... Wald. Rudolph Wald... that's his name."

"Rudolph Wald... Does he ever go by 'Ralph Waldo'?" Christi asked.

There was brief silence, then Richard said, "I don't think so. I've never heard that name."

"Interesting.... I hope your children are all right. Can you be here by eleven? I'll go over the case and we may be able to get an emergency hearing in a day or two."

"I'll be there. Thanks," Richard said sounding relieved.

Christi heard June reading the Sunday paper to Hap in his office across the hall. She got the recipe and joined them.

"Here's the infamous cookie recipe," she said cheerily, handing June the card. June laid the Sunday paper aside and read the list of ingredients aloud.

1 cup oil	*1/2 tsp. soda*
3/4 cup liquid Sucanat	*1 cup pecans*
2 eggs	*1 cup chocolate chips*
1 1/2 tsp. vanilla	*1 cup sunflower seeds*
grated rind of 1 orange	*1 cup raisins*
2 cups organic rolled oats	*3/4 cup grated coconut*
1 1/2 cups spelt flour	*1/3 cup sesame seeds*
1/2 tsp. baking powder	

Mix all ingredients and bake at 380 degrees for 15 min. or until brown.

"What is liquid Sucanat and spelt flour?" June asked, making a quizzical face.

"Sucanat is unrefined cane syrup," Christi explained. "I learned of it through a friend from Louisiana. It has a good flavor, plus it has iron, but you can use sorghum instead. I use spelt flour, similar to whole wheat, just to vary the grains in my diet. I figure with such healthy ingredients, the cookies must be good for me. It helps soothe my guilt over eating sweets," she said jokingly.

"Why doesn't this recipe have a name?" inquired June.

"Well, I never thought about it. Do cookies have to have a name?"

Hap interrupted the women. "With the variety of grains, nuts and fruits in them, you should call them 'Harvest Cookies'."

June disagreed. "I was thinking they should be called 'Mr. Washington's Cookies'. Let's compromise," she suggested, reaching for a pen on Hap's desk. At the top of the card, above the recipe Christi had written, June wrote:

Mr. Washington's Harvest Cookies

"Mr. Washington's Harvest Cookies," June announced proudly.

"I think we can reach consensus on that," Christi said, happy to have the fuss over her cookies concluded. "By the way, Mr. Washington came yesterday. He gave me the Fourth Principle—the power of the People shall be inviolate."

Hap and June both looked stunned. "Those were the very words used in an article about the Berlin Wall in yesterday's paper—written to commemorate the anniversary of its fall. I was just reading it," June said. "Listen to this," she said picking up the paper.

> The Berlin Wall may mean many things to many people. It taught me a poignant lesson about the power of the People.
>
> Easter 1963, when I was twenty years old, I traveled to West Berlin with a student group. Our access to the city was limited to travel by air over Communist East German territory which surrounded this small island of freedom. Upon our arrival, we toured West Berlin by bus. We were then dropped off at Check Point Charlie, the main point in the Berlin Wall through which Americans gained entry into Communist East Berlin. Another student and I ventured into the walled city together.
>
> As it was Easter Sunday, my friend and I decided to find a church to attend mass in East Berlin. When we began to make inquiries, the response was one of fear on the part of all whom we asked. They hurriedly walked away, saying "nicht, nicht." In East Berlin

there was no church for us to attend.

When we took photos of a street scene, the East Berliners quickly darted from view. The sense of fear permeated the air we breathed. Bullet holes remained in many of the walls and numerous bombed buildings had not yet been repaired. We were thankful to be Americans.

We found a small restaurant, not an easy task in this dismal enclave. Our waiter couldn't speak English, but through sign language informed us it was imperative that we keep a small note on which he had written how much we had paid for our meal. We understood his insistence when we recalled the East German guards who had counted the money we had with us when we entered. When we left, they would again count our money, no doubt to assure we had left none to assist a citizen of East Berlin with dreams of escape.

On November 9, 1989, the Berlin Wall fell. During the brief six-month window before it was dismantled, I returned to Berlin with my son, 16, and my daughter 14. It was Easter, 1990. This time I took photos of my two children standing on that wall, with no fear, chipping off souvenirs with hammers and chisels rented from a nearby hawkster.

In 1963 I had seen the power the Berlin Wall had over the People of East Berlin. In 1990, I saw the Berlin Wall for what it truly was—mortar and sand, a wall that had no power at all. I understood that this wall that had separated friends and loved ones in fact never had any power, other than the power the People it was meant to entomb had surrendered to it. When the People set aside their differences and acted in unity, no tyrant could contain them behind this or any other wall.

When the People of East Berlin reclaimed their power, in honor of their new-found freedom, they danced on the wall that had imprisoned them. Those in government stood helplessly by, unable to exert their will over a People who would no longer succumb to fear.

People of all nations can dance on their walls, those imagined barriers that imprison us, that separate us from our neighbors and turn us against one another. To proceed on this course, we must first recognize that those who govern have no power except that which the People willingly entrust to them. The power of the People is inviolate.

June and Christi looked at one another and then at Hap. "It's a paradox, isn't it," Christi said, "that Communism was to have guaranteed equality for all. But it defined equality only in terms of material goods. It refused to acknowledge even the existence of the soul, so was doomed to failure from the start."

"You know," Hap said as he leaned back and swiveled slowly in his chair, "when I was a child we were dirt poor, but I didn't know it. Our friends and relatives all lived just like we did, in shanties. They drove old cars, if they drove cars at all. But as a family and as neighbors, we shared everything we had. When someone was sick, or out of work, others pitched in. Oh, we had our differences, but they never separated us when things were tough. We loved each other too much for that to happen. I learned that material wealth is insignificant compared to wealth of the spirit. It's a sense of belonging, knowing you are one with those around you, that creates happiness and makes a community strong."

"Maybe that's the key," Christi said excitedly. "Could sharing one's wealth be a natural expression of love and equality? Think of the Third Principle, that the equality of every citizen shall be honored. The Communists failed, but when equality of the spirit is honored, perhaps the equitable distribution of material goods will be a natural consequence, without the use of force or even a sense of sacrifice. But when we live in fear, we try to cure that fear by hoarding our wealth. It relates to the Fourth Principle, as well—the power of the People shall be inviolate. Mr. Washington said the power of a People springs from the spirit, not its physical might. When the citizens of a Nation love one another, they are able to act in unity and are so powerful they can do anything, even create abundance. It all ties together. I'm beginning to see the bigger picture."

Hap sat up in his chair. "I just had an idea. June, please pull out the Declaration of Independence in that book of historic American documents," he requested. "Let's see if it mentions any of these Principles."

June quickly found the document that announced to the world on July 7, 1776 that the American Colonists had terminated their allegiance to the King of England. She read the opening statement.

> When in the Course of human events, it becomes necessary for one people to dissolve the political bands which have connected them with another, and to assume among the powers of the Earth, the separate and equal station to which the Laws of Nature and of Nature's God entitle them, a decent respect to the opinions of mankind requires that they should declare the causes which impel them to the separation.—
>
> We hold these truths to be self-evident, that all men are created equal, that they are endowed by their Creator with certain inalienable Rights, that among these are Life, Liberty and the pursuit of Happiness.— That to secure these rights, Governments are instituted among Men, deriving their just powers from the consent of the governed.— That whenever any Form of Government becomes destructive of these ends, it is the Right of the People to alter or to abolish it, and to

institute new Government, laying its foundation on such principles and organizing its powers in such form, as to them shall seem most likely to effect their Safety and Happiness. Prudence, indeed, will dictate that Governments long established should not be changed for light and transient causes; and accordingly all experience hath shewn, that mankind are more disposed to suffer, while evils are sufferable, than to right themselves by abolishing the forms to which they are accustomed. But when a long train of abuses and usurpations, pursuing invariably the same Object evinces a design to reduce them under absolute Despotism, it is their right, it is their duty, to throw off such Government, and to provide new Guards for their future security.—

June and Christi again looked at one another and at Hap.

"The power of the People shall be inviolate.... The equality of every citizen shall be honored," Hap said slowly and deliberately.

"And Mr. Washington was right," Christi added. "Whether it was the British Colonies or the Communist Bloc, when life became intolerable, out of that struggle came the power to gain even greater freedom than had been known before. Evolution. All was in Divine Order."

Just then they heard the front door open and close. "Oh, I have an eleven o'clock appointment. That must be him. Please excuse me," Christi said as she quickly stepped toward the door. "We'll have to continue this discussion as soon as we can."

Richard Selander was an exceptionally handsome man, about forty, with blond wavy hair and broad shoulders. Considerably taller than Christi, she had to look up to meet his deep blue eyes as they shook hands.

"I'm sorry about what has happened to your children. Please come in and we'll see what can be done about it," she said as she led him to her office.

Richard sat facing Christi in the chair in front of her desk. "Several people referred me to you. It was as though all roads led to you. I decided I had to meet this woman." Christi didn't respond to his flattery.

Richard described his troubled marriage, with a wife that went from one man to another, the latest being a private investigator. He was visibly moved as he described his close relationship with his son, age ten, and his daughter, age eight. He said both he and his wife worked, but he primarily cared for the children in the evenings, supervising homework, and on weekends when he spent time with them riding horses and playing tennis. When he told his wife he was going to seek a divorce and petition for custody of the children, his wife flew into a fit of rage and she and her boyfriend took the children. He had spent much of the night at the police department and calling family and friends, looking for them.

Christi called the court and scheduled an emergency hearing at 9:00 a.m. Wednesday morning. She promised to file the papers by tomorrow.

"In case I need to get in touch with you, can I call you at home?" he asked.

"Of course," she said jotting her home phone number on a slip of paper.

"I'm supposed to be at a Masonic meeting tonight," Richard said, "but I don't plan to go. I'll stay close to home in case anything develops."

"A Masonic meeting?" Christi asked in a surprised tone. "Are you a Mason?"

"Yes. Followed in the footsteps of my dad," Richard said modestly.

"I'd love to know more about the Masons. I take it you have been a member for a long time?"

"Probably close to twenty years. Say, it's time for lunch. Any chance I can take you to lunch? I can tell you a little about it."

"Why not?" Christi replied. "There's only one restaurant in town, but their meat and potatoes are reasonably good."

"Great. May I use your phone before we go?" Richard asked, motioning toward her phone. "I need to make a personal call."

"Sure. I'll wait for you in the reception area," Christi said, picking up the two clients' files that were lying on her desk. She closed the door behind her as she left.

Within minutes Richard joined her. "All done," he said smiling.

Over lunch Richard quizzed Christi about her interest in the Masons. She told him she had read a little about their history, and was especially interested in their role in founding the Nation. She described the Masonic artifacts she had found in the hidden compartment by the fireplace. He offered to come to her home and help her decipher their meaning, an offer she eagerly accepted. There was little time for her to ask about his involvement in the Masons before he said he had to leave for another appointment.

As they parted, he looked at Christi and asked, "Why is such an attractive woman like you practicing law way out here?"

Christi smiled and replied, "It was better than the alternative."

Early that evening Richard called Christi at home. "I have good news," he said sounding upbeat. "My wife brought the kids back. We're going to try to work out a settlement, perhaps with shared custody. You can cancel the emergency hearing, at least for now."

"That is good news. I know you're relieved," Christi said, wanting to conceal her disappointment. "But... is the offer still on to take a look at the Masonic artifacts I have? You're the only person I've met with first-hand knowledge."

"Sure. How about next weekend?"

"I can't do it then. I'm going to North Carolina with a friend. Can you come the weekend after that? Maybe around three or four Saturday afternoon. We can roast chestnuts and talk about the Masons."

"It's a date. I'll be there," Richard said enthusiastically. "What are you going to do in North Carolina with your friend?"

"We're going to visit her grandfather. He's some sort of official in their Indian tribe."

"Sounds intriguing. I hope you'll tell me all about it," Richard requested and Christi agreed.

Tom called later that night, excited about a new development he felt might be pertinent. "Remember the discussion you had with Washington about the crucifixion of Christ? There's a speaker coming to Boston, a pathologist who lectures on the Shroud of Turin. You know, the cloth that covered Christ when he ascended. It's supposed to have healing powers. This doctor's an expert on the pathology of Christ's death as it's reflected in the Shroud. He'll be here weekend after next and I have two tickets. Can you come?" he asked eagerly.

"Weekend after next? Gee, I'm sorry, but I can't make it that weekend. I'm doing some research on the Masons. I think I've found a source that can help decipher the meaning of the things that we found in the secret chamber."

"Oh, that's a shame... that you can't come," Tom said sounding disappointed. "What's the source you have found?"

"Oh, well... it's a man I met as a client. But he doesn't need my legal services any longer. He's just a friend. He's coming here... to look at the things I found. He's a Mason."

"I see.... Maybe I can get a tape of this speech. I'll at least take notes for you."

"You're sweet, Tom. You know I'm going to North Carolina with Shenan next weekend to see her grandfather. I'll give you a full report of that adventure when I get back. We can share notes."

"When I come for Thanksgiving... if I'm still invited."

"Of course," Christi quickly replied. "You, Shenan, Hap and June—we're going to share the first feast at the table since it was returned to the meeting place."

CHAPTER TWENTY-SIX

T hursday night it was late before Christi was finally able to fall asleep. As she drifted off, she was certain, though she didn't know why, that Mr. Washington would be waiting for her in the morning. She tried to recall if she had a supply of cookies on hand. She was sure she did.

As she descended the stairs the next morning, her hunch was confirmed. Mr. Washington was standing by the large bay window watching a gentle rain.

"Good morning," Christi said as she entered the dining room. "I thought you would be here this morning."

"Yes," he said. "I come when you are ready for a new Principle, and we are progressing quickly. Perhaps you now sense when that time arrives."

They were soon at the table enjoying tea and Mr. Washington's Harvest Cookies in their customary manner. Mr. Washington wasted no time in getting to the lesson. "The Fifth Principle is practical," he began. "Its mastery will pave the way to lasting change. It is about changing one's perception, one's fundamental beliefs—you must change yourself in order to change the world. **CHANGE ONLY COMES FROM WITHIN.** This is the Fifth Spiritual Principle for Governing a People."

"Change only comes from within?" Christi questioned. "What about the politicians who promise to deliver change, as though we need do nothing?" She paused. "Perhaps the change they're interested in is that of getting themselves elected, since that's the change that results."

"You are a good student," Mr. Washington chuckled. "It is just such promises that lead many citizens to believe that government is in control of their lives and if things are not right today, they must wait for government to fix them. But when people project fear and hatred upon their world, no manner of government policies can fix the world they see. The Fifth Spiritual Principle is directed at the citizens, to assure each does his or her part in bringing the Nation to unity of consciousness so that peace and prosperity may flourish in an atmosphere of love."

Christi reflected momentarily. "Through our work together I have come to understand how important—and how difficult—it is to change oneself. But knowing what a difference it is making in my life, I can see the importance of this Principle. If the Fifth Principle can lead to harmony of consciousness, as it is learned by greater numbers of citizens, change will occur within the Nation with increasing speed, until it appears effortless," she said smiling, pleased with her growing understanding.

"It will achieve just that. When the Fifth Principle is learned, one is not subject to manipulation through fear, justice can be delivered without judgment, it is the root of the equality of all citizens and the key to the power of the People being inviolate. And yet it will be resisted by those who believe their present belief system to be good."

"What do you mean?"

"For example, those who are attached to their wealth and believe more and more wealth is good, will find it hard to give up this belief. They see their physical possessions as a reflection of themselves. It is this lesson they must unlearn, for they are not their physical possessions, or even their body, for nothing physical can last forever, as they shall. But because they do not recognize their belief as faulty, they are likely to experience fear at the prospect of change."

"I know how attached we can become to our possessions," Christi said with an embarrassed grin. "Does this Principle apply to the poor, as well?" she asked. "Do they identify themselves with the belief they have no choice but to be poor and fear change as well?"

"Yes," Mr. Washington replied. "They must accept the truth that they are equal, that they are empowered and responsible for change within themselves, as is everyone. The prospect of unlearning the limitations they believe about themselves and accepting new responsibility is likely to cause fear, at first."

"Is it ever easy?" Christi asked, smiling at her teacher.

"For some, it is," he replied. "For those who know they have lived outside the law, conversion is much easier. To them, discarding their beliefs doesn't seem such a great sacrifice as it does to those who perceive their beliefs to be good."

"So how does someone begin to change her beliefs, when they seem to be good and are operable in the world she has constructed to accommodate them?"

"Change can only come at the level of the mind," Mr. Washington answered. "What you want to achieve is love, and only fear stands in the way. Because fear arises from the belief in separation, it is at the level of the mind that you must correct the perception that you are separate. It is useless to pray that you may overcome fear, as this only affirms its power over you. God cannot release you from fear because it exists only in your mind. You must ask, instead, for help with what caused the fear in the first place—your perception of separation. Only in this way can you break the endless cycle of fear and come to experience love."

"But this unlearning must begin somewhere. How is the first step taken in breaking this cycle?" Christi asked.

"To do so, you must witness your choices," he explained, moving his finger through the air. "*Before* acting, ask if your choice is based on the perception of separation. If you are experiencing any fear, you will know that it is. But only your mind can produce fear. It does not arise from a threat outside of yourself. When you experience fear, you must say to yourself that you have somehow chosen not to love, or fear could not have arisen. Then the process of correction becomes nothing more than the determination to change your mind."

"We fail to appreciate the real power of our mind," Christi said laughing. "Every instant it is creating."

"Yes," he agreed, "it never loses its creative force; it is never sleeping. To know love and experience peace, you must recognize the power of the mind. All thinking produces form at some level, so you must be ever vigilant about what you think."

"I often wondered as a child," Christi said, "why God made it so complicated. Why can't we all just ascend into Heaven because God says so, instead of having to endure this seemingly endless struggle within ourselves?"

"Because you are an aspect of God," Mr. Washington replied. "How could any part of God not have the power to create? To do what you suggest God would have to take your free will and power to create from you, but then you would no longer be an aspect of God. You would be diminished to a mere pawn of God, which would destroy the Oneness of all."

Christi laughed. "You mean we are doomed to accepting responsibility for our thoughts and the actions that result from what we think? We can't blame God?"

"That is your lot," he said smiling.

"So, are you saying that the solution to salvation lies just in changing our mind? Is this the crux of the Fifth Principle?" she asked.

"That is precisely the point," he confirmed. "You do not condone insane behavior. Why do you condone insane thinking? You may believe that you are only responsible for what you do, but your first responsibility is for what you think, because it is only at that level that you exercise choice about what you do."

"But so often fear takes over. It's hard to control it," she bemoaned.

Mr. Washington shook his head. "Being afraid may seem to be an involuntary act, beyond your control, but it is not. It appears involuntary only because you have become so accustomed to submitting your will to fear that you have forgotten that it is under your control. Fear cannot be controlled by God precisely because it is something you impose upon yourself.

"When you are fearful, you are responsible for this experience and must change your thinking. To do so, you must become consciously aware of the choices you make," he explained. "Step back and witness those choices. Through the act of witnessing you will change what was previously an unconscious reaction into a conscious action. Don't look to others to create change for you. You are in total charge of this process."

"But old patterns are so deeply ingrained, such change is fearful to most of us." Christi tried to envision herself teaching such a concept to others, then said, "I need to know if it can be introduced in a way that is less threatening."

"Even though a good teacher understands that only fundamental change will last, she does not begin the teaching at that level. The motivation for change must be instilled first. In fact, to assure change, all the teacher need do is increase the student's motivation for change, for a change in motivation is a change of mind," Mr. Washington pointed out.

"But how does the teacher plant the seed of motivation so the student will desire to change?" Christi asked.

"Always extend love and never project fear. Begin with the fundamental truth that giving and receiving are one. And giving must not be confused with bargaining, for to bargain is to limit giving. You see, having is *not* the opposite of giving. You may find this is where conflict first arises on the path to fundamental change, while your motivation to change is yet conflicted. Eventually you will see that to have all you must give all."

"I'm still at the stage of experiencing conflict," admitted Christi. "That happens a lot. My heart knows the Principles are true, but my mind wants to go another way. As I learn this new system of beliefs, it seems I have not yet relinquished the old ones and I get caught in the middle. For those of us who are mortal, this can be a difficult journey. And teaching these Principles to others seems impossible when I cannot master them myself."

"So it seems," Mr. Washington said smiling kindly. "Because you identify yourself with your belief system, if you accept two conflicting belief systems, peace of mind is impossible. To avoid such conflict you must be vigilant and witness your acts in every moment. But chaos and consistency cannot coexist for long. The desire for love is inherent in your nature, so you are propelled toward truth. You will eventually recognize there is but one choice, so you need not choose after all— you cannot undo what has been irrevocably made for you. In time, this understanding will be achieved and easily taught to others."

Mr. Washington sipped his tea. "This is excellent tea, and the cookies as good as ever. Yet another of our meetings has achieved its purpose and now must end. There are few remaining, and I shall miss them," he said wistfully.

A mixture of sadness and urgency came over Christi "There are only two Principles left. Before we meet again, I will focus on today's lesson. I'll practice observing my actions, before I act, and devote more energy to changing myself from within."

"You are preparing yourself well," Mr. Washington said approvingly. "Change is manifesting from within."

CHAPTER TWENTY-SEVEN

The cold November morning sky was still dark when Christi and Shenan headed south on I-95 to North Carolina. They expected to arrive at the home of Shenan's grandfather by early afternoon. This was precious time together and the friends conversed happily as they crossed the miles.

"Grandfather Moses is probably the most significant person in my life," Shenan told Christi as the conversation turned to the object of their mission. "I stayed with him and Grandmother a lot when I was a child, because Mom was kind of unstable—a drinking problem that made the visits to my grandparents especially welcome."

"Is your grandmother still alive?" Christi asked, absorbed in the details of Shenan's family history.

"No. She died about ten years ago," Shenan said. "Grandfather has lived alone ever since."

"Does he mind living alone?"

"I'm sure he misses Grandmother, but he never complains about anything. He doesn't consider his wants and desires to be all that important."

"What does he do," Christi asked, "I mean, to keep himself busy?"

"He takes care of the sun," Shenan replied without hesitation.

Christi was intrigued. "What does that mean?"

"He lives on a tiny peninsula surrounded on three sides by a swamp near the edge of a river. He has a clear view of the sun as it rises in the east and sets in the west, although he can't see much else because of the dense woods all around. Developers tried to take the land, to fill in the swamp and build a waterfront development, although it has belonged to the Indians from the beginning of time. The only reason the white man didn't take it before is because it's in the middle of a swamp. It was saved by the Wetlands Act, so it's safe a little longer."

"What does he do to take care of the sun?" inquired Christi, prodding for details.

"He greets the sun as it rises in the east. He believes—actually my people believe—that the sun would be forsaken if this wasn't done. And each evening he bids the sun farewell as it sets in the west. The sun would be forsaken if this wasn't done, as well. So he lives alone in this remote place, nearly self-sufficient, living on the fish he catches, the animals he hunts and his garden. He lives a simple life all by himself, but believes that the welfare of the entire world depends on him."

"What will happen when he's no longer there?"

"Many years ago I told him I never wanted him to die. He said that he couldn't die until there was someone with his special powers to take over his responsibility of caring for the sun. I often pray there will be no one else with such powers," Shenan explained, blinking away tears.

"What are the special powers your grandfather has that makes him able to carry out this ominous responsibility?" Christi asked.

"He has been trained since childhood in the Indian ceremonies that have been passed down from generation to generation. There's a different ceremony for every important event in life, such as naming a person, or even a place or thing. And of course, for death, but also for healing people who are ill. There are rituals for purification when something or someone has become defiled. And there are the rites of manhood which usually involve a quest, an exploration of a young man's inner space. Girls approaching maturity now have such rites of passage, too. There must be careful preparation for each of these sacred journeys, as well as the process of integration once each has been completed. Most white people don't seem to know this inner space exists, but native people treat it with great respect. They know it is more powerful than anything on the physical plane."

"Change only comes from within," Christi said, looking out the window across the fallow tobacco fields. She looked at Shenan. "That's the Fifth Spiritual Principle for Governing a People. Mr. Washington came yesterday." Christi explained this Principle in detail, and how change can only occur in the mind. Shenan said that was what Grandfather Moses had always told her, that if she assumed responsibility for her thoughts, her actions would never be a problem.

They soon began discussing the meaning of reality, and how their views were changing.

"I used to think Grandfather Moses was crazy," Shenan said. "I never told anyone about him when we were in college. Now I'm convinced the rest of the world lives in a delusional world, not him. I'm proud of my ancestor. He'll tell you that you're not crazy either, that you're just on an extraordinary journey. You'll see."

It was early afternoon when Shenan turned off the interstate, onto a smaller state road. After some distance she turned onto a narrow two-lane road that was paved, but not well maintained. It was not long before the next turn took them to a dirt road on which they traveled through dense oak woods for some distance. The car ride terminated at a small clearing where the dirt road ended.

"We have to walk the rest of the way," Shenan said as she parked the car at the edge of the clearing.

For miles there had been no electricity lines or other indication that civilization had encroached this far. Christi saw no sign of anyone else around. "Does he know we are coming?" she asked, looking up at the tall oak trees that closed in on them.

"Probably. I've been sending him messages every day since I decided to make this trip," Shenan replied.

"How did you send them?" Christi asked, noting the absence of any evidence of means to communicate.

"Mentally. You know… telepathy."

"Did he send you an answer?"

"Not that I know of," said Shenan. "But I'm not all that good at it. You get out of practice when you live in the so-called 'developed world' where people would perish if they had to depend on their subtle senses to survive. Most people have lost their ability to communicate the way we were meant to, using our mental abilities. That's why they believe they are separate, unconnected to everyone and everything around them. They have lost the ability to experience that connection."

"I didn't know you were ever proficient at this type of stuff," Christi said, as they walked down a narrow path leading deep into the woods. "This is something you never told me, even though we lived together for four years."

"I was ashamed," responded Shenan sadly. "I didn't want to be different from everyone else. I didn't want anyone to think I was weird, and in the white man's society, this is weird. In our tribe, Grandfather Moses is the wisest of the wise. But in the white man's world, he would be diagnosed as having a delusional disorder, a schizophrenic whose contact with the 'other world' is nothing more than hallucinations brought on by some sort of dementia."

"How well I know. Don't ever send him to Dr. Lumpkin!" Christi said, as they joined in laughter.

"Remember when we studied general psychology our sophomore year of college?" Shenan asked.

"Sure, I remember you hated the class and I had to force you to study for the exams."

"When I read that stuff, I knew I could never tell anyone about Grandfather Moses. I was afraid they would arrest him or put him in an insane asylum." Shenan's solemn face imparted the pain of the experience. "That's why I never mentioned him to anyone, not even to you." Then Shenan laughed heartily. "Not until you started exhibiting the same type of symptoms!" she said gleefully, as Christi joined in the mirth.

Their laughter filled the woods as they strolled briskly along the path, acorns crunching beneath their feet. After walking for some time they came to an opening in the woods and a small white frame house, more accurately described as a shanty. Dense swamp outlined with cypress trees surrounded the house on three sides, just as Shenan had described. They passed the garden plot behind the house. No one seemed to be home.

"I wonder if something has happened to Grandfather," Shenan said, sounding alarmed. "If he knew we were coming he would be here to greet us."

Just then an elderly man with the most wrinkled face Christi had ever seen came around the side of the house. His long white hair was tied in a pony tail and he wore a red plaid flannel shirt and well-worn blue jeans.

"Grandfather Moses!" Shenan exclaimed with joy as she raced into his arms. "I was afraid you were not here."

"I was just inside, stirring the fire to heat water. It needed a little encouragement," he said, with a lightness of spirit that Christi found welcoming.

"This is my friend, my very best friend in the whole world," Shenan said, introducing Christi. "She wanted to meet you because you have something in common."

Moses Adkins looked at Christi with penetrating dark eyes that, to her surprise, did not intimidate her. In his presence, she felt a glow and knew this was a person she could trust.

"Welcome to my mansion," he said with a grin that revealed spaces between the teeth he yet had. "Won't you please come inside?"

"Thank you, Mr. Adkins," she said.

"You must call me Moses," he directed. "Or Grandfather Moses, if you like."

"Thank you... Grandfather Moses. I'm pleased to be here," she said as they entered the larger of the two dimly lit rooms of the house. In the middle of the room sat a small table covered with a brightly colored cloth decorated with Indian designs. Three cups and saucers were sitting on the table, none of which matched.

"Shenan has told me this is an especially important place," Christi said, as she accepted Grandfather Moses' offer to sit at the table.

"Its importance means many things to many people," he replied. "Like beauty, it's in the mind of the beholder."

Grandfather Moses took a speckled blue enamel pot off the stove and poured a black liquid into the cups on the table. "Coffee," he said. "Do you like sugar?"

"No, thank you," Christi said. "I take mine black."

Shenan laughed. "Maybe not this black," she said.

"In our eyes, the gods live here," Grandfather Moses said, smiling as he put the blue pot back on the stove.

Christi couldn't help but smile back at his jovial, mischievous face. "I can believe that," she said, scanning her surroundings and beginning to feel its energy.

"Then you must be able to see, not only with the eyes of the body, but with the eyes of the spirit," Grandfather Moses said, as he sat at the third place at the table. "Do you also hear with the ears of the spirit?" he asked. "Only those ears can hear the message of the wind, or the real song the birds sing."

"Maybe," Christi said. "I want to hear in this way."

"The voice of Mother Nature is clear to those who hear with such ears," Grandfather Moses said as he continued to assess Christi with his deeply set eyes. "With such eyes and ears you can awake from the dream and leave the world of illusion, but you can no longer live in the white man's world—a world so dense people see and hear only lower vibrations." He paused and sipped his coffee. "Now, tell me, what do we have in common?"

Christi felt no fear. She launched into her description of the unusual events in her life, confident Grandfather Moses would understand. She related how she had been an attorney in D.C., first working for the Justice Department and then for a large firm. Grandfather Moses made agreeable but unintelligible sounds continuously as she spoke. She told him about her attraction to the special table at the firm, a fact he took in stride. She told him how she became dissatisfied with the practice of law and the dishonesty that she experienced, how she bought an old house in northern Virginia, not too far from where George Washington had lived, and opened a small law practice.

"George Washington," Grandfather Moses said, that being the first intelligible words he had spoken since she began to tell her story. "He was not always good to the Indians. . . . But he has healed, as we all do, and is forgiven," he said shaking his head.

Christi looked at him, sensed his approval and continued. "One night I awoke hearing voices in a room downstairs in my house, in the room where the table is," she said. "It was people from the past."

"Oh, the ancestors were meeting in your house!" Grandfather Moses exclaimed. "This means you are special, for the ancestors make such a choice with great wisdom. They know you are a dreamer of the future, that you will hold the vision."

Christi was surprised at how closely his words paralleled those of Mr. Washington. She continued with even more confidence. "After that meeting, George Washington wrote me a note and asked if I would meet with him."

"And I hope you agreed. Please tell me you agreed to see him," Grandfather Moses said with concern that she may have rejected the offer.

"Yes," Christi said. "I agreed and we began to meet regularly. He is delivering Seven Spiritual Principles for Governing a People to me."

Grandfather Moses looked at Christi with his black piercing eyes. "Tell me, what do these seven principles say?"

"Some of them sound like the old Indian teachings," Shenan interjected. "The equality of all people shall be honored; the power of the People shall not be violated; change must come from within."

"The first had to do with fear, that fear shall not be used to manipulate the People," Christi added. "The second was about justice without judgment."

"Such spiritual principles for governing a people... being delivered to the white man by George Washington?" Grandfather Moses said as he looked at Christi, then Shenan with surprise. "Shennie... you didn't tell me you were bringing the messenger of such news. This is what we have waited for."

He leaped up and spryly danced around the room, spinning several circles around the table, making sounds like a chant of some kind. "How can we thank you?" he said patting Christi on the shoulder so hard she nearly slipped off her chair. "You have brought the message we have been waiting for. The white man's time has come! We knew it would happen, and there were many signs that the time was near. But my Shennie has brought you to tell us the time is now! It is the time of change. We will soon begin to speak the same language, the white man and us!" he exclaimed as he continued to dance around the table.

Shenan smiled joyfully at her grandfather, excited by his response to her friend's report. Christi sat silently, watching Grandfather Moses dance, wondering what would happen next.

"We must send the ancestors our message of thanksgiving," he said, as he danced toward a cupboard in a dark corner of the room. "Please come with me to the ceremonial pit." He motioned for the two women to follow. "We will offer thanks." He directed Christi and Shenan to their appointed positions next to a fire pit near the edge of the swamp, then blew into the live coals, feeding them small twigs until fire leaped forth. He piled on larger sticks and wood until the flames in the pit soared.

Grandfather Moses began singing in a language Christi did not understand, but she assumed it was a song of thanksgiving. He lit a small bundle of sage that he waved in the air, spreading its pungent odor throughout the site. Then he took a bundle of dried tobacco and held it toward the sky before placing several leaves on the fire, as an offering to the ancestors.

After some time the tone of his chant changed and Shenan whispered to Christi that Grandfather Moses was now offering a prayer for new life. He made an offering of tobacco to the four winds.

When the ceremony came to an end, Grandfather Moses invited Shenan and Christi to share a meal of fish stew, coarse cornbread, and berry pudding at the small table in the house. As they ate, Shenan told her grandfather that Christi had come to consult him about whether or not she was crazy, since she's been meeting with someone who's dead.

Grandfather Moses looked intently at Christi. "In the white man's world you are crazy. The white man has created a culture full of meaningless distractions so the inner world can remain hidden. Many live behind walls they are afraid to peek over, for they don't know how to look into their inner space. Native people, in many parts of the world, have preserved the Ancient Wisdom, and now our so-called 'conquerors' may share this powerful knowledge. You have brought the message that the time has come.

"In the world of native people, things such as you have seen are not crazy, they are real," he continued. "What you do at your job is crazy. We have people who are doing this for us too, this going to court... you know, to get back our land. But how can a judge say who owns the land? The land belongs to Nature. We just take care of it for the time we are here—that is our duty. You, friend of my Shenandoah, you are blessed, not crazy. And George Washington has come to be your guide; how lucky for you. He will guide you in your times of need," Grandfather Moses said with the same gentleness she felt in the presence of Mr. Washington.

When the meal had ended, Christi and Shenan prepared to leave. Christi was satisfied that her mission was accomplished—she had received confirmation that what was happening was significant and fit into a much larger picture.

It was late afternoon as Shenan hugged her grandfather goodbye. Unexpectedly, he told Shenan he had good news. A younger man, in his sixties, had agreed to take his place and assume responsibility for caring for the sun.

Upon hearing this news, Shenan burst into tears and held Grandfather Moses tightly in her arms. "Grandfather, does this mean I will never see you again?"

"Shennie, I'm not leaving you. I will visit often from the other side."

She knew this was a promise he would keep.

Shenan and Christi made the return walk to the car in silence. It was cold and nearly dark as they approached the car. Shenan peered inside. The glove compartment door was open and papers were strewn on the floor. "Someone has broken into the car!" she cried. "Who would do that? Who could have found it in this remote place? Let's get out of here."

Christi looked around, then jumped into the car. Shenan turned the ignition and was relieved when the motor started. She put the car in reverse, pushed on the accelerator, then shifted gears and sped down the narrow dirt road. Shots rang out behind them. "Let's hope they're hunting deer, and not us," Christi said as they sped through the dense woods.

CHAPTER TWENTY-EIGHT

For several days Christi continued to hear the sound of gunshots firing in the woods. Each shot remined her of the break-in of Shenan's car. Her anxiety was increasing. She was relieved Richard was coming on Saturday and she would not be home alone.

Saturday morning she drove into town and bought local chestnuts at the farmers' market. On the way home she struggled with her attraction to Richard. He was more handsome than Tom, but that wasn't it. Tom had become so much a part of her life, she was feeling confined. With Richard there was no commitment.

She had just placed the Masonic artifacts on the table when Richard drove up to the house. "Please come in," she said. "May I take your coat?"

He took off his leather jacket and rubbed his hands together, blowing on them to warm them up. "It's cold out there. Say, you have a nice place here. Who lives with you?"

"Oh, I live alone. Have for years." Christi led him into the dining room. "You can warm up in front of the fire," she said motioning to the fireplace that was crackling with well-seasoned hickory logs. "I have hot mulled cider on the stove. Would you like some?"

"Sure. That must be what smells so good."

As Christi prepared mugs of hot cider in the kitchen, Richard began to examine the artifacts in the box. "I take it these are the things you found in the hidden compartment you were telling me about," he said as she set the silver tray on the table.

"Yes. These were the beginning of a mystery I have yet to solve. I assume they were used in Masonic meetings that may have been held in this room. I hope you'll be able to tell me more about them."

"Who have you had look at them?"

"I took them to a friend at the Smithsonian, but she couldn't help. A man I met there said they belonged to a demonic sect, or something. I don't plan to take them back."

"Have you ever used them for anything?"

"No, except one time a friend came..." She hesitated. "A friend came and we put them out. Maybe they have magical powers. We heard some voices, here in this room."

"Could you tell what they were saying?"

"Oh, you know, we were just playing around. I think it was something about forgiveness. We have to forgive everyone."

"That doesn't seem like significant information. Has anything else happened?"

"Are you interested in government?"

"Government? Do you have anything to do with government? Has anyone from the government seen these things?"

Christi laughed faintly. "Why are you asking so many questions? Tell me about the Masons. How did you become a Mason?"

"My father was a Mason. I think I told you that. And his father was one too. It goes back to the Civil War in my family. The Masonic lodges were important in the Confederacy's effort to defeat the North. Brethren fought together in many units. If we'd just had a little more time, we would have won. As it was, my family lost their fortune in that war. I have no use for Yankees."

Christi cleared her throat. "What can you tell me about these artifacts? Do you know what these symbols mean?" she asked, unfolding the floor cloth.

"They represent different teachings, about the psyche and the soul— that sort of thing. Some of the others are more into that than I am."

"Look at this Bible," Christi requested, handing it to him. "The inscription talks about Washington's healing as an Antient Mason in the Grand Lodge of Ireland. Does that mean anything to you?"

"This is old. It must have been given to him when he became a Mason. I see you have a picture of Washington hanging over the mantel, in his Masonic apron. Are you interested in Washington?"

"I'd like to know more about his involvement in the Masons and how that influenced the founding of the Nation."

"Oh, that's probably blown out of proportion."

"If the Masonic lodges were important to the Confederacy during the Civil War, why wouldn't they have been important during the Revolutionary War, in the same way?"

"I never thought much about it."

"You haven't?... How about some roasted chestnuts? I got some this morning."

"That sounds good. Can I help?"

"You can turn the wire basket... see that they don't burn."

Richard took the basket with the chestnuts and began turning it slowly in the fire. Christi sat on the floor near him sipping her cup of hot cider.

"Sometimes I feel like that picture of Washington is real," she said. "Like he can see me and watches what I'm doing. Have you ever had that type of experience?"

"Naw, I don't think much about such things. Not since we told ghost stories when I was a kid."

"Sometimes I think he talks to me. Do you think that's crazy?"

"I guess it depends on what he tells you. What do you think he says?"

"He's teaching me about government. How to make it better.

Certain principles that we should implement in order to move into the next millennium."

Richard looked at Christi. "Tell me what these principles are."

"The first one has to do with fear. That fear should never be used to manipulate the People."

"That would put a lot of politicians out of business," Richard chuckled. "How would they win elections if they didn't use fear to manipulate the voters?"

"That's the point. The Principles are introducing a new paradigm. The second one is about judgment—that we must deliver justice without judgment."

"Sounds like that might put the judges out of business. The unemployment rolls would swell," Richard said and they laughed.

Christi rubbed her finger in circles on the rim of her cup as she gazed into the fire. "The Third Principle says that the equality of every citizen must be honored, but it refers to spiritual equality, not material possessions. The Fourth Principle is about the power of the People, that it shall be inviolate. Mr. Washington says the power of the People springs from the spirit..." Christi stopped.

"Sounds like you and Washington are pretty friendly. Where are you getting this stuff?" Richard asked, looking suspiciously at Christi.

"I'm not sure. It's just information that comes to me," she said hesitantly.

"Are there any more of these principles?"

"I know of one more. It says that change can only come from within."

"These are radical-sounding ideas. Is some group trying to start a revolution? Who is giving you this information?" he asked sternly.

"It just comes to me," she insisted.

"Someone must be giving it to you. Are you in some group, some secret order where these things are taught? You must be," he said angrily. "Why won't you answer my questions?"

"I don't have answers to your questions. I don't know where the information comes from—it just comes."

"I need to know your source. Who are you working with?"

"Who are you working with that wants to know?" Christi demanded.

"No one," Richard said taking the chestnuts from the fire. "I think these are done."

"I invited you here to talk about the Masons, not to interrogate me."

"Sorry. I didn't mean to get angry. I've been upset recently."

Christi smiled and put her hand on Richard's shoulder. "It's understandable, with what's happened recently with your children, and all. I'll put on some music," she said as she went to the CD player. "That helps me stay calm when I'm upset." She played a series of slow melodies performed by the Berlin Philharmonic.

She refilled their cups with hot cider, then joined Richard by the fire. "Tell me about your kids, what are they like?" she asked.

He proudly described his role as a parent as they ate the roasted chestnuts. "I like this music," he said as he poked the fire making the flames crackle. "Would you like to dance?"

"I'd love to. I haven't danced in ages."

The sun was setting and the ceiling shimmered with color as the couple slowly danced around the table. When the music stopped, Richard bent down and kissed Christi on the forehead. She looked up and they kissed, arms tightly embracing one another. A warm feeling flowed through Christi.

"I've stayed longer than I planned," Richard said, pulling away. "I have to pick my kids up at seven."

"Can't you stay for dinner?" she asked longingly.

"Another time. I have to meet someone. Can I use your phone before I go? I need to make a business call."

"It's in the kitchen, above the counter. Just pull the door shut."

Richard soon emerged from the kitchen. "Thanks, I took care of it," he said, then quickly left.

CHAPTER TWENTY-NINE

Christi rose early Thanksgiving morning to prepare for the celebration, but her holiday spirit was dampened by her new attraction to Richard. She was not eager to face Tom, who would soon arrive
with Shenan. They were riding together from D.C. where Tom had
spent the last couple of days on university business. She hurried to the
kitchen to prepare squash from her garden, cleaning out the seeds and
filling each half with nuts, raisins, cinnamon and maple syrup.

Shenan soon drove up the long drive, and she and Tom came in
with their bundles of groceries. Tom brought the turkey he had
promised to prepare and Shenan brought Virginia wine. Christi gave
each of them a hug. Tom quickly set about stuffing the turkey and
putting it in the oven to roast while Christi went to the garden to
pick kale, pull carrots and dig potatoes for her vegetable dishes. The
house quickly filled with the aroma of Thanksgiving dinner in-the-
making.

"Tom, tell me about the lecture on the Shroud of Turin," Christi
asked as she finished making fresh cranberry-apple-orange relish.

"It was excellent! The doctor who spoke is convinced the Shroud
is genuine and certain it helped him heal incurable arthritis. I'm
convinced it's genuine as well, based on the pathological evidence he
presented. He's coming to D.C. in January. You must hear him speak."

"Did Shenan tell you about our trip to her Grandfather's?" she
asked as she and Tom joined Shenan in the dining room where she was
setting the table.

"She did. What an experience that must have been!"

Tom and Christi sat on the small couch by the bay window.

"One I'll never forget. By the way, was your trip to D.C. for the university productive?"

"More so than I had anticipated. And... I have something to tell you."

Christi looked surprised. "What? What do you have to tell me?"

"Well, I'm going be a visiting professor at Georgetown University next semester and work on a special project, a colloquy on evidence of God in recent scientific discoveries. There will be several physicists, which includes myself, theologians, scientists and medical doctors gathering to exchange ideas on this topic. That's why the pathologist who's an expert on the Shroud will be in D.C. in January. He's working on the project as well."

"Oh..." Christi said looking blankly at Tom. "What an interesting opportunity. So... you'll be much closer... in D.C."

"That's one reason I was eager to get this job... so we could be closer together. You don't seem pleased. Perhaps I assumed more than I should."

"I didn't say I didn't want you closer. It's just such a surprise."

Shenan looked at the couple. "Is there something I can do in the kitchen?" she asked.

"I have to baste the turkey," Tom said, getting up. He walked briskly to the kitchen.

"What's going on?" Shenan whispered, sitting next to Christi on the couch. "Have you met someone else?"

"It's nothing.... Not yet, anyway."

"Who is it?"

"This handsome guy I met at work. He just separated from his wife and may not even be interested. It's just that... well, I'm not ready to make a commitment to Tom. I thought eventually life would become simpler, but that doesn't seem to happen. Not to me."

"We each bring the lessons to us that we need. Some of us like to learn the hard way," Shenan said puckering her mouth in a grimace.

Hap and June drove up as Christi and Shenan were heading to the kitchen to put the finishing touches on the meal. Christi ran to the door and hurried down the steps to assist Hap. Tom and Shenan followed close behind.

"Shenan," Christi said. "I want you to meet two of the most important people in my life, Hap and June Hayes." They shook hands and exchanged pleasantries.

June handed Tom a pumpkin pie. "Don't drop that. I got up at six this morning to bake it just for this occasion."

Everyone gathered in the warm kitchen while the final touches were put on the numerous dishes. "Tom, that turkey smells like Heaven," Hap said, breathing in the aroma. "You'll sure make someone a good husband."

Shenan coughed. "Would everyone like wine to drink with this feast?"

When the food was on the table the guests took their designated places and Christi sat at the head of the table. "Everyone please hold hands while we pray," she requested. They joined hands and bowed their heads. "Today we offer thanksgiving... that God is as near to us as we are to one another, and even nearer... dwelling in the heart of each of us. We give thanks for our friends and families, those who are with us and those who are apart, recognizing we are all one.... And we ask a special blessing for Tom's work in D.C. next semester. Amen."

Shenan raised her eyes at Christi as the others said "Amen."

Tom carved the turkey and served scoops of dressing while Christi passed the gravy and vegetables and Shenan poured wine.

"Tom, tell us about the work you're going to do in D.C.," Hap said. "This is the first I've heard of it."

Tom glanced at Christi. "I have to be there first thing in the morning to finish up the details. But it looks like I'll be spending next semester in the Capital, teaching at Georgetown and working on a project that may in some way be related to the information Christi is receiving."

"How is that so?" Christi asked.

"I'm participating in a colloquy among physicists, theologians, scientists and doctors who are gathering to exchange ideas about recent theories in their respective fields that may relate to God. I'll be looking for evidence of God, from a physicist's point of view, in conjunction with quantum physics."

"What evidence of God do physicists have?" June asked.

"We're not sure, but I have an idea where to start. At the level of the quantum field there is only energy and information, no physical matter. I surmise that this level of pure consciousness is the level of pure potentiality from which the world was created. This has to relate to God in some fashion. There is even evidence that the level of the quantum field can be influenced by *our* intent, a revolutionary discovery in physics that may relate to our free will and power to co-create."

"How will physicists and priests find a common language?" Shenan asked.

"Well, for example, yesterday I had breakfast with one of the priests I'll be working with, Father Johnson. You know those pictures with dots that you can look at one way and see one thing, but if you turn it just a little, you see a different image?"

"No," Hap answered, causing everyone to laugh.

"I do," Christi said. "They were fun when we were kids."

"I told Father Johnson I had been working on a physics problem using the intersection of two perpendicular lines that we use to designate 'real numbers' and what we call 'imaginary numbers'—numbers that were devised to make certain calculations work. But instead of seeing an intersection of the horizontal line with the real numbers and the vertical line with the imaginary numbers, there was a shift and I saw the intersection of these perpendicular lines as a cross, like the cross of Christ.

"The horizontal bar of the cross with the real numbers represented the physical plane, what we now perceive to be the 'real world.' I saw the vertical bar, where the imaginary numbers are placed, as a representation of the spiritual world, what some would deem to be the 'imaginary world.' I realized if the vertical, or spiritual line, is extended, it reaches far beyond the physical plane. On the other hand, on the physical plane, we can stray far from the axis that connects us to the spiritual. The ideal is to remain directly at the intersection of the two and thus constantly in the present moment, both physically and spiritually. Father Johnson and I agreed it is here we are most likely to hear God's Voice."

"That's an interesting concept," Hap said. "What is most intriguing is that only those of us who are in physical form can experience being at that intersection."

"Interesting point," Tom said. "Father Johnson pointed out that a horizontal physical plane intersected by a vertical spiritual plane is also a good way to conceptualize miracles. He says miracles are love expressed in action, emanating from the spiritual level but manifesting on the physical level. There's a shift into a vertical perception, away from the physical and invisible to the eyes of the body. There's no relationship between the time a miracle takes and the time it covers because time is collapsed, so learning can occur during a miracle that otherwise may have taken thousands of years. This sudden shift from horizontal to vertical perception causes the giver and receiver to both emerge farther along in time than if this hadn't happened. Father Johnson says miracles are the only way we can affect time while we are on the physical plane."

"That makes sense," Hap said. "Because miracles are governed by the law of God, they can't be constricted by time or matter. By taking us beyond the laws of the physical plane, they raise us into the spiritual sphere where God's law governs and all is perfection."

Tom nodded. "I was intrigued by this concept of miracles. Father Johnson says they are an expression of love which unites us directly with our brothers and sisters in a space beyond ordinary space and outside of time. By experiencing miracles our minds become conscious of the Oneness—that we are all one. He says we create a miracle each time we forgive another."

"That certainly relates to the Spiritual Principles being taught by Mr. Washington," Christi acknowledged.

"I'm certain there's a link between what Mr. Washington is teaching you and this project," Tom said. "I just don't know what it is."

"Well..." June said smiling sweetly, "at least with you a little closer, maybe this romance can gather some steam."

"Did someone say there was pumpkin pie for dessert?" Shenan asked.

CHAPTER THIRTY

Christi's efforts to integrate the Spiritual Principles into her life were erratic. She was conscious of her growing distaste for the courtroom battle where one party is ultimately vindicated and one is vilified, but her alternatives seemed limited. She encouraged clients into mediation whenever possible, but even this often failed to cure the animosity that arose from judging the acts of another. Something more fundamental—even revolutionary—was needed.

But the greatest difficulty came in her relationships, especially with those closest to her. Her old patterns tenaciously held on and her bulwark of defenses were slow to dissipate. She was irritated with herself for feeling confined by Tom and blaming him when she knew he was not the cause. On one hand, in resisting a commitment to Tom she was fearful of losing him, but on the other knew this was not justified. By all indications he was loyal and committed to their relationship. It was she who was interested in dating someone like Richard, even though his life was in turmoil and he lacked many of Tom's qualities. She wondered if it was Tom's goodness, the probability he *would* make a good husband, that frightened her.

"Why can't I see more clearly what's in my best interest?" she asked herself as she sat at the table, enjoying a warm fire and watching an early December snowfall. She reflected on how her life had changed since she and the table had moved from the Capital—not an easy journey. And yet, the times when she experienced a peace she had never known before were increasingly frequent.

As she gazed out the window she saw a figure wearing a long dark coat and a colonial hat emerge from the snow. "Mr. Washington!" she exclaimed and raced to the door. "Please come in and warm up by the fire. I'll put the teapot on," she said as she invited him in out of the cold.

"I assume it's time for the Sixth Principle," Christi commented as she set the silver tray on the table and began to serve the tea and cookies.

"Yes," Mr. Washington replied. "It's time to talk about love. But to understand the power of love, you must first examine what other defenses you believe are available to you."

Christi sat down and began to sip her tea as she listened intently.

"To begin, I ask that you again consider the crucifixion of Christ, for it holds many lessons that are not yet well understood." He took a cookie then began to question Christi. "First, please consider the defenses that Christ had available to him as he hung, crucified, upon the cross on Calvary Hill. What did he have to defend himself?"

"Well..." she said as she contemplated Christ's circumstances at that infamous moment in history, "his hands were spread apart and nailed in place, so he couldn't bring them together even to protect his body, much less strike another. His feet, too, were nailed firmly to the heavy wooden cross, so he couldn't flee or even crawl from his attackers. He couldn't kick or strike them with his feet, as someone being attacked would instinctively do. And of course he had no gun or protective armor as he hung, nearly naked, for all to see that his accusers were in complete control. He was totally defenseless," she concluded, saddened by Christ's vulnerability in that condition.

"Your analysis does not go deep enough. In his defenselessness, what was the source of his great power? What did he *say* as he hung upon the cross?" Mr. Washington asked, encouraging her to search further.

"He said... 'Forgive them Father, for they know not what they do.'"

"Yes. His defenses were not weapons, or even judging those who persecuted him. He recognized the insanity of their acts, but also that their insanity deprived them of the capacity to see any other way to address their fear. He knew they believed their attack upon him to be justified. So he implored God to *forgive* them, just as he did. Forgiveness does not attempt to use fear to undo fear, which is futile. In response to their attack upon him, he extended love, and with the power of love he set both himself and his persecutors free. His accusers were redeemed and Christ ascended into Heaven—everyone won. And Christ was not the exception, Miss Christi; he was the example."

She nodded as she listened attentively, weighing the significance of his words.

"Every mind projects fear or extends love; which defense you choose is a choice that is renewed each instant," advised Mr. Washington. "Every attack is a cry for love. When you extend love to those who attack you, you are answering the real plea your enemy has directed at you. Love is empowering. What could be more empowering than to give to everyone, even your enemies, what they truly demand? If you defend against the attack of your enemy by extending love, you totally disarm him. His arsenal is immediately demolished."

"That means our enemies cannot harm us," Christi said thoughtfully. "It means our only enemy is ourself, when we choose to project fear instead of extending love."

"Exactly," Mr. Washington said. "It was the power of love that distinguished the crucifixion of Christ from all others, and resulted in the miraculous events that followed."

"He defended himself only with love," Christi said, considering the defensive tactics she had been taught in law school and had perfected as a trial attorney. "So this is why our courts cannot heal relationships. They only determine winners and losers, but in God's justice there can be no losers. Christ defended himself with the power of love and by that act changed the world forever. . . . But despite the lessons he taught us. . . we seem to fall so short," she lamented.

"You can only witness the power of love and justice if you abandon the belief that any of God's children merit vengeance," Mr. Washington explained. "Each citizen is asked to recognize the innocence in everyone, so love and justice may no longer be separate. What cause can there possibly be to warrant attack upon the innocent? In justice, it is the power of love that corrects mistakes. It is this truth that is reflected in the Sixth Spiritual Principle for Governing a People. **LOVE IS THE ONLY SOURCE OF POWER.**"

Christi was silent. She felt the power of this Principle, but it seemed incongruous that it was being delivered in such a simple setting, at this old table in her dining room, and to someone as unworthy as she. Then she recalled the birth of Christ, in a manger among lowly animals, witnessed by simple shepherds.

Christi sighed. "Mr. Washington," she said as her hand rested on the warm grain of the table, "the Principles require that the world as we know it be turned upside down. It seems such a monumental task."

"You do not fail if you cannot practice the Principles at all times," Mr. Washington reassured her. "Your experience in this world is but a shadow of all that occurs within yourself. You need only hold the intent to call upon the Holy Spirit who knows your innocence and not your sin, to assist you in seeing the innocence of others, and not their sin. You are not alone in this task, and you need give so little for the Holy Spirit to respond to your mere thought."

Christi resisted the notion that dramatic change can come so easily. "It seems that mere thoughts will take such a long time to heal the insane beliefs that encompass much of the world."

"An insane belief system cannot be healed by thoughts that share in it," Mr. Washington advised. "When a brother behaves insanely, you cannot heal him by judging his errors. It is not up to you to change him—you must accept and love him as he is. If you want to give your errors over to the Holy Spirit, you must also do this with his. God's law does not permit contradictions. Neither God's light nor that of your brother is diminished because it is not seen.

"The power of love comes from God who is love," he said placing his hand on his heart. "When you extend love, you are exercising your power to co-create with God, and that is your only assigned task. It is a task that is critical, for the reign of love can only be restored upon Earth through you and your brothers and sisters. Through you, not by you."

Christi offered Mr. Washington another cookie. "Our relationships with others are often our greatest source of pain," she said with regret. "Restoring love through us, when we so often fail to treat even those closest to us in a loving way, makes this seem such a formidable task."

"Let love teach you that you are not separate. Envision a holy circle of love. Each person, animal, forest—all that you encounter—you judge worthy of crucifixion or redemption. If you place each within the holy circle, you share that circle as one. If you place any outside the holy circle, you are barred from within as well and can only experience separation. Giving and receiving are but different aspects of the same universal flow of energy. Therefore, to be in balance, what is given must be received. The power of love lies in God's gentleness, which you share because you are of God. The choice to restore the gentle reign of love is yours alone."

"Then we must undertake a gentle revolution," Christi boldly declared, looking directly at Mr. Washington. "We must overthrow the tyranny of fear and restore the reign of love. Our armor is God's love and our plan of attack is to change *our* minds. And in our defenselessness we are impervious to attack!"

Christi quickly reflected upon her words and retreated. "Mr. Washington, it's so easy for me to speak with such resolve when I'm with you. But this is a different world. When I return to the 'real' world, acting upon what we discuss is hard," she complained, her shoulders slouched. "Overcoming my attachment to material possessions; existing in the world without attack; it all seems so contrary to my nature."

For a moment Mr. Washington was silent. "While on occasion you glimpse the progress you have made, you fail to recognize how far you have truly journeyed," he said quietly. "You forget where you were when we began—in a world of illusion, unaware of reality. You will succeed. Those who have tried to banish love have failed, but those who choose to banish fear shall succeed. Love is the only source of power, and it gives you everything. When you have love, you want for nothing.

"Soon you will see how foolish it is to substitute the tyranny of fear for the power of love. You will soon learn that the triumph of fear, which is truly weakness, is so distorted that it imprisons all that you want it to release."

"The funny thing is, it's easier to tell someone 'I hate you' than it is to say 'I love you'," she stated.

Mr. Washington concurred. "Many still associate love with weakness and vengeance with strength. They cannot imagine love as a powerful defense. They believe love can be slain by hate. They imagine they have become prey to the dark forces and are but a little life easily snuffed out by death."

"What are these dark forces?" she inquired.

"The dark forces have given their power to the material world. Because of this, they exist in a primitive state of consciousness and are consumed with fear. They fear those who can destroy their world by teaching them love as much as they fear those who would pillage their hoarded treasures. Because they believe in separation, they cannot distinguish one form of destruction from another.

"But as long as you defend yourself with love, not fear, you will be safe in the circle of love," he instructed in a cautioning tone. "The power of love will be the wind under your wings. It will lift you, and those who are to join you, effortlessly to the heights you are destined to soar."

CHAPTER THIRTY-ONE

In the waxing daylight of mid-December, Christi's alarm sounded in the darkness. She hurried to get ready to drive Hap to Federal Bankruptcy Court in Richmond.

Christi drove up to the small white frame house, parked the car and walked toward the door. As she approached, Hap opened the door before she could knock. "I had a feeling you would be here any minute," he said, as he slipped into his coat and pulled the door shut behind him. Christi helped him into her car, and they were on their way.

"I've been looking forward to this time together," Christi told Hap as they came to I-95 south. "My discussions with Mr. Washington have raised several practical issues I want to discuss." She drove onto the six-lane highway. A long black car pulled in behind them. It reminded her of Harp—a thought she chose to ignore.

"I've been thinking about my experience as a kid, growing up in the midst of the religious wars between the Protestant and Catholic sides of my family," Christi began. "My father's family was Irish Catholic, while my mother's family was Brethren. Each said the other couldn't go to Heaven. For the Brethren, the Catholics couldn't go to Heaven because they hadn't been dunked three times when they were baptized, and for the Catholics, the Brethren couldn't go to Heaven because they didn't believe in papal infallibility. All they did when they were together was fight over religion."

Hap smiled. "Thank goodness for separation of church and state. Imagine what it would be like if one side of your family had had the power to govern the other." They both laughed.

"That's the danger when religious institutions are in control of government," Christi declared. "Vengeance is carried out on a national scale, and unfortunately, in the name of God."

"What do you think of prayer in public school?" Hap asked.

"My personal experience is instructive. As a child I was raised Catholic and sent to catechism. I was taught which sins were venial sins that would just send me to purgatory and which were cardinal sins, a direct path to hell—like eating meat on Fridays, which all my Protestant friends did. I also learned the Catholic version of the Lord's Prayer. Among the innumerable sins that I was warned against was saying the ending on the Lord's Prayer that Protestants say, you know, 'For Thine is the kingdom, the power and the glory forever.' That was a cardinal sin. I'm sure I worried about my Mom going to hell because she was Brethren and they always said it that way.

"My best friend, who was Presbyterian, told me she had been taught in Bible School that Catholics didn't believe in the Bible, so we couldn't go to Heaven. She meant we didn't use the King James Bible that has the Protestant version of the Lord's Prayer in it. When I was in grade school, each morning we said the Lord's Prayer in school— the Protestant version, as they were in the majority. So before we even opened a textbook, I was confronted with the fearful prospect of going to hell if I said the Protestant ending of the Lord's Prayer, or going to hell if I didn't. And you know what, Hap? The very people who put me in that untenable position believed they were acting in my best interest by making me say the Lord's Prayer in school each morning. It was well-intentioned people who have left me with scars that I now revisit every time I hear either version."

"Makes you wonder how Buddhist, or Islamic, or Jewish children would be scarred by being in that situation, when their religious beliefs are even more distinct from Protestantism than yours," Hap observed. "You know, I've always considered abortion to be another issue, that, when you get to the bottom of it, is an issue of separation of church and state. I was raised Methodist and taught that when a decision to have an abortion is made prayerfully, in consultation with one's minister and doctor, it is not immoral. Some other mainstream Protestants, as well as the Catholics, disagree. When mainstream religious denominations don't agree, it becomes an issue of dogma," he asserted. "I think this distinguishes it from other issues upon which there is general consensus. To use the power of the State to impose the religious dogma of some denominations upon others is a misuse of that power and can only create dissension in the Nation. Why can't people just agree to disagree?"

"Mr. Washington says that people identify themselves with their belief system and when you don't agree, this weakens it," she responded. "Since they believe in separation, the only response they know is to attack. When you have people who believe that every attack deserves another, I guess it becomes endless, generation after generation, like the Protestants and the Catholics."

Christi changed lanes and tried to distance her car from the black car that continued to follow dangerously close behind them.

"Mr. Washington said there are no secrets, because we're all one," Christi continued, watching in the rear view mirror. "Once you understand this, the politicians can't dupe you into being their pawns any longer. We had a long discussion about how this works with gun control."

"Do you know old Sam Taylor?" Hap inquired.

"You mean the man who gives everyone water when their plumbing doesn't work?" Christi asked, recalling those days.

"Yeah, that's him. He's a fanatic about his guns. One day he said the solution to criminals who take their uzies into fast food restaurants to mow everyone down is for everyone in the restaurant to be armed with their own weapons so they can mow the criminals down first. And he was serious."

"Oh, great," Christi said sarcastically.

"I said to him, 'Well, Sam, what about some blind guy like me, or little kids? What are we supposed to do in the midst of this shootout?' Of course he hadn't thought about that. I told him that in his fervor to protect his right to bear arms, he was going to destroy everyone else's right not to bear arms. People wouldn't be free to take their kids out for a hamburger without packing a pistol, and even then, they'd be less safe than before."

"Mr. Washington says to determine the real intent behind a policy, all you do is consider what it actually does, not what it's supporters say it will do."

"That's an interesting way to analyze an issue," remarked Hap. "Take the dispute over homosexuals in the military. How do you think this approach would work in that case?"

"Let's try it. First, what are the reasons given for wanting to exclude homosexuals from military service?"

"They say they run a higher risk of having AIDS, so on the battle-field they might contaminate others with their blood. Another is that they might commit sexual assaults on other soldiers. And they also say they will cause discord among heterosexuals who don't like homosexuals."

"Can these objectives actually be achieved by excluding homosexuals from military service?"

"Of course not," Hap quickly replied. "Some heterosexuals have AIDS or engage in illicit sex that exposes them to the risk of AIDS. To protect soldiers on the battlefield from exposure to blood contaminated with AIDS you would have to exclude all heterosexuals who commit adultery, for example, or frequent prostitutes. That would achieve the objective of reducing the military budget!" They again laughed.

"Let's see," Hap continued, "the next argument is about possible sexual assaults. I'll bet heterosexuals engage in sexual assaults more often than homosexuals. It's certainly not uncommon. And the last argument about avoiding discord among heterosexuals who don't like homosexuals—the fairest way to solve that is to court-martial the heterosexuals who cause the trouble."

"Now then," Christi said, "if the objectives the supporters say they're promoting can't be achieved by the policy they want implemented, you have to ask what actually would be achieved, because that's the real purpose."

"That's easy," Hap said. "What would actually be achieved is a massive hate campaign against homosexuals."

"There you have it," Christi said. "That has to be the real purpose. They just disguise their real intent with arguments that sound logical, and fool a lot of people."

"It seems reasonable that if the center of a belief system is true, only truth can extend from it. But if it is based on lies, only deception can come from it," Hap noted.

Christi looked anxiously at the black car that remained so close behind them they would crash if she stepped on the brake, even lightly. "They're trying to intimidate me," she thought. "I won't let them," she promised herself.

"Hap, we're coming into Richmond now, so we'll be at the courthouse soon," she said. She took the I-195 exit off of I-95, and the car she was watching stayed right on their tail. She turned onto the downtown exit and drove to Main Street where she found a parking space near the courthouse. The black car drove by without stopping.

Christi aided Hap across the street and into the elevator to the floor where the Bankruptcy Court was located. He was eventually heard on a motion regarding the exemption of a creditor from the discharge of a bankruptcy petition. He introduced into evidence a fraudulent financial statement that had been provided to an unsuspecting farmer who thought he was doing all he needed to protect a loan he was making to the friend of a relative. The judge quickly granted the motion.

As they exited the courthouse, Christi looked about but saw no one who appeared to be following them. Once on the road, it was not long before she and Hap were again immersed in discussion that continued the duration of the trip.

"Hap, you grew up in a poor neighborhood, right? What do you think about welfare?"

"This is the way I see it," Hap said jokingly. "People who are poor believe they have no choice, that they are trapped without money and without opportunities to earn money. The problem is not their lack of money so much as it is their belief about their power to change their circumstances. If a poor person is given some money, that may temporarily change his ability to purchase material goods, but it doesn't get at the root of the real problem—his faulty belief system."

Christi again spotted the black car in the traffic behind them. It soon pulled directly behind her car. "But wouldn't poor people be angered by that analysis, since it blames them for their condition?"

"Yes and no. Forces outside themselves have contributed to the poverty they experience. Social forces, laws, economic policies, there are many causes to blame, and they are real. So society must accept joint responsibility for changing the perception of the poor, to diminish the power of the obstacles poor people believe stand in the way of greater affluence."

"Are you saying it is the beliefs of the poor or the conditions imposed upon them that have to change?"

"Ultimately," Hap began, "it is the beliefs that poor people have about themselves that must change. But those beliefs didn't arise out of thin air. They are the result of experiences from which the beliefs were learned, and people other than the poor share responsibility for creating those experiences. They must now share responsibility for creating new experiences that support the poor in overcoming the negative beliefs that trap them in poverty. We have to see that we're all in this together."

The discussion ended when Christi took the exit off of I-95 and began the drive down several country lanes to Hap's home. "We have to do this more often, Hap," she said as she watched the black car following closely behind.

As Christi told Hap goodbye, the black car turned down an alley a few hundred feet from Hap's yard. She got in the car and locked the doors. "What now?" she thought as she tried to focus her mind over the pounding of her heart. "I can't go home and let them terrorize me throughout the night, manipulating me with their fear tactics. I won't surrender my power to whomever is trying to take it from me.... I've got to get myself in the present moment and listen... for God's Voice."

She closed her eyes and breathed deeply. "How can this be an opportunity?" she asked. The answer came instantly. "It is an opportunity to confront my fear, to see that it is an illusion, like the Wizard of Oz, just smoke and noise.... But how?... I have nothing to fear.... What if I die? I can't see what opportunities would come to me or others if I died.... God is the strength in which I must trust...."

Christi opened her eyes. "I'm going to find that car!" she said aloud. She started the engine and sped around the corner, into the alley where she had seen the ominous vehicle turn. It was nowhere in sight, but she continued to search until she spotted it parked just outside of town. She pulled up behind it and got out of her car.

As she walked toward her adversary, she felt her heart still pounding in her chest. "Just extend love," she told herself. She approached the driver's side and mustered her courage to knock on the window. She could see a man sitting inside. As he rolled the window down, she saw it was Curtis, Harp's driver at the firm.

"Good evening, Ms. Daniel," he said, looking ashamed.

Christi was stunned. "Curtis! Why were you following me?"

"I'm so sorry, Ms. Daniel. What can I say?" He fumbled nervously for words. "I was just following Mr. Harp's orders. It's part of my job.... I gotta have my job—my son's in college and I want him to be somebody, not a driver like me. Mr. Harp is helping that happen, even if it's by making me do what I don't want to do. Sometimes, Ms. Daniel... I think the world is upside down. I don't try to figure it out; I can't. I just want my son to finish college so he doesn't have to live in a crazy world like I do. Please, Ms. Daniel, don't fight 'em. They're bigger than all of us put together."

"But Curtis, how can we..."

Someone approached Christi from behind and before she could turn around, she felt a metal object pressed in the middle of her back.

"Hello, Christi."

She recognized the voice. "Richard? I didn't plan on meeting you here. Is that a gun you have greeted me with, stuck in my back?"

"Compliments of Willard Smith—just for this occasion. Curtis, put the handcuffs on her, behind her back. Then tie this scarf around her eyes," he ordered.

"Is there something you plan to do that you don't want me to see?"

"Shut up and get in the car. Face down on the floor."

When Christi was handcuffed and blindfolded she indignantly obeyed. Richard sat on the seat above her, his foot resting on her hip. They began a ride that seemed endless.

As the trip became monotonous, Christi directed her thoughts to the Principles. "Extend love.... They don't know why they're doing this," she silently told herself. "In my defenselessness, love is my power. I must trust my brothers with whom I am one." She repeated these thoughts over and over and noted their calming effect.

Christi was certain they traveled on the highway for miles, then turned onto country roads. After some time, Curtis stopped the car and got out, probably to open a gate. The ride soon ended and Christi was led into a house. Richard took Christi to a small room where the handcuffs were removed and she pulled the scarf from her eyes. The room was square with a tiny window. Against one wall was a bed, opposite a toilet and sink on the other side of the room. "This room was designed to hold prisoners," she thought, then wondered, "Who do they imprison here?"

"Make yourself at home," Richard sneered. "Win will be here in the morning. He has some things he wants to discuss with you."

"Is this what you learned from the Masons?" Christi questioned with disdain.

"You were even more gullible than we had hoped," he retorted. "I've never been in a Masonic Lodge."

Richard brusquely shut the door and Christi heard the key turn in the lock. She looked out the small window and saw a large river in the moonlight. "The James?" she wondered. "This could be in Goochland County."

She stared at the moon, so far away but seemingly so close. She reflected on her faulty perception, her ineptitude at witnessing her own actions. "Why is my judgment so poor?" she ruminated. "How could I have been attracted to Richard, blind to what he really is? Am I just as blind to what Tom is?" She thought of Tom's embrace and how safe she felt when she was in his arms. She wished he was here, but knew this was a lesson she must learn on her own. She renewed her determination to trust the Principles.

Christi dreaded the long night before her. She lay down on the bed and began to breath deeply. "I am sustained by God's love, even in these circumstances," she said quietly. She was surprised by how calm she felt. She mused at how harshly she often judged herself. "The problem is... I don't love myself," she concluded. She closed her eyes and continued the deep breathing. "Before I can extend love to others, I must extend it to myself. Only when I forgive myself, can I forgive others. I must know the security of truly loving *myself* before I can be secure enough to truly forgive others. I must believe in my own innocence before I can believe in the innocence of others."

Her breathing was deep and even. She focused on perceiving her light within, seeing it within her mind's eye, consciously experiencing how it felt. "That light has always been there, undiminished by the fact even I could not see it," she whispered.

Christi soon slipped into a quiet place. Waves of light began to slowly flow before her, first green, then blue, then violet. She relaxed into the flow.... Then, out of the misty light, a beautiful angel appeared before her, a more magnificent being than any she had ever seen. The angel bowed. Christi wondered who she was bowing to, then realized there was no one else in the room. In her mind, she reverently bowed back.

"Why am I here, a prisoner to these dark forces?" she asked the angel, in thought, not spoken words.

"Your journey through time and space is not at random. You can only be at the right place at the right time. Such is the love of God," the angel replied.

"But what lesson am I to learn in this place?"

"You are studying a unified thought system in which nothing is lacking that is needed and nothing is included that is contradictory or irrelevant. You are where you are needed. I come to express gratitude for your willingness to prepare yourself well. Your time to lead is soon."

The angel was so real, Christi concluded it must actually be present in the room. She opened her eyes. Except for the ray of bright yellow moonlight shining through the small window, the room was dark. She pulled a blanket over herself and fell asleep. . . .

There was a sharp knock on the door that startled Christi from her sleep. She heard the key turn. Winston Harp stood in the door.

"Did you sleep well, Christi?" he asked sarcastically.

"Actually, I did," she replied calmly.

"Put the ankle cuffs on her, Dick, and bring her out here to the table."

Richard cuffed her ankles and Christi stumbled to the table as Curtis brought her a cup of hot coffee and a plate of scrambled eggs and toast. She sat down across from Harp and stared into his eyes.

"Eat your breakfast," he ordered, looking away.

She picked up the cup of coffee and warmed her hands on it. "What do you want of me?"

"I want to know who you're working with. Who is this 'Mr. Washington' guy that you talk about all the time?"

"How do you know who I talk about?"

"Don't take me for a fool. Dick bugged your phones. You're the fool, not me. We know everything you have said on the phone, at your office, at your home. Even to Dick. He was wired when you and he had your little rendezvous. So cozy. . . like two lovebirds."

Richard shuffled nearby. Christi saw the gun tucked in his belt. She sipped her hot coffee and began to eat the eggs and toast. "God is the love in which I forgive," she said to herself as she swallowed the food.

"Now tell me, who are you working with," Harp demanded when she finished eating. "We know it's some secret order, some cult that is consumed with gaining power."

"There's no cult," Christi said. "There's not even a group. Mr. Washington comes from the future—a figment of my imagination, you would say."

"Don't play games with me. Where does he live? You must know his address."

"I have no idea. He visits me, I don't visit him."

"We've concluded he's a pretty high operative. You're probably too low to be privy to such sensitive information. Why does he meet with *you?*"

"He's someone who comes to supply a lack, to give guidance on how to emerge from darkness. He teaches that to praise God we must praise one another whom God has created. Freedom is love. Anyone we want to imprison we do not love."

"I've heard you talk about love a lot on the tapes. Is that a code word? What does it really mean? Maybe they don't let you in on that either. Where do you meet Washington?"

"Only at my house, at the table."

"When is he supposed to meet you again?"

"I never know for sure. He just comes when it's time."

"He's giving you some Principles. You tell everyone they have something to do with government. Are you trying to subvert the government? Is that the plan?"

"No. The Principles are guidance for a new era."

"How many Principles are there?"

"There will be seven. I have only been told about six, so far."

"I know what those six are," Harp snapped. "We have our experts working on decoding them; we'll find out what they actually mean. We're going to get to the root of this scheme. You and your kind aren't going to take over *my* government. When is Washington bringing you the Seventh Principle?"

"I don't know. Soon, I suppose."

"Can you have him meet you here?"

"I have no way of contacting him from here. I have to be at home. But I assure you, all this is unnecessary. I'll tell you the Seventh Principle when I know what it is. You already know the other six, so why shouldn't I?"

"How can we trust you to tell us the truth? You might try to lead us off track—modify the code, or something."

"What can I do to make you trust that I will tell you the truth? If you choose to doubt it, I can't change that."

Richard stepped nearer. "She's the only one we know of who has access to this guy, Washington," he interjected. "They never talk on the phone. We believe they only meet at her house. We can stake the house out."

"I don't trust her, but a stakeout might work," Harp quipped.

"You needn't bother to do that. I'll tell you when I know. It's information that will soon be public. I'll give it to you," Christi stated.

"Win, I don't see that we have much choice," Richard added. "How can we contact Washington without her?"

Harp paused, agitated. "Damn it, you might be right." He looked at Christi hesitantly. "All right.... I want an answer by the end of this month. New Years Eve—that's the deadline. If we don't hear from you by then... your life isn't worth two cents."

"Even if I'm not alive, I'll still get the Seventh Principle to you. I promise. We're not nearly as limited as you believe. If you don't see the body as necessary for communication, then communication remains unbroken, even if the body is destroyed. And anyway, the last Principle may be something simple. Perhaps you already know it."

"Get her out of here, I'm sick of her gibberish. December 31st at midnight—that's the deadline. If we don't hear from you, there's no where you can hide that we can't find you. We have contacts everywhere. And don't bother reporting that you were kidnapped. We're all in another state right now, and we have witnesses. You have no one."

Richard put the handcuffs back on Christi and tied the scarf over her eyes. He led her into the sunlight outside, then pushed her onto the floor of the car and threw a blanket over her. The silent ride began again, but this time it passed more quickly. When the car stopped and the blindfold was removed, they were in the woods near a country road.

"That's the road to your house," Richard said, motioning toward the road. "Your car is parked beside the road, about a ten-minute walk from here." He removed the hand and ankle cuffs, then jumped into the car and he and Curtis sped away.

Christi looked up at the sky. An eagle soared majestically overhead.

CHAPTER THIRTY-TWO

Upon her release, Christi's immediate concern was to protect client confidences by removing Harp's bugging devices from her phones and arranging periodic checks to guard against such future invasion.

Hap took the news of what had happened in stride, but cautioned her to be careful. She told Tom of the events, but rejected his plea that she report them to the police. By the time her phones were checked, all evidence they had been bugged was gone. Harp had again committed perfect crimes for which the courts could provide no redress. Only a higher power could secure justice in this instance.

She then sought a much-needed break by spending Christmas week with her family in Colorado, returning to Virginia two days after Christmas. The afternoon of her return she busied herself with a list of household chores: laundry, housekeeping, and baking Hap a batch of Mr. Washington's Harvest Cookies as a belated Christmas gift.

It was late afternoon when she stopped to rest. She took the morning paper to the table, but once she relaxed, she realized how fatigued she was from the trip. She rested her head on her arms and soon dozed off. After resting a short time, she became conscious of someone else in the room. She lifted her head and saw Mr. Washington standing at the opposite end of the table.

"Good afternoon, Miss Christi. Do you know what day is today?" he asked, smiling in his usual gentle manner.

She hesitated. "It's December 27th. Oh… it's the Feast of St. John the Evangelist. I had wondered if you would come today."

"Yes. As the sun begins its journey from the winter solstice to the summer solstice, the seeds that have been sown will soon germinate and begin to mature. It's time to conclude this chapter of our work by considering the Seventh Principle. You are now ready for our final lesson."

As she rose to prepare their tea and cookies, Christi was caught in a fulcrum of emotions. Sadly, her meetings with Mr. Washington were coming to an end, but there was also the exciting prospect of unforetold events that might now unfold. But was she ready? She returned shortly to serve her guest who had remained standing, waiting for her, before taking his place at the table.

They sat down and Christi was silent as she poured tea while Mr. Washington began the lesson. "Many people are coming to an awareness that they are spiritual beings, not mere physical objects called bodies, but they do not yet understand that Nations, too, have a spiritual presence. Just as individuals come into the world with a special purpose, Nations, too, have a *destiny*. Wherever a collective consciousness exists, it must have a purpose." Mr. Washington sipped his tea. "In order to introduce into consciousness the concept of spirit in Nationhood—the idea that this Nation has a spiritual purpose to fulfill—symbols of the spirit were employed wherever possible, as insignia of this New Order of the Ages."

"What is the purpose, the destiny of this Nation?" inquired Christi, her curiosity instantly piqued.

"Just as with individuals, a Nation's purpose can evolve," he replied. "Before the American Revolution, this land was carrying out the purpose of the British Colonies. The Colonies served the purpose of uniting peoples of the world by developing a common language. Laws and customs became more uniform, and even similar religious traditions were shared in diverse parts of the world. But the American Revolution marked the end of that era.

"From the moment of its founding, the United States of America was meant to foster a major step in human evolution. To lay a strong foundation for this purpose, spiritual principles were made an integral part of the very structure of government, following closely the precepts used by the Medieval stone masons in building their majestic cathedrals—physical metaphors of the spiritual realm. The pinnacle of power was built upon a broad and solid base that incorporated within it the concept of balance among equals. A powerful central government composed of a federation of strong states was balanced by the guarantee made to each citizen of protection against the abuse of either federal or state power."

Mr. Washington and Christi each took a cookie.

He paused, then continued. "All citizens are equally endowed with the right to life, joyous and complete in every way; to deliverance from the effects of guilt; to forgiveness and recognition of their total innocence; to perfect peace; and to love. This is the only justice Heaven knows. It is our vision that the laws and governments of Nations shall be employed to facilitate the realization of such justice. The ultimate purpose for which the United States of America was founded was to be the example of how such can be achieved."

Christi looked wide-eyed and gasped. "To realize *God's* justice?" she asked in awe. "This purpose is so grand... I'm so insignificant and inadequate by comparison. How can I have a role in achieving such a purpose?" she asked in a near whisper.

"No, Miss Christi! You are as God created you. You are the light of the world. It is not a demonstration of humility to deny what you are. For the Destiny of this Nation to manifest through you, you must step forth from the crowd, a spiritually enlightened leader, to hold the vision until the dream is realized. You must lead the People to the collective manifestation of the dream on the physical plane by teaching them to see that they, too, are as God created them. They are not the pathetic beings they create in their illusions. They, too, are the light of the world."

"But... if you're leaving, how can I do this... alone?" she asked almost inaudibly.

"You are never alone." Mr. Washington shook his head slightly. "It is only your limited ability to perceive that you tenaciously cling to that creates such an illusion. When you see with true vision, you will see that your brothers and sisters are your constant companions on this journey to know God. Their needs are your own and your needs are theirs. Without you, they would lose their way. Without them, you would forever be lost."

"I've learned so much from you," Christi said appreciatively. "And yet, overcoming my perceived limitations is still a challenge. I rationalize that what I have regarded as injustices that I thought warranted vengeance must now be understood to be misperceptions that call for redress through gentleness and love. I tell myself that I have no need for defenses because, where there is no attack, there is no need to defend... and sometimes I'm even successful. But telling myself is not the same as knowing."

"I understand," Mr. Washington said patiently. "However, it is an important beginning from which the motivation to discipline the mind arises. The manner in which the body is used is a choice—a choice of the mind, not the body. It is the spirit that is the altar of truth, not the body. The mind must be trained to use the body only to communicate love. This is the real purpose for which it was intended and it will be invulnerable so long as it is needed for this purpose. And so it is with Nations, as well. The physical wealth of this Nation must be used only to communicate love. This, too, requires discipline. But it is in so doing that it will be invulnerable—and its destiny shall be achieved.

"The goal is to achieve Heaven—a state of consciousness in which perfect love, peace and joy are achieved, knowledge of God is complete, and the journey to the Source comes to an end because the destination has been reached. But none can achieve Heaven until all do, for the many are one. So long as any part of consciousness has not yet achieved Heaven, none can, for the many are one. It is this truth that is the Seventh Spiritual Principle for Governing a People. *E PLURIBUS UNUM*—THE MANY ARE ONE."

"The motto of the United States," Christi said softly, glancing at Mr. Washington with surprise. She had seen it many times in many places; inscribed on the ribbon held in the beak of the eagle on the national seal; on every dollar bill and on many coins. *E Pluribus Unum*. She had paid it little heed.

"What you pay attention to will flourish," Mr. Washington said. "What you ignore will wither. It is the exchange of energy created by your attention, guided by your intent, that nourishes that to which you attend. It is now time to pay attention to this Nation's motto. When Americans accept their Oneness, they shall be known by the fruits of their labor. Their Brotherhood shall be crowned from sea to shining sea.

"The many are one, Miss Christi," Mr. Washington repeated with emphasis. "Therefore, the journey of every soul to Heaven is your journey. The search of every soul for love, peace and joy is your search. It is your mission that every soul's knowledge of God be complete so you can know God completely. The children of God are indivisible. As you unite, you unite in God."

Christi poured more tea for Mr. Washington and tried to conceal the tears that welled up in her eyes as she listened silently.

"When you recognize the holiness of your companions on this journey," he said, "you will realize there is no journey—only an awakening. The journey to God is a journey without distance, to God who has never changed. There is no road to travel on and no time to travel through."

Mr. Washington took another cookie from the plate that Christi offered him.

"It seems reasonable," she began tentatively, "that just as the body is a physical expression of the condition of the soul, the condition of a Nation reflects the condition of the collective consciousness of its People. Just as a sickness can provide important information regarding changes needed in one's life, a crisis or imbalance in a country can signal the need for change in governmental policies necessary to heal the collective consciousness."

"Yes," he agreed. "An environmental crisis is a good example. It reflects policies based solely upon a desire to take from the Earth, with no concern for balance. But because giving and receiving are an integral aspect of the circle of life, when the intent is only to take, the measure of the loss thereby experienced is equal to what has been consumed with nothing given in return. You set the value on what you receive; you determine its price by what you give. But remember, in this moment, you can choose anew."

Mr. Washington looked directly into Christi's eyes. "When you see only with the eyes of the body, you are blind. When you see with the eyes of the spirit, this is true vision. Then you see strength instead of weakness, love instead of fear, unity instead of separation. When you listen only with the ears of the body, God's voice seems distant and difficult to hear. When you listen with your spirit, God's voice is unmistakably clear. Anyone who chooses to listen in this way cannot be deaf to the messages of love and hope. They will eagerly exchange the misery they have created for the joy of Heaven."

Mr. Washington paused. "You know, I am going to miss having your nice cookies and fine tea," he said as he finished the tea in his cup.

"I'm going to miss sharing them with you. I've become fond of this blend of tea," Christi said, fighting the tightness in her throat.

Mr. Washington smiled at her. "You will be occupied with your work. But as you set upon this mission," he continued with a tone of caution, "I must warn you. As is often the case, things may seem to get worse before they get better. There are still those who serve the lord of death, who come to worship in a separated world, each with his tiny spear or rusty sword, to keep his ancient promises to die. If the mind uses the body for attack in any form, it becomes sick and decays, as does a Nation that uses its resources for attack. But there is a better way and it has now been shown to you."

Mr. Washington took the last cookie on the plate then contemplated the multitude of rainbows dancing on the ceiling. He looked at Christi. "The power to work miracles has been given to you, Miss Christi. The opportunity to work miracles will be given to you, as well, soon. But the will to work miracles must come from within, from a mind committed to assisting God in attaining Heaven for all of God's creations. The miracle worker recognizes the distortions that result from misplaced loyalty, but blesses them, nonetheless. This undoes such distortions and frees them from the prison of illusion. When you look out from the perception of your own holiness, you see only the holiness of others."

Mr. Washington placed his hand upon Christi's. "Know at all times that you are safe and have all of the tools necessary to succeed. There is nothing you will be asked to accomplish that you cannot accomplish. Do not set limits on what you believe can be done through you. If you believe your part is limited, you must believe others are likewise limited, for the many are one, and all are equal."

Mr. Washington sat back in his chair and Christi knew the lesson had come to an end. As he rose to leave, he took an envelope made of thick parchment from inside his vest. "Please place this in a safe place, as a remembrance of me," he said, handing it to her. Mr. Washington and Christi stood for a moment looking at one another, each with admiration for the other. As Mr. Washington walked toward the door, Christi accompanied him.

"The world is not as most people now see it," he said. "All that they see will perish, but all that God created is eternal. Therefore, the world they see cannot possibly have been created by God, and there *must* be a world they do not yet see."

Mr. Washington stepped outside then turned toward Christi, extending his right hand which she immediately clasped with both of hers.

"Go now," he said, "and teach others to see… so that love can replace fear, laughter replace tears, and abundance replace loss. This is the real world, for your will and the Will of God are one.…" He pulled his hand away, looked to the west, then again at Christi and saluted her. "You are an able soldier. My peace I give to you."

"My peace I give to you, as well," Christi replied, tears falling from her face.

Mr. Washington turned to the west and walked toward the hill as she stood in the doorway watching, while images of their special times together flooded her memory.

When her kind and gentle friend was out of sight, she returned to the table and carefully opened the envelope he had given her. Inside was a letter written in his distinctive hand.

Dear Miss Christi:

Our work together may appear to have come to an end, but, in truth, it has yet to begin, for eternity has but one dimension—always.

On your journey to know God, always remember—

When you meet another, it is a holy encounter.

As you see another, you will see yourself.

As you hear another, you will hear yourself.

As you treat another, you will treat yourself.

It is in others that you will find yourself or lose yourself.

Whenever two children of God meet one another,

they are given yet another chance at salvation.

*Never leave another without first giving salvation and
receiving it yourself.[6]*

*The place in which you meet another is the meeting
place of God.*

Your humble servant,

Geo. Washington

Christi could not imagine what she should now do to commence her assignment. She went to the kitchen to keep busy finishing her tasks as she sorted through her thoughts and feelings. She worked busily and it was dark before she again stopped to rest. She turned on the evening news.

"... thirty percent chance of light snowfall in the western part of Virginia. Cold winds but clear skies toward the east," the weather reporter announced.

A newscaster interrupted the report. "We interrupt this broadcast to bring you a news update. This afternoon federal agents and Washington D.C. bar officials entered the offices of the firm of Harp, Harrison & Humphrey, a well-known D.C. law firm, and seized all banking and accounting records pursuant to a search warrant obtained late last night from a federal judge. Reportedly, an investigation spanning several months and involving numerous undercover agents found evidence that the firm was laundering money from illegal Chinese gun sales on behalf of several clients of the firm. In return, the clients reportedly made major campaign contributions to the Rebel Republic, the conservative political party founded last year by the senior partner of the firm, Winston Harp, contributions that were also being laundered through accounts maintained by the firm. We will keep you advised as further developments occur."

Christi pushed the off button on her remote control. It was moments before she realized the phone was ringing. It was Tom.

"Christi, you will never believe what has happened!" he said, nearly breathless.

"I just heard the news on the TV. It's no surprise something like that was going on. They were raising money too fast for it to be legitimate, even with all the fear-mongering they were doing."

"What are you talking about?"

"Aren't you calling to tell me about the bust at Harp, Harrison & Humphrey? I just heard the report on TV. The firm's books were seized based on evidence they were laundering illegal Chinese gun money and campaign contributions," Christi explained.

"No, I'm not calling about that," Tom said. "You know they'll probably be acquitted."

"Then... what are you calling about?"

"You'll never believe this! Father Johnson, this older priest at Georgetown—he must be about seventy. He's one of the theologians on this interdisciplinary project. We began casually talking about the project and its potential, just in a general way. But we soon became fast friends. This is too extraordinary to be true!" he said, his words spilling out like a broken dam.

"Slow down for a second, Tom, and catch your breath," Christi admonished jokingly.

Tom chuckled. "As we got to know each other better, our discussions became more personal. We quickly grew to trust one another, and continued to reveal more about ourselves. I began to tell him about the information from Mr. Washington, but I didn't mention that you were actually meeting with him. This afternoon when we met—just a little while ago," he said with continued excitement, "he asked me point blank what has been happening. He wanted me to tell him details about the Seven Spiritual Principles. I had a sense he had spoken about them to someone else, and whomever he had spoken to wanted the information. When I was reluctant to go into further detail, he confided that there is a public policy aspect of this project," Tom disclosed, hushing his voice, "but it's being kept very quiet. Father Johnson said that he and several other people at the University have been working with a secret committee in Congress, a committee chaired by the Vice President— can you believe it—on how to incorporate spiritual principles into public policy and law! I nearly fell off my chair."

"Why are they keeping it so quiet?" Christi inquired, beginning to appreciate Tom's excitement.

"They're afraid the media would ridicule everyone involved, accuse the politicians of having seances, or being into cult stuff. They don't want this aspect of the project to be discredited as being anti-religious before they even begin, so it's top secret."

"Are they having much success? The secret committee, I mean."

"No. Father Johnson said they keep bogging down in religion, disputes over dogma. They apparently haven't been able to keep specific religious doctrines separate from universal spiritual principles. He wants to meet with you. . . tomorrow, if possible. He thinks the information you have may be an important key to what they are trying to do. Can you come to Washington tomorrow? I have tentatively arranged for us to meet Father Johnson at his office at ten in the morning."

She considered her schedule, ignoring her racing heart. "Sure... I can do that. Tomorrow I'll tell you about the Seventh Principle which I now have."

"That's terrific," Tom said. "We have a lot to talk about. I can't wait to see you."

There was a pause. Christi cleared her throat. "Tom... it's hard for me to admit... and I've fought it. But I now accept that our work is related and we were brought together for a purpose. We'll be together a long time."

Her heart felt like it stopped beating as she listened to Tom's silence. At last he replied, "I love you, Christi. I always have. Forever."

She sighed in relief. "I love you, Tom," she said softly. "I'll be there tomorrow."

Christi sat for a moment, gathering her thoughts. She must trust the Principles. She picked up the phone, this time to dial the firm of Harp, Harrison & Humphrey.

"We are unable to take your call at this time," a recorded voice said. "The firm is temporarily closed. If you have an emergency, please leave your name and number and which attorney your call should be directed to."

Christi waited for the beep. "This is Christi Daniel. I have an important message that must get to Mr. Harp. Please tell him the Seventh Principle is 'E Pluribus Unum—The Many Are One', our national motto. Also... please give him this message. Tell him... that during these difficult times... I will remember him in my prayers."

It was late when Christi placed the three candlesticks, the square and compass, the old Bible and the worn floor cloth in a large briefcase and set it on the table in preparation for her trip to Washington in the morning. She packed a few clothes in a garment bag, showered, and got ready for bed. It was a clear, crisp night.

Christi had not knelt by her bed to pray since she was a child, but this night she felt compelled to do so. "Dear God... let me see that I am as You created me... that I'm here because I am the light of the world. Grant me the will to practice forgiveness—to see there's nothing to forgive—which is my function as the light of the world, so that I may have peace of mind. Speak to me as I teach others to see that they, too, are the light of the world, that forgiveness is their function, and peace of mind their right. And... forgive Winston Harp. Bless both him and me.... I entrust my life to You."

After Christi fell asleep, she began to dream of a broad plain that was nearly barren. The only structure that disrupted the flat plain was one huge, vertical stone outcropping some distance away. She felt drawn to this unusual structure and walked toward it. As she approached, she saw a deep niche in the massive edifice. As she drew even nearer, she saw that there was a person who appeared to be mad chained to the stone within the niche.

In her dream, she decided to extend love to try to heal this prisoner, to break the chains that bound this pathetic human and to heal the tormented mind that cried out for help. She positioned herself some distance from the prisoner and began to focus her intent on sending the energy of love, intending it to be as powerful as possible. She watched intently to observe if her efforts were of any effect. As she scrutinized the face of this prisoner more closely, she realized she knew this person to whom she was extending love. It was herself.

At that moment, a golden moon emerged from behind the pine trees. As Christi lay asleep in preparation for her journey, a radiant beam of light streamed through the window, illuminating a path beside her bed. The Angel of Destiny stood nearby.

NOTES

1. MacNulty, W. Kirk, *Freemasonry, A Journey through Ritual and Symbol*, Thames and Hudson, 1991.

2. See John Dove, *The Virginia Text-Book*, pp. 106-107, 7th Ed., Press of Fergusson & Son, Richmond, VA, 1895.

3. Morgan, Marlow, *Mutant Message Downunder*, Harper Collins Publishers, 1994.

4. *The Living Bible Paraphrased*, Guideposts Associates, Inc., 1971.

5. Ibid.

6. See *A Course In Miracles*, T-8.III 4:1-7, Foundation for Inner Peace, Inc., Glen Ellen, CA (1975).

A Course in Miracles is available in bookstores. *ACIM* may be ordered on computer disk from Centerlink, 3 Miller Road, Putman Valley, NY 10579. Telephone: 914-528-7617

Readers interested in obtaining further information on the subject
matter of this book are invited to correspond with
The Secretary, Sunstar Publishing, Ltd.
116 North Court Street, Fairfield, Iowa 52556
For more Sunstar Books: http://www.newagepage.com